SHRAPNEL

by

Marie Manilla

*To The
Bridgeport Library —*

Marie Manilla

august 2012

"Caving" first appeared in the Fall 2004 issue of *New South* (formerly *GSU Review*).

"Always In My Heart"
English lyrics to "Siempre En Mi Corazon" written by Ernesto Lecuona
English lyrics by Kim Gannon
Copyright © 1940, 1942 by Southern Music Publishing Co., Inc.
Copyright Renewed.
All Rights Reserved.
Used by Permission

Published in the United States by River City Publishing
1719 Mulberry Street
Montgomery, AL 36106

Interior book design by Lissa Monroe
Jacket design by Jack Durham

First Edition—2012
Printed in the United States of America
1 3 5 7 9 10 8 6 4 2

ISBN 13: 978-1-57966-084-0
ISBN 10: 1-57966-084-3

Library of Congress Control Number: 2012941682

SHRAPNEL

Marie Manilla

RIVER CITY PUBLISHING
MONTGOMERY ALABAMA

For veterans and patriots of all political leanings, especially my father,
Lieutenant Charles E. Manilla,
United States Army Air Forces, World War II.

CAVING

Bing Butler hunkers over in the breakfast nook scraping butter across burnt toast, black crumbs speckling his plate, his eggs. He jabs his knife into jelly and starts slathering, but his hands are so trembly a glob drops on his lap.

"Son of a bitch." He stands to blot at the mess with a napkin, only smearing it deeper into his tan jumpsuit, his standard uniform for the last fifty years. "Well, shoot," he says, heading to the bedroom to change, maneuvering around packed boxes scattered like landmines. Before he gets to the hall, a fan belt squeals out front. "Already?" He squints at the oversized wall clock: 6:42.

"Newspaper said eight!" He opens the front door, running fingers through hair not yet sculpted into the pompadour he's been sporting for half a century, his only vainglory. Three cars are parked on the skirt of his lawn. The occupants head up the driveway toward Ping-Pong, picnic, and card tables set out the night before and covered with sheets to hide the jigsaw puzzles and state park ashtrays Bing and his dead wife collected during their fifty-two-year marriage.

"Paper said eight!" he hollers, sliding thick glasses higher up the bridge of his nose. The scavengers ignore him, lifting sheets to scour vases and checkerboards and meat thermometers. Bing lopes toward a lug of a man who turns and asks, "Got any tools?"

Bing looks at the man's meaty hands, grimy fingernails, healed-over nicks. "This way," Bing says, resigned. He bends to open the garage door, but his back is stiff and the door won't budge.

"Let me," the man says, hoisting it up with one hand.

"Thanks," Bing mutters. He pulls the frayed light string, illuminating his workshop. How many tabletops has he planed and varnished in here? How many chair legs has he turned on the lathe? Impossible to calculate. He looks over at his neglected torch and visor lying at the end of his workbench, folded leather cape pockmarked with burns. Dust-coated chisel, hammer, and brush lined up waiting for him to chip slag and make a seam so smooth a blind man could never feel it. Bing feels like the blind man now.

A lady in foam curlers points toward the front door. "Anything inside?"

"Yep," Bing says. "Everything goes except what's boxed up or in the master bedroom." He watches her enter, suspicious, but her purse is too small to steal anything of consequence, and besides, last night he hauled his valuables next door to Dillard's for safekeeping: Barbara's jewelry box; stack of photo albums; Safeway sack full of important documents.

For three hours a stream of yard salers parades across his front lawn, knocking over the SOLD sign twice. Bing takes low offers, too embarrassed to haggle over fifty cents for one of Barbara's purses or a pair of her house slippers. One lady buys a whole box of aprons and dish towels, worn thin from years of use. Bing reckons he should have washed them since they are likely crusted with spaghetti sauce or pie filling from the thousands of meals his wife prepared over the years.

"Need a break?" Dillard makes his way over with a coffee mug in each hand, trying not to spill.

"Thanks." Bing grips a cup, his knuckles aching. He forgot to take his arthritis medication again. And his heart pills.

"How's it going?" Dillard asks.

A man skinny as a golf club bangs out the storm door with Bing's living room curtains looped over his shoulder. A woman follows with the rods. Bing tries not to think about the day twenty-odd years ago that he and Barbara hung those flowery drapes he never really liked. Home furnishing was Barbara's department, so he never said a word.

"Vultures," Bing says. "They're like a bunch of vultures picking at a carcass."

"It'll thin out soon," Dillard says, "when the sun gets too hot."

Bing tugs a kerchief from his hip pocket and wipes the back of his neck. "Pretty hot already. That's one thing I won't miss. The heat."

"I hear West Virginia can get pretty hot, too."

"Can't be like Texas heat," Bing says. "Hard on the ticker."

"Yep." Dillard scratches his shirt over the scar from his own open-heart surgery.

Two burly women haul out Bing's sofa. He forgot to check under the cushions.

Dillard grunts. "Neighborhood won't be the same without you."

"Hasn't been the same neighborhood for years." Bing nods across the street at José Córdova just stepping out to scoop his newspaper from the front porch. He waves the paper in greeting, and the men hold up their mugs in reply.

"Know what you mean," Dillard says. He looks at the SOLD sign, the trumpet of grass around the pole that the mower couldn't get. "The couple that bought the house. They're not—"

"No," Bing says. "I wouldn't do that to you."

When he and Barbara first looked at this house, the subdivision was brand-new with scrawny saplings planted in every yard, spotless concrete driveways. Bing just a year out of the Navy. Barbara two months pregnant and tired of living in her parents' garage apartment. "It's a great starter home," the realtor had said, and they had planned on outgrowing it, having more children than this house had bedrooms.

A boy darts over with a shoe box full of baseball cards; he looks back over his shoulder at his mother who urges, "Go on."

"How much?" he asks.

Bing scratches his chin.

"Could be some real gems in there," Dillard says. "Cal Ripken. Wade Boggs."

"Could be," Bing says, but he knows better. Roger stopped collecting in the sixties, when he was a teen. Before Vietnam.

"They're not for sale," Bing says, wrestling the box from the boy's grip.

The boy's lower lip juts out and his eyes water up. He walks back to his mother, who sneers at Bing before strapping her arm around her son's shoulder and steering him toward the street.

Dillard looks at the shoe box in Bing's hands. "Those Roger's?"

"Yeah." The mother and son get in their car, fasten their seat belts, start the engine. Bing looks at the cards. "Oh, hell," he mumbles. "Wait!"

The boy rolls down the window, and Bing hands him the box, waving off any payment. The boy smiles, both front teeth missing.

"That was nice," Dillard says after the mother and son drive off.

"No time to get sentimental. Whatever I don't get rid of I have to move."

Two women fight over a wooden salad bowl set. The mustachioed one wins and presses three quarters into Bing's palm.

"I can't believe Susie finally got you to move up there," Dillard says.

Bing nudges a lump of crabgrass with his boot. "She's been after me for two solid years."

A teenage boy hands Bing a twenty for the lawn mower. He wants the gas can and weed whacker thrown in free. Bing agrees, watches him push the mower toward his truck, lift it in one smooth arc onto the truck bed.

"I just can't keep the place up anymore." Bing looks back at his one-story rancher, the sagging porch roof, leaf-filled gutters, overgrown azaleas. This is a mighty confession, and he can't look at Dillard, who is friend enough to look away.

"I imagine your house looks a sight better than what you'll see up in West Virginia. They even got plumbing up there?"

Bing laughs. He has been trading these hillbilly barbs with Dillard ever since Susie announced she would be marrying that West Virginia boy she met at U.T.–Austin. The boy she started bringing home for Thanksgiving, though all they did was bicker over everything from Dick Cavett to George Wallace. Their voices rumbled so loud one night Bing wanted to send Glen packing, but Barbara said, "You leave them be. She's finally met a man who can hold his own." Bing agreed, but that didn't change Glen's ancestry, and in the twenty-five years since his daughter became a hyphenated Butler-Babcock gal, Bing and Dillard have used up all the good ones about pig-toting, barefoot, gap-toothed, inbred holler-dwellers.

"He a coal miner?" Dillard asks.

Bing chuckles until he realizes it is an earnest question—often the first thing people ask when they hear where Susie's husband is from. Dillard's memory is failing.

"No," Bing says. "He and Susie teach at the university up there. Marshall, you know, where Randy Moss came from."

"Randy Moss. Hell of a football player."

Bing says, "That's a fact."

Dillard pours the last of his tepid coffee into the grass. "They got blacks up there too?"

"Reckon so."

"Huh." Dillard juts his chin toward José Córdova's house. "Least you won't have to contend with them."

"Amen to that."

Bing considers the number of houses on his street where white people still live. Used to be all of them until 1967 when the Bradfords moved in, a colored family just stubborn enough to ignore the cold shoulders and veiled threats. No one would really *harm* them, Bing felt sure, but a few late-night phone calls to shake them up was all right. And they had a passel of children, of course, with big Afros and slouchy walks, which was bad enough, but even worse when his Susie started hanging out over there. Going right inside that colored house like it was a regular thing to do, and didn't that make Bing want to lock her in a hole somewhere, and himself while he was at it, out of shame.

In the seventies the Mexicans started moving in. By then there were four colored families, and they were none too happy about the wetbacks taking over. Made their own obscene phone calls, or so rumor had it, but it didn't work any better for them than it had for Dillard and Bing a decade earlier. The place had gone to hell. Property values so low Bing couldn't get nearly enough out of the old place to move into a new one. And really, Barbara had said, she wouldn't feel right living any place else. This was her home, she said, after all.

"You think West Virginia's ready for the likes of you?" Dillard asks.

"They better be. I'll have to teach them a thing or two about big-city living."

"Hell," Dillard says, "you could probably run for office. Mayor Butler. I'd vote for you—twice."

Dillard's wife, Tootie, traipses over with a plate of sandwiches.

"Mighty kind," Bing says. "I've got something for you, too." He shuffles to the front door and leans in to scoop up the egg basket just inside the hall closet. "Barbara would want you to have all this." He hands over an assortment of Texas memorabilia that collected dust on a shelf in the china cabinet: plates with scenes from South Padre Island, the Hill Country, Big Thicket; a six-inch replica of the San Jacinto monument; sand dollars from Galveston.

"Don't you want to take all this up to Susie's?" Tootie says. "Something to remember us by?"

"Naw." Bing takes a bite of sandwich and shoves it to one side of his mouth. "I'm sure she's got her china cabinet filled with all kinds of West Virginia doodads."

Dillard snorts. "Imagine what kind of junk that is. Outhouse penny banks. Flip the handle and the penny shoots into the crapper."

"Rolls of toilet paper made out of the Sears catalogue," Bing says, "so they can read while they're at it."

"Except none of them can read."

"Now you all quit," Tootie says. "I'm sure they're fine people up there same as here. Susie wouldn't have married in if they weren't."

"That's a fact," Bing says, feeling scolded.

"Little turd paperweights made out of coal," Dillard says.

Bing laughs so hard he nearly chokes.

Tootie shakes her head. "I swear," she says. "You two."

That night, after Goodwill drives off with all the junk nobody would buy, Bing walks through his naked house. Every carpet stain, every plaster crack exposed, every nick in the kitchen linoleum from Roger's football cleats and Susie's aerial darts, though he told her a million times not to play with them in the house. There's the splotch on Susie's bedroom ceiling from where she burnt incense night after night, smoke wafting up, the sweet strawberry smell that finally made Bing so nauseous he barged in and threw a glass of water on it, drenching all the incense cones lined up. He imagines the new couple will paint all these walls, every room, and rip up the shag carpet while they're at it.

Isn't that what he's doing? Starting fresh? A new life with his daughter, the last place he ever figured he'd end up. But what else can he do? He can't see anymore, for God's sake, not without his Coke-bottle glasses that he regularly misplaces. He hasn't told Susie that. She'd never let him make this trip all by himself, and his gut tells him he has to do this one last thing before surrendering to old age.

For supper, Bing settles in bed with a glass of milk and a pack of Oreos. He'll eat the entire package if he wants, never mind the crumbs—*sorry, Barbara*—and he does make it through a whole row before falling asleep, chocolate spittle covering his teeth, his chin, and by morning his pillowcase too.

The day before he leaves, Bing slides into a booth at Rosie's, where he's eaten five nights a week since Barbara died—cholesterol be damned. He orders red beans and rice, Frito pie, and chicken-fried steak.

Janey, his favorite waitress, says, "Now where in the world are you gonna put all that?"

"I'll make room." Bing pats his belly. "No telling what all they'll feed me up there."

"I hear the food's real good," Janey says. "Pinto beans and cornbread. Buttermilk biscuits and redeye gravy."

"Maybe," Bing says, doubtful. Janey sashays to the kitchen, backside swaying from side to side. That's another thing he'll miss.

He pulls out his road map and starts tracing his route, using salt shakers and sugar packets to highlight attractions. The restaurant gradually fills with regulars. He counts four tables of Mexicans, rowdy men and their cackling wives and crabby babies. The men order for their families in chopped-up English, and Bing doubts there's a green card among them. Janey is just as polite as always. She has to be, Bing figures, if she wants a decent tip. He has noticed that Mexicans are generally good tippers.

Bing's food arrives, and he savors every forkful, working a blend of beans and corn chips around his tongue, all to the accompaniment of those Mexican families laughing and whooping it up. Bing would never admit this out loud, but he's grown so used to the din—toddlers babbling, wives scolding, the melodic chatter of Spanish and English—that it has become difficult for him to enjoy a meal in his own kitchen by himself. Too quiet. But he doesn't expect that to be a problem at Susie's. That was third on his list when he tallied all the reasons to pack seventy-seven years' worth of Texas living and move up there: *No more quiet dinners.*

In the morning Bing clears the odometer before starting the two-thousand-mile trip to Huntington. He wants to see how close AAA is to actual mileage. He lays the TripTik on the seat beside him, packs his lip with his morning Skoal, and settles an empty Coke can between his legs for his spit. "So long," he says, throat achy.

It's difficult backing out of the driveway with the U-Haul trailer hitched to his Olds. He wishes Dillard could see how expertly he handles the turn. Doesn't even scrape the fire hydrant, a regular mishap these last few years that's kept his glove box full of rubbing compound and spray paint.

Dillard's windows are dark, so Bing clicks his tongue and drives four blocks out of his way to pass Shorty's, his favorite bar. No more tossing back a Lone Star on Saturday afternoons with Dillard and the boys, no more dart games. Bing's eyes blur and he blinks to clear them, something he's had to do more and more since Barbara died.

I-10 East is already crowded. The U-Haul drags Bing down and cars whiz by, but he's in no hurry. He admires Houston's skyline, concrete and glass and brick reaching into the sky. All that oil-boom money. Then the bust. Now Enron. And the general fear of attack since 9/11, though thirteen months have passed since then. All those oil refineries so close makes people fidgety, it seems. Bing included, and he imagines West Virginia might be a safe bet, nothing much to target up there. He feels like a coward, abandoning his home state when the going gets tough.

When the urban sprawl thins, Bing drives over a bayou and spots a gang of boys crossing the bridge. Skipping school, probably, to look for turtles and fishing bait. One of them has a crabbing net slung over his shoulder, reminding Bing of the weekend Barbara coaxed him into going crabbing in Galveston with Roger's Cub Scout troop. "You need to spend time with your son," she had said, so Bing loaded the Dodge with four carsick boys—chubby Roger the greenest of all—and caravanned down with all those gung ho fathers who knew nothing about crabbing.

Bing knew, and the scouts gathered around him on the back-bay dunes, sea wind whipping their hair, crusting their eyes and ears with sand. "Grab you a chicken neck," Bing instructed, "and tie a long piece of string around it."

The boys grimaced as they reached in the ice chest for chilled pieces of poultry, hands slippery with fat, making the knot tying difficult. The scoutmaster and fathers did most of the tying, but not for Roger, Bing insisted. He wanted his son to tie his own knot, but by the time Roger secured it, all the good crabbing spots were taken. Bing steered him to a quiet place where he could plop his bait in the brackish water and wait for the first tug. And when it happened, Roger got so excited he tried to whip the crab out and flop it into the sand, but as soon as the crab hit air, it unclenched its claws and fell back into the water.

"You have to scoop him out," Bing said, handing over the net.

It was rough going at first, Roger trying to coordinate the bait and the net that was as tall as he was. He dropped it and dropped it, crabs scattering, until he found the delicate balance, the net's sweet spot, so that he could tug his string with one hand, hold the net at the ready with the other. Finally, after an hour of hard work, he got a firm nibble.

"Take your time," Bing said.

Bing's scrutiny made the boy's hands shake, the net wobbling in his grip. "I can't."

Bing crouched down and put his hand on his son's shoulder. "You're doing fine," he whispered. "You can do it."

Roger pulled in a big lungful of air that stilled his hands. He tugged the crab closer and closer, dipped the lip of the net in the water, slipped it under the crab and scooped him up.

"That's a doozy," Bing said, squeezing his son's neck, a big grin spreading across Roger's face.

When they joined the other boys showing off their piddly five- and six-inch trophies, neither Bing nor Roger felt inclined to brag about their eight-inch whopper. They didn't want to suffer the attention. Besides, Bing was teaching Roger another lesson: the potent value of secrets.

Hours later a white sign looms in Bing's windshield, growing larger and larger as he rumbles toward it and can finally read the letters: WELCOME TO LOUISIANA. Bing's chest thunks so hard he jams on the brakes and veers off on the berm, the contents of the U-Haul dangerously shifting. Bing gets out and leans over, gripping his knees as he takes deep breaths, remembering his cardiologist's warning to pull over every few hours to move around, keep his blood circulating. When he straightens, he looks up at the billboard, the Mardi Gras masks smiling down at him.

Bing turns around and looks at the black ribbon of asphalt he just traveled. To the soil he loved so long and so well. Only other time he left was during the war, and he wrote letters home daily while he floated around the Pacific, anxious for the return envelopes from his mother, from Barbara, all sporting that treasured Texas postmark. "Shit." Bing wipes his eyes, gets back in the car, doesn't bother to look as he squeals onto the road, gravel spraying off his back tires, the horn from a passing big rig wailing its displeasure.

Bing pretends to enjoy the new sights. Crossing the Port Arthur bridge gets his vertigo going, so high above the water, cars so close he expects their side mirrors to touch. He drives by Lake Pontchartrain, wishing Barbara could see it. She always ordered trout Pontchartrain from that Cajun restaurant with the name that sounded like a sneeze. Remembering Barbara calms him. He pretends she's sitting beside him, pouring coffee from the silver thermos, stirring half a Sweet'N Low into hers. Settling a quartered ham salad sandwich between them, reading aloud from *Reader's Digest* to pass the time.

The memory works, and soon Bing pulls into the parking lot of the Motel 6 in Hattiesburg, Mississippi, his destination for the day. Dairy Queen is next door, and Bing looks forward to eating a chili dog while perusing the Battle of Vicksburg pamphlet he picked up in the motel lobby. He pushes through the heavy door, happily inhaling the aroma of frying meat, until he sees that every counter person, cook, customer is black. Nappy heads swivel in his direction as he drops his keys. *Holy shit*, he thinks, eyes sweeping the room. Eating in a room full of Mexicans is one thing, but this, well, *holy shit*. He bends to scoop up his keys, trying to word an excuse to back out the door: *Left my lights on; forgot my billfold*, except that it's conspicuously bulging from his breast pocket.

When he stands, the counter girl urges him forward with a smile, teeth whiter than his daily Bayer. "May I take your order?" she asks. Bing squints at her nametag but doesn't say a word. Lavonda juts her face forward. "Help you?" she says louder as Bing's eyes bounce around the neon menu above her head.

"I, uh, want," Bing says. The cook in the back looks at him, spatula teetering in his hand as he waits to hear what kind of meat to slap onto the grill. *Working up a gob of spit to hawk into my food*, Bing thinks. *Eat this, Whitey.*

"Are you here for ice cream?" Lavonda nods. He echoes the motion even though that's not what he wanted at all. "Cone or a sundae?" Lavonda says, head still wagging.

"Sundae," he says, because he has to say something.

Lavonda opens her mouth, probably to offer choices of butterscotch or chocolate, wet nuts or dry. She must think better of it because she closes her mouth and rings up a hot fudge sundae, fingers clicking the register keys, drawing Bing's attention to her inch-long nails, a perfect ocean sunset painted on each one.

Bing pays and leaves, chest heaving as he crosses the parking lot, unlocks his motel room door, and lunges into the darkness. He sits on his bed looking at the ice cream in his hands. He picks off the cherry, sets it on the Gideon Bible, and digs into the unwanted whipped cream and soft serve. "Damn," he says, remembering the chili dog he'd meant to order. "Damn." He scrapes chocolate sauce and nuts from the Styrofoam cup.

In the morning, Bing drives even slower than the day before. Cars pass him, honking, drivers shaking their heads. Bing doesn't care. This may be his last bit of peace. Soon he'll be squeezed into Susie's guest bedroom, or maybe on a foldout couch. Her wild kids, Reenie and Brian, playing loud music at all hours. Back-talking him the way teenagers do. But he has no choice, he reminds himself. He hasn't told anyone about setting a fire on the stove twice. About leaving his car running in the garage. He prefers to let Susie think he is doing this for her, that he finally gave in to her pleading: "Do it for me, Dad. I promised Mom I'd look after you."

Bing wonders how his wife finagled that deal. Bing and Susie weren't close. A distance that only increased when she turned fifteen and started reading all that women's libber crap. Stopped wearing a bra—which embarrassed Bing to no end whenever she bounced into a room blathering on about Gloria Steinem, and suddenly everything about Bing was wrong-wrong-wrong.

This dismal thinking slows him even more. That night he stops in Bowling Green, Kentucky. He calls Susie to tell her he'll be a day late.

A staticky pause. "That's okay, Dad. Just drive safely. Please."

"Always do."

The next day he's back on the road, up to full speed to make up for lost time. Not twenty minutes later he sees the sign for Mammoth Cave. "I'll be jiggered." He marvels that he overlooked this portentous highlight during his trip preparations. It's an omen he cannot refuse. Two weeks before Barbara died, when she was back in the hospital for good, he had pulled the visitor's chair up beside her and held her hand as they watched a documentary on Mammoth Cave. Enthralled, Barbara said, "Next summer, I want to go there."

"Sure thing," Bing said.

"And while we're at it we'll visit our Susie," Barbara said, tears streaming, knowing full well there would be no next summer.

"Whatever you want," Bing had said, nodding. He's nodding now, in the car by himself, feeling Barbara's presence so thickly he can smell her Pond's. Bing settles into the line of cars and campers heading in. "I told you I'd bring you here."

He swings into a NO PARKING zone at the end of a row and worries about leaving the U-Haul unattended. He checks the padlock and follows the blond couple who parked beside him with their four wheat-haired children. They're going to buy tickets,

Bing hopes, since the park signs are so small he can barely make out their instructions. The family gets in line, and Bing falls in behind as the children complain about having to pee. "You just went," Mom says, her words tinged with some foreign accent, maybe Scandinavian. Bing feels a twinge in his groin at the mention of piss, but the people are already twenty deep behind him, and he doesn't dare detach himself from the Swedes. They are his North Star to find his way back to the Olds.

Inching forward, Bing remembers all the lines he and Barbara had waited in, in car and on foot, as they traveled around Texas: Big Bend, Enchanted Rock. She even coaxed him to tube down the Comal River in water so blue he felt certain they must have added dye. He can feel her beside him now, her forearm against his to steady whatever reading material she picked up to enlighten their visit. Her presence so palpable he forgets to listen to what cave the Swedes are touring. When it's Bing's turn he says to the ticket lady, "Same as them."

"How many tickets would you like?"

"What's that?" Bing asks, trying to unscramble the Kentucky phonetics that sounded something like *Hayow minny tikits wud ya lak?*

"Two," Bing says, the number engrained, and he doesn't even blink as he swaps his money for two stubs.

"Tour starts in five minutes right over there," the ticket lady says, pointing.

Bing makes his way toward a cluster of bodies, looking for yellow hair, wondering if he has time to go to the bathroom. But a ranger waves his arms to gather the group in, randomly passing out flashlights, directing their steps. Bing can't find the Swedes and decides he is on the wrong tour, but he's carried along by the mob as they march to the cave entrance. He tries to relax, breathe deeply, enjoy this experience, if not for himself, for Barbara.

He trots down a dozen or more steps toward the mouth of the cave. It does look like a mouth, ominous, gaping. Someone shouts, "Maybe we'll find Bin Laden!" a joke that sinks like an anchor, the wound still too fresh.

As they near the entrance a chill wind rushes over them. Bing's forearms pimple, and he pictures his jacket on the backseat of the Olds with his ball cap and umbrella. He wants to rub his arms to warm them, but the teenage boy behind him does that and his girlfriend calls him a pussy, making Bing's face redden.

The ranger delivers a history of Mammoth Cave—at least that's what Bing guesses since he can't hear much from his stance at the back of the group. The teenage couple makes fun, tossing around words such as salt*peter* and stalac-*tits*. Finally they enter the cave and sunlight disappears, rock walls narrowing as it becomes darker and they become flashlight reliant. Bing's nose grows cold, and he feels the damp chill in his bones, hears the drip-drip of water, feels the sympathetic twinge in his kidneys. The ranger flashes his light on features formed by thousands of years of water, one drop at a time. Columns and straws. Underground channels splitting off, walls smooth and glistening. The slender septum of earth separating two paths, looking so much like the laparoscopy Bing watched on the Discovery Channel, trachea branching off into the bronchial tree.

"And now let's see what real dark looks like," Ranger says, instructing all flashlight holders to turn off their lights.

Sudden, complete, absolute blackness. A dark so penetrating Bing opens his eyelids wider and wider, waiting for his pupils to adjust, but there's nothing to adjust to, nothing to see. No hint of edges or shoulders or heads. And the pure quiet except for the ever-present drip-drip. Bing imagines water pooling in a concave depression in the rock, or his bladder, one drop after another, stretching the thin skin taut.

The teenage boy lets out a ghostly "Oooooooo," and the group chuckles, needing that relief from the immobilizing blackness.

When the lights are back on, Bing inhales and feels his belly tighten against the waistband of his jumpsuit. He has to pee—now. He tries to squeeze down the urge even as a few warm drops seep. *Damn incontinence.* His body's lingering protest against prostate surgery, an utterly shameful betrayal. The group moves forward around a craggy bend, and Bing pretends he's fascinated by a guano splat so the teenagers will pass him, which they do.

As soon as he's alone, light and chatter fading, he wedges behind a stalagmite and unzips. *Keep watch,* he thinks, his standing orders to Barbara whenever he had to perform this private act in public places. How she tricked him—once. Yelled "Look out!" so loud he sprayed an arc of urine on a statue of L.B.J. in some rose garden. Bing was furious, but Barbara couldn't stop cackling at the former president's sopping shoulder. "If Susie were here she'd kiss you on both cheeks," Barbara said, recalling the fiery debates during those Vietnam years.

Bing strains to empty his bladder, pushing harder and harder, eyes latched onto the hint of light in the distance, fainter and fainter as the group recedes. Then he is once again thrust into blackness.

"Shit." Bing tucks himself back into his jumpsuit though he isn't quite through, zipping his fly with dribbled-on fingers, banging his knee against the stalagmite as he bumbles forward, hopefully forward, both hands against the damp curving walls as he inches along. The cry *Help!* forms in his brain, on his tongue, but he can't spit it out. He imagines those teenagers' rude remarks. Besides, if he keeps moving, he'll catch up. How far could they have gotten?

Bing follows a whoosh of cold air, deciding it must lead to an exit, even as his feet slant downward, toes gripping the soles of his boots, one hand on each side of the tunnel for balance, until suddenly the walls disappear and Bing pitches forward, banging his knees, palms in the sand. He stands with a grunt that echoes off distant walls, claps his hands free of sand and hears running water, an underground stream. Bing is drawn toward it, arms out for balance as he slides one foot forward, then another, until he feels frigid water seeping into his right boot. He withdraws it, shaking it against the wetness saturating his sock.

He tries to back up, find the tunnel he just came from and worm his way to the entrance. Arms straight out in front, feeling blindly, he hits wall and works his way along until he feels an opening, a glorious opening, and he ducks in. The ceiling seems lower, walls narrower, but this has to be it. Has to be.

Bing propels himself forward, outracing the scary thought, the probability that he is in the wrong shaft. "Help!" he calls, heart quavering, the word blunted by the close ceiling that drops lower and lower until Bing bangs his head against something that breaks loose and crunches beneath his feet. Bing puts his hands on his knees, trying to decide what to do. "Go back," he says, awkwardly turning around in the cramped space to head back to the stream. He drags his knuckles along the cold walls, trying to remember how many steps he took, how many minutes. He keeps walking, and walking, banging his knees, his head, his shoulders. It's taking much longer to get out than it did to get in. He must have veered down another opening, is in yet another shaft leading to who-knows-where. The uncertainty makes him run, as much as he is able to run with his bad knees and the geologic booby traps he continually scrapes against. His lungs labor, and he pictures his own trachea, his own glistening pink septum quivering against chilled oxygen. People probably get lost in these caves all the time, he figures. Dozens of them. Hundreds. They must have emergency plans. Do headcounts of tours. Surely his ranger will notice they have one less body. He'll send a search party with flashlights and flares and blankets. Or at the end of the day someone will notice the lone U-Haul in the parking lot. They probably have to deal with this all the time.

He bursts into an expanse of room, listens for gurgling water but does not hear it. Still, he is no longer in that cramped space, and he inhales thin air until his heart steadies. He takes a step forward, his foot landing in a depression. His legs crumple as he folds to the damp earth, going face-first into the dirt. Stunned, he lies there, listening, hearing only his own wheezing breath, the rustling of jumpsuit as he rolls off a sharp something and lies flat on his back, arms beside him, legs stretched out. His body settles into the moist earth, and he feels the chill from his heel to his scalp.

"Barbara," he moans. "Barbara."

He pictures her in that bronze coffin. Her placid face, skin waxy, the wrong lipstick, hair too pouffy. He imagines her in that box in the cold earth right now. How dark it must be. Just like here. He sees her eyes fluttering, pulling against whatever glue they use to keep them closed. The embalmer's fingertips squirting or dabbing it onto her hazel eyes, eyes that he loved to peer into when she wasn't looking, only when she wasn't looking. *Barbara.* He pictures a road map with two red Xs, one on the spot in Texas, one in Kentucky, marking the earth where they both lie, peaceful. And it does feel peaceful. He could fall asleep right now, right here, and maybe never wake up. Never, ever have to move into a house where he suspects he is not really wanted. Forfeit the humiliating end that surely awaits him, in a hospital room with tubes and beeping machines, and an empty visitor's chair beside him because there is no Barbara to wait patiently and hold his hand and watch a PBS special about caves where old people go to die.

Minutes, hours, days later Bing feels warmth on his face. He opens his eyes and the light insults him, so he seals them fast and feels his shoulder being jostled. "Old man. You all right? Hey, old man!" He opens his eyes to the sun, but it isn't the sun; it's a flashlight, and behind it a silhouette, no, two of them, tilted over him, jabbing their mean fingers into his shoulders, his side, until Bing says, "Stop it!"

"Shit!" one of them says. "We thought you were dead."

Aren't I? Bing thinks, chest sinking. *Aren't I?*

INCOMING

It takes him awhile, his pride more bruised than his body, but eventually Bing settles back into the rhythm of driving. The steady thump-thump of the road under his tires makes his eyelids droop, jaw sag, and he repeatedly drifts into other lanes. He blinks at the scenery, Kentucky's sloping horse farms, the white fences, clusters of mahogany horses flicking black tails. He's heard about Kentucky poverty, but it just can't be like West Virginia poverty—a view confirmed when he passes mansions around Lexington and the Keeneland Racetrack. All the Kentucky Derbies he watched over the years. How genteel it all seemed. The silly suppers Barbara and Tootie cooked up with their homemade hats covered in bird nests and silk flowers. Serving Hot Brown Sandwiches and Derby Pie.

Bing's heart ka-thunks when a road sign warns: *Huntington WV 127 miles.* He looks up at the hills on either side, worn ridges revealing their advanced age. Suddenly he feels penned in by mounds of earth, by having his view blunted. He can't see around the next curve, or over the next mountain. Not like Texas where you can see in all directions for miles. Except the Hill Country, of course, but those hills offer a different kind of closeness. Security. Protection.

Something high in a jagged crevice catches Bing's eye: a proper Appalachian shanty. "Ha!" He starts counting dinged-up trailers with mud yards. Chicken coops and weathered tobacco barns. Valleys turned into landfills. It's just as he expected, but in his mind the images were black and white with barefoot, rag-clad children standing in front of caved-in porches or outhouses. Dogs rooting for scraps. Malnourished women holding bare-bottomed babies. Dull-eyed coal miners coated in soot. He thinks these images come from watching those TV commercials in the sixties during President Johnson's War on Poverty. Appalachians suddenly became everybody's poor relation, however backward. And hadn't there been a few ads about the Mexicans scraping by in south Texas? Barefoot brown children in front of outhouses. Not dogs, but goats rooting for scraps. Migrant workers picking pecans until their fingers bled. All this in Bing's very own backyard, but nobody wanted to claim Mexicans as a relation, poor or otherwise.

Two hours later Bing pulls Susie's directions from the ashtray. *Exit Hal Greer Boulevard.* Bing does, and soon he's stuck in four lanes of cars at a traffic light. *Sparse congestion.* The license plate on the Buick in front of him reads: *Almost Heaven, West Virginia.* "Some heaven." On his right, Meadows Elementary is letting out. Children bolt across the lawn to crossing guards who ensure their safe passage. All of them shod and hauling bulky backpacks, just like the kids back home. Same goofy haircuts and ridiculous pants. Mouths full of metal and bubble gum.

Bing turns left at the light and drives through Ritter Park. His eyebrows arch at stately homes lining wide boulevards, the canopy of tree limbs overhead, vast lawns with manicured gardens, and statues, and fountains that spit blue water—not a doorless refrigerator or stack of bald tires. *Pretty as River Oaks,* he thinks, Houston's posh neighborhood. Bing finds his daughter's street, which is a bit more modest than the ones he just traveled. Driveways lined with late-model Camrys and Volvos and Subaru wagons. Houses three stories at least. Something inside Bing tightens up, like a fist clenching, or an overwound watch.

Bing pulls into the driveway, and there's Susie watering pots of geraniums on her porch.

"Finally," she calls, ambling to him.

"Little girl," he says, getting out, popping his spine right and left before offering a loose hug. She looks so much like her mother. Same round face and sharp dimples, same middle-age paunch. Same fine-textured hair, though at least Barbara colored and styled hers. The bags under Susie's eyes, the purple crescents, are all her own.

Glen bangs out the front door. "You made it!" He's as lanky and stooped-shouldered as ever.

Bing says, "I can read a map."

"Welcome home." Glen waves at the brick fortress that could fit two of Bing's Houston houses inside.

"What do you think?" Glen says.

Bing stoops to pluck the lone weed from a crack in the driveway. "It's no River Oaks."

"Well, what is?" Glen goes for a hug, but Bing thrusts out his hand. Glen takes it without flinching.

Bing follows them up the steps to the porch with terra-cotta tiles, wrought iron furniture with thick cushions. Porch swing big as a Chevette. Inside, Bing is too busy estimating the ceiling's height—*thirteen feet?*—and he nearly trips over a fat cocker spaniel heading toward the fireplace. No fire.

"Frida!" Susie calls. The dog stops and slowly retreats.

"She's blind as a bat," Glen says. "Can hardly walk across the room without her hind legs going out."

"How old is she?" Bing stoops to count tumors bulging on Frida's back, inhaling the unmistakable stench of old dog.

"Fifteen," Glen says.

Why don't you put the poor animal down? Bing bends to offer a perfunctory pat. The dog growls.

Susie says, "It takes her awhile to warm up to people."

"Point taken." Bing avoids the Persian carpets, stepping only on the hardwood floors. The living room is crowded with a tapestry sofa and love seat, crystal lamps, tables inlaid with mother of pearl or topped with pink marble. Bing clasps his hands behind his back so he won't knock over any vases or figurines. *Not a room you could just kick your feet up in*, he figures. *Always need a coaster under your drink.*

There's the china cabinet in the dining room, and Bing covers his mouth to keep from smiling. *Turd paperweights made out of coal.* He saunters over, boots heavily thumping. He is sorely disappointed. Stacks of china, gold candle holders, tiny coffee cups on dinky saucers. Not a West Virginia spoon rest or toothpick holder in sight.

"Fancy shmancy," he says.

Susie leans close to his ear. "Not exactly my taste either, but we inherited all this from Glen's grandmother, so what can you do?"

"I hear that." Bing pictures his Grandma Lottie's butcher-block table in the back of the U-Haul, concave surface worn smooth from a century of use. He had intended to pass it on to Susie. He studies a porcelain egg with tiny arched doors that open. Inside, a pink-cheeked woman plays a delicate harp. Grandma Lottie's table no longer seems like a good idea.

Suddenly a rumbling thump-thump-thump from above, rattling the egg, the stacks of dishes, the chandelier over the dining room table.

"What in blazes?" Bing says.

Susie shakes her head at her husband. "Your turn."

Glen grimaces and leaves, shoes pounding the stairs as he makes his way up.

"What's going on?"

"Reenie," Susie says, as if that should explain everything.

Bing looks at the chandelier trembling on its chain, feels the stereo vibrating through the walls, and he can't stop smirking.

Once the music is turned down, Bing tours the rest of the house, running his fingers along the banister spindles as they make their way to the second floor. Two bedrooms are offices: one for Glen, one for Susie. Glen's looks like a professor's ought to, Bing thinks, with a cherry desk, green banker's lamp, leather chair. "Real tidy," he says about the line of diplomas hanging on the wall. Glass-fronted bookcases loaded with literature books. Bing leans in and squints at shelf labels: *Native American*, *Slave Narratives*, *Chicano*, the lowest shelf tagged *Literature of War* with Civil War diaries and commentaries on the Great War, World

War II, Korea, Vietnam. Short stories, poems, essays, and letters. Vietnam letters.

Somewhere in the U-Haul is that Safeway sack crammed with birth certificates, Bing's Army discharge papers, notarized will, and a bundle of fragile blue airmail letters from Vietnam.

Susie's office is a disaster: mounds of books and journals and student papers stacked on heater vents, windowsills, the reading chair. Posters on the wall of the homeliest women Bing ever saw. One of Fidel Castro. Bing is not shocked and expects Susie to call him a pig for sporting Republican bumper stickers as soon as she sees them. He may not agree with all of Bush Jr.'s policies, but Texans stand up for each other.

Susie points to a closed door. "Brian's room. I'd show it to you if he were here, but we try to respect the kids' privacy."

Bing wonders what a seventeen-year-old boy needs to keep secret. At that age, Bing was selling war bonds, collecting scrap metal and rubber for the cause. Much too concerned about real threats like Hitler and Hirohito to care about his mother finding pin-up posters of Rita Hayworth or half a pack of Lucky Strikes.

The one door Bing knows not to open still vibrates from the music pounding inside.

Susie nudges her foot against the door. "The attic is now Reenie's room. I wouldn't—"

"I won't," Bing says, again noting that bleary look in Susie's eyes. He sported a similar droop about thirty-five years back.

"We've got your room all ready," Glen says, leading Bing to the basement.

Bing imagines a concrete floor with a furnace in the corner and duct work overhead. He is wrong again. Wall-to-wall carpet, striped wallpaper. Besides a bedroom he's got his own den with a big screen TV. Beyond the laundry room is a full bathroom, and Susie says, "I'll only come down on Saturdays to wash clothes. The rest of the time this is your space, Dad. You decorate it any way you like, though I did hang a few pictures."

Susie nods at the photos above the mantle: Bing's and Barbara's twenty-fifth anniversary. Susie's and Glen's wedding. Reenie and Brian dressed up as Dorothy and the Scarecrow for Halloween. Roger's Army picture. Bing eyes it, and Susie says, almost as a dare, "I hope it's okay I put that up."

Bing stares at the image of his son in uniform. Roger trying to conjure a hard Army gaze, not quite successfully. Roger was a mushy boy, which is why Bing pushed him into football. Turn the boy's belly flab into muscle. Teach him some aggression because *it's a jungle out there.* Even Coach said Roger was too cautious, though he could bulldoze a tank if he wanted. When Bing posed for his own military photo he looked into the lens and imagined a Jap on the other side: *I'm gonna kick your yellow ass.* Nothing soft about him. He looks at his daughter, can easily imagine her in a dress uniform, shoulders back as she stares into the camera with a piercing look that says: *Go ahead, make my day.*

"There's the phone," Glen says, pointing, "so you can call your buddies back home and tell them we have indoor plumbing."

"And electric," Susie says, smirking.

Bing forces out a stunted laugh. "That's a good one."

"Dinner's ready anytime you are." *Dinner*, Glen called it, not *supper*.

They tromp to the kitchen. As Bing pulls in his chair he says, "What about the kids?"

"Brian's at the arcade," Susie says. "Reenie prefers to eat in her room."

Bing prefers it that way, too. "What'd you fix?" he asks Susie.

"Glen cooked Thai."

"Thai," Bing echoes. "Never had it before, but I hear it eats like Chinese."

It's not like any Chinese Bing ever had. Milky soup with lemon grass. Spaghetti noodles mixed up with peanut butter.

"Delicious," Susie says, slurping every bite.

"I wanted something special your first night," Glen says. "I don't cook like this every day."

"I appreciate that," Bing says.

He tries to slip Frida some under the table, but the dog growls and sneezes.

"Frida doesn't get people food," Glen says.

Bing looks at Susie who shrugs, suggesting she has lost this battle, too. "When I was a boy they didn't even make dog food. It was table scraps or roadkill." Nobody laughs and Bing tries hard to fill the silence. "How's Reenie like Marshall?"

"Fine," Glen chirps.

"I was surprised she turned down a scholarship to that fancy school," Bing says. "What was the name of it?"

Glen mumbles, "Swarthmore."

"A full ride," Susie adds.

A full ride, Bing thinks, imagining the price tag. "Well, there's no place like home."

"It's all because of Junior," Susie spits.

"Reenie's still dating that fella?"

Susie groans. "She could have done so much better."

Bing doesn't know if she's referring to Junior or Marshall. Before he properly weighs it, he says, "Brian planning on going to Marshall, too?"

"Hah!" Susie snorts.

Uh-oh. Bing is afraid her outburst is a reflection on the boy's brain power.

Glen is more diplomatic. "He's weighing his options. He still has a year to decide."

Susie chews her food like she's grinding glass. "He says he's decided! He says he's already decided!"

Decided what?

"Anything can happen in a year," Glen says.

"You don't know that. You just don't know!" The vein in Susie's temple throbs.

Here we go, Bing thinks, recognizing that vein as a signal that he's in for fireworks.

Instead, Glen stands and says, "When you're right, you're right."

Bing sits there, bewildered, wondering if after all these years Glen and Susie have forgotten how to fight.

After supper they unload the U-Haul, grunting as they heave the mahogany headboard down the basement steps. The end table Bing made in high school shop. Barbara's sewing lamp. Mattresses and suitcases and box after box secured with duct tape. They fit the bed together and dress it with Bing's own linens, the bedspread Barbara ordered from Penney's.

"If you find any of Reenie's stuff down here just leave it on the kitchen table," Susie says.

"Reenie's stuff?"

"This was her room," Glen says.

"I don't want to take the girl's room."

"No trouble," Susie says.

Glen snorts.

Bing pulls four jumpsuits from his suitcase and opens the closet door, EAT SHIT written on the back wall in fat, black letters. Susie comes in with a stack of towels, and Bing quickly shuts the door. The one piece of advice Dillard drilled into Bing's head before he left was *Don't make waves.*

Later, after he combs his hair, Bing settles into his pillow that still smells like home. He clicks off the light and pretends he's back in Houston. The lump of blankets beside him is Barbara. Susie, maybe six or seven years old, sleeps down the hall with an agate shooter clenched in her palm. In his own room, Roger is sleeping, too, wad of pink gum stuck to his bed post, the first thing he'll pop in his mouth when he wakes.

K RATIONS

Bing is dreaming about desserts. Slender hands with red fingernails set a whole pecan pie before him. Bing pierces the center of the pie with a fork, steam rising up. He leans in for a sniff of caramelly sweetness, oven-roasted pecans, but when he inhales, what he smells is shit. Regulation latrine crap, pungent and stifling. He coughs, which wakes him, and when his eyes pop open he sees a fuzzy shadow looming.

"Barbara?" he whispers.

"Shit." The figure drops something on the floor before darting away.

The stench lingers, so Bing fumbles for his glasses and looks around his room until the pieces clank back into place. Susie's basement. Bing swings his legs out from under the covers, bare toes groping for slippers. He finds one, then the other, lines them up to shove his feet inside, and when he does, something warm and squishy oozes between his right toes. "What the hell?" Bing pulls out his foot now coated in dog shit. At least he hopes that's what it is, recalling Frida waddling around upstairs.

He picks up his slipper and looks toward his closet with his granddaughter's greeting inside. Bing stands and hops to his bathroom to rinse the slipper in the bathtub and give his foot a good scrubbing. *Some welcome.*

He pulls on his robe, wears the dry left slipper, and creaks upstairs to the kitchen. Susie stands at the counter wearing a t-shirt with a picture of Marilyn Monroe with her front teeth blacked out. Susie looks at Bing and down at his feet, the one slipper. She blinks twice and points at the coffeepot. "Want some?"

"You betcha." Bing sits at the table.

The coffee is strong and steams his glasses so that he has to peer over them to watch Susie pull boxes of cereal from the cupboard. She sets them on the table and goes for the bowls, the milk. *Moves like her mother*, he thinks, *slipshod and loose*.

"Grape-Nuts?"

"Sure," he says, disappointed, wondering how long to let the pellets soak before they're soft enough to chew.

Susie settles beside him and peels a banana. "Sleep well?"

"Yeppers," Bing says. The October chill bites his right foot, his ankles. He wishes he'd pulled on socks.

"You smell something?" Susie leans toward Bing, sniffing.

"Like what?" He wants to tell her about his weird morning greeting, the fuzzy visitor, but under the café light dangling over the table it doesn't seem like a good idea.

"Like shi—" Susie stops and screws up her face, looking at her father's robe, his pajama bottoms, probably wondering about his bathroom etiquette.

"I don't smell anything." Bing tries to end the scrutiny without stirring up the family stew. "Glen up?"

"He showered and shaved and left hours ago."

Shit-shower-shave, Bing thinks, looking at the spot on his wrist where his watch would be. "When do you leave?" He tries not to sound anxious, but he is not a morning person. When Barbara was alive, she knew to set Bing's Folgers and Egg Beaters before him and back off, let the caffeine slough off his morning irritability. Texas manners take real effort this early.

"Soon." Susie scans the front page of the *Herald-Dispatch* lying flat on the table. The headline reads: *Weapons Inspectors Want More Time*. Underneath is a picture of Colin Powell pointing to an aerial photo of some undisclosed Iraqi location. *That's one impressive military leader*, Bing thinks. The first black man he might have voted for if Powell had thrown his hat into the presidential ring. No one was more shocked to come to that realization than Bing, a nugget he firmly kept to himself.

A clamber on the stairs and Brian darts into the kitchen, Joe Boxer shorts, t-shirt hanging from his bony frame, hair shorn to a nearly regulation cut.

"Morning, young fella," Bing says, amazed at the height of his grandson, whom he hasn't seen since Barbara's funeral.

Brian was fifteen then, half a foot shorter and newly equipped with a learner's permit. He sat up front with the limo driver on the way to the cemetery and quizzed him about gas mileage and horsepower. Bing sat in the back between Susie and Glen, feeling small, pressed into the leather seat. Directly across from him sat Reenie, her pudgy knees nearly touching Bing's. She was already seventeen but not interested in getting permits for driving or anything else. That morning he had found her rummaging through

Barbara's closet, pulling down 1960s dresses that Barbara had refused to part with.

"Take whatever you want," Bing said.

Reenie had and was wearing one of those orange polyester dresses with an empire waist. Cropped, pink hair wisping from under a pillbox hat. The only mismatched accessories were the combat boots.

"Who the hell are you supposed to be?" Brian had asked when Reenie stepped from Bing's porch.

"Kiss my ass," Reenie said, giving him the finger.

"I think you look nice," Glen said, ushering his daughter to the limo. "Like Jackie Kennedy. Or a stewardess."

"That's not the look I was going for."

"I bet Junior would like it." Brian made such a sourpuss face even Bing wanted to strike him.

"Who's Junior?" Bing asked, too dazed by his horrible circumstances to register the answer.

A month later his phone bill told him. Nearly four hundred dollars' worth of long-distance phone calls to Junior, Reenie's boyfriend back home.

Now, in Susie's kitchen, Brian reaches in front of his grandfather for a cereal box, and as he does, Bing sniffs for lingering excrement. He smells nothing.

Brian fills a bowl, splashes on milk, and turns to leave when Susie stops him.

"Don't you have anything to say to Grandpa after he's just driven across half the country to live with us?"

Brian shifts from one foot to the other. "Why did Roger join the Army?"

"Brian!" Susie says.

The boy says, "What? I mean he could have chosen the Air Force or Navy, right?"

"I warned you a million times we don't talk about that." Susie's face is splotchy.

"Why not?" Brian says.

Susie swings her head around to glare at Bing. "Because we don't, do we, Dad?" Her eyes flame exactly as they did years ago when Susie sat at a different kitchen table and seethed, "How come we never talk about him?"

"Because we don't," Bing had said, before tromping to his workshop out back.

Brian says, "Whoa," and leaves, abandoning the mess he started.

Bing wonders where in the hell this is coming from so early in the day, in his tour with this family, but Susie runs her hand over her face. "I'm sorry. I'm just . . . I'm sorry."

Bing isn't sure what just happened. He reaches for the Skoal in his robe pocket and twists off the lid.

"Dad," Susie says, straightening a place mat. "I'd appreciate it if you wouldn't chew in the house."

"What's that?" Bing says, fingers poised to scoop up a dip.

"You can do it on the front porch, or in the backyard. And we put a special garbage can in the alley for your spit cans."

"No problem," Bing says, mind reeling. He gets up and enters the living room where the dog lies on her bed by the front door. Frida's bloodshot eyes follow him as he crosses the room. "Thanks for the gift," Bing says, reaching a hand toward her. Frida draws her lips back, gray teeth worn down to nubs, growl grumbling in her throat. Bing pulls his hand back. "Careful, or you'll wind up suckin' on a tailpipe."

Outside, Bing sits on the porch swing and packs his lip, lone slipper scraping terra-cotta tiles as he sways back and forth. He calculates the time down in Houston. Imagines Dillard at his window watching the new neighbors unload. Tootie probably fixed them a pineapple upside-down cake, or a whole supper. Lasagna, maybe. Big pot of gumbo.

Two squirrels chitter at the base of a tree in the front yard. Bing is impressed by the trunk's stout girth. It's the tallest sycamore he's ever seen, three times bigger than the ones back in Texas. Seeds the size of Ping-Pong balls. Bing looks at the other trees lining the street: thriving sugar maples and sweet gums all dwarfing their skimpy cousins back home.

The front door opens and Brian bangs out, hops down the steps, backpack slung over his shoulder. Bing raises his hand in greeting, but the boy ducks into a primer-gray Camaro parked at the curb. Soon the engine screams and the car rumbles down the street.

Susie comes out next wearing a gauzy dress, leather tote dragging down her forearm. She hands Bing a house key and a leash.

"Could you take Frida out about noon?" she asks. "Just up and down the block. She can't go too far anymore."

"Sure thing," Bing says.

She hands him a wad of sandwich baggies. "And you have to pick up after her."

Bing looks at the plastic wad springing open in his palm. "Okay." He wonders if Frida's got anything left after the impressive load in his slipper.

"I'll be home around six." After a pause she adds, "We're all really glad you're here, Dad."

Bing doesn't know if he believes her, but he's comforted by the silver earrings dangling from her lobes that he gave Barbara one Christmas. Out of his mouth pops, "Where's the girl?"

"The girl?"

"Reenie," he says, pulse quickening, an irrational fear. It was a harmless prank, after all, but if Susie had pulled that decades back she'd get a ringing earful.

"She has an early class. Left even before Glen."

Before Susie gets in her car she hollers, "We're going out for Mexican tonight. All five of us."

"You don't have to do that," Bing groans.

"Enjoy it now, Dad. Tomorrow we'll be back on Glen's weedy salads."

Bing ambles to the kitchen where he finishes the paper, a third the size of the *Houston Chronicle*, the local section devoted to illegal methamphetamine labs, a thriving career choice apparently, except that one exploded over the weekend blasting a car-sized hole in the side of a house.

He scours the kitchen for something to eat besides cereal and finds rice cakes and bean sprouts. Desperation sends him snooping under the sink where he spots a box of MoonPies tucked behind the Brillo pads. He knows it's not safe to mix edibles with cleaning products, but that doesn't stop him from snarfing down four marshmallow pies in a row without even sitting down. When he finishes, he shoves the box back where he found it.

At noon, precisely, Bing grabs the leash and baggies.

Frida is still stretched out on her pillow. "Let's go," he says, reaching down to fasten the leash. Frida draws back her lips and snaps at his hand. Or gums it, really, since she no longer has the teeth to back up her bad temper.

"That's what I thought," Bing says, running his tongue over his partial.

Frida eases off the porch one step at a time.

"You walk like you got a stick up your butt," Bing says, noticing crap flakes around her rear. As they inch down the street she smells every grass blade and leaf. At the end of the block she nearly bumps into a fire hydrant. "Look out," Bing says, tugging her out of harm's way. This is the first time he's walked a dog on a leash, and he feels self-conscious as Frida dribbles pee on people's lampposts and monkey grass.

Eventually Frida circles, squats, and unloads a long strand of poop. Bing turns his back to her and looks at the sky. He doesn't quite know how to pick the stuff up, but he manages, and holds the bag daintily between finger and thumb, hiding it behind his back when cars drive by, feeling a gush of relief when he nears Susie's house. He lifts his foot to ascend the front steps when a voice calls, "You must be the grandpa."

Bing looks right and left, but there's no one in view. He climbs one step, and another, urging Frida to follow.

"Reenie told me you'd be moving in."

Bing backs down the steps.

"Up here."

Over at the neighbor's house on the right, a woman leans out of a second-floor window, her two-foot silver braid dangling onto the windowsill.

Bing's neck creaks as he leans backward for a better view. "That would be me," he says, hiding the crap behind his back.

"I'm Ellen Foley."

"Howdy do," Bing says, trying to recollect the name of that fairy tale damsel with the long hair. This crinkled-up woman is certainly no princess.

"Had lunch?" Ellen shouts.

Bing feels the MoonPies lying heavy on his stomach. Mostly he considers the jittery feeling in his veins that makes him want to run away from this strange person hanging out of her window. "Sure have," he says, taking a step toward Susie's porch.

"I've got cold meatloaf."

Bing pictures a thick slab of meatloaf between white bread, heavy on the mustard. Slice of Velveeta cheese.

"You're sure you've had lunch?"

"Yep," Bing says, ignoring his grumbling belly, wishing his wife were here to make small talk, leaving Bing free to hang back a step or two and nod, or slink quietly away.

"You look like a man who enjoys home cooking."

Dammit, Barbara. Bing takes another step toward his daughter's house so he can no longer see Ellen. "Surely do," he hollers, climbing up, wanting this conversation to be over, wanting to toss Frida's bag of crap in the bushes and dart inside.

"Lord only knows what Glen's feeding you."

Will this woman never shut up? Bing drops the shit in the recycling bin and shoves open the front door.

Ellen yells, "If you ever get tired of—"

"Much obliged," he shouts, yanking the dog inside.

The thought of meatloaf makes Bing hungry for Barbara's recipe with crunchy bits of celery and green pepper. He heads to the kitchen, wondering how many MoonPies he can eat in one day, if he should replace them so their rightful owner won't get rattled. But he doesn't even know where a grocery store is. Or a gas station. Post office. Xerox machine for his tax forms. He draws a map in his mind of his old stomping ground, everything he needed within a five mile radius. He knew all the cashiers and gas station attendants. Which bank teller was prone to mistakes. After Barbara died he had to learn which supermarket aisle had tomato soup and saltines. Preparation H. In the deepest crevice of his brain is a disturbing fear that he no longer has the mental capacity to start over.

The doorbell rings and Frida howls. For fifteen minutes Bing has been standing in the kitchen holding a can of mushrooms. Frida barks more furiously, and Bing can't decide whether to answer or not. It's not his house, after all. The doorbell is followed by a burst of knocking, so Bing heads for the door, mushrooms still in hand.

It's Ellen Foley.

"You're not getting away that easily," she says, arms straining under a tray draped with a kitchen towel. "Will you let me in before I drop this thing?"

"Oh," Bing says, stepping aside. Ellen rushes past him wearing what look like pajamas. Calf-length green tunic with matching bottoms. Chinaman slippers. Frida follows on Ellen's heels, still yapping. "Hush!" Ellen barks. The dog turns around and heads back to her pillow. Bing waits at the door for Ellen to deposit the goods and return, but she doesn't.

"Are you coming or not?" she calls.

In the kitchen, Ellen eyes the can in Bing's hand. "Looks like I got here just in time." She pulls the towel from the tray.

Bing could almost cry. Two thick slabs of meatloaf on crusty French bread. Cottage cheese and cling peaches. Plate full of frosted brownies.

"Catsup or mustard?" she asks.

"Mustard."

Ellen finds the bottle in the fridge and sets it on the table with a napkin and silverware.

"Thank you," Bing says, staring at the food, wanting Ellen to leave so he can dive in.

"Go on," Ellen says, nodding toward a chair.

"But—"

"I've already eaten," Ellen says, sitting down.

Bing feels acutely self-conscious as he sits and slathers on mustard, but his food drive kicks in and soon he's got a mouthful of meatloaf, no crunchy bits of celery, but it's good eating.

"I love Glen dearly," Ellen says, "and I love his cooking, but I can't imagine a man like you surviving on it for long."

Bing nods and munches away.

"This must be quite unsettling for you," Ellen says. "Moving all the way up here."

"Naw," Bing says, shoveling in a forkful of peaches.

"Susie's been worried about you living down there all by yourself."

"I wasn't by myself."

"I know that. I'm sure you have dozens of friends."

"That's right." Bing would have trouble finding a foursome for golf—not that he plays.

"Susie tells me you're a welder."

"Yep. Learned it in the Navy and did it for forty-two years."

"I weld," Ellen says.

Bing's head jerks up as he tries to envision this, well, not *dainty*, exactly, but woman nonetheless in the heavy hood and gloves. It takes real muscle to hold that torch for long.

"Sculptures mostly. My backyard is crammed full of them. I make jewelry, too." Ellen lifts a pendant dangling from her neck, big as a playing card, all silvery swirls with bronze inlay. Green and blue stones peppered throughout. Her hand goes to her earlobe, and Bing follows it to see a matching earring. He takes this opportunity to scour Ellen's face, and aside from the wrinkles, she's a handsome woman. Not pretty, like Barbara. Might be if she put on makeup. Did something with that hair, the thick braid hanging over her shoulder, the curly bit at the end resting on the kitchen table. He spies a ring on her finger, an inch thick with geometric shapes cut out all around.

"I made that, too. It's my wedding band."

"That's real special," Bing says. "You make one for your husband?"

Ellen looks over at Bing. "I did."

"What's he do?" Bing hopes that he might also weld, though he can't imagine talking shop with any man who would wear an artsy fartsy ring like that.

Ellen blinks twice. "I'm a widow."

"Sorry about that. I'm a widower myself."

"I know."

Oh shit. Bing realizes he's about to step into one of those jagged-toothed bear traps Dillard warned him about.

Not two weeks after Barbara's funeral, Bing and Dillard had cleaned up the kitchen cluttered with sympathy casseroles and pies. Bing scrubbed pans while Dillard wiped the table, avoiding the stack of thank-you cards Bing was working through. After thirty minutes Dillard stammered, "Bing, as your friend, I feel it's my responsibility to have a certain conversation."

Bing fished around mucky dishwater for serving spoons. "A conversation?"

"Yep," Dillard said. "Let's see. How do I put this? You see, there's these gals, buddy."

Bing turned to squarely face his friend, soap suds dripping off his fingers, hoping to God Dillard wasn't about to suggest that Bing start dating.

Dillard picked a blob of something from the table top. "Barbara had a lot of women friends. At church. In her sewing circle. From that Jazzercise class she and Tootie take—took."

Bing's fists clenched.

"A lot of these women are widows," Dillard said. "Living off their husband's pension."

"You better get to the point in a hurry."

Dillard folded his dishtowel and looked at Bing. "Some of them aren't at all happy about the size of their husband's pension, if you know what I mean. Some of them want a man to hold the door for them. Pull out their chair. And there are a lot more widows than there are widowers, so you do the math."

"*You* do the math. What the hell are you talking about, Dillard?"

"You're a hot commodity, that's what I'm getting at. Pretty soon you'll start getting calls from these ladies who want to bring you pot roast and sew on your buttons to help you get over your loss."

"I don't want to get over my loss."

"I know that," Dillard said. "Won't nobody replace Barbara, ever. I'm just warning you to be on the lookout for Black Widders."

Now here sits Ellen Foley trying to weld her sly fingers around him. *Not a chance*, Bing thinks, abruptly standing to shove the empty tray toward her.

"Thanks for lunch," he says. "I have to finish unpacking."

"Oh! Of course. I'm sure you have a lot of settling in to do." Ellen stands and takes the tray. Bing follows her to the front door, green tunic tucked slightly in the crease in her behind. Bing looks away.

Ellen turns before leaving. "You come on over whenever you need a stout meal. I don't know how to cook for just one person."

"Mighty kind."

Ellen shoulders out the door and starts down the steps. "Don't be a stranger," she calls. "It's not easy to make new friends at our age."

Bing nods and closes the door, watching her cross the lawn and disappear out of sight. He grouses to the dog, "I'm not about to make friends with some woman."

RELIGION

Downstairs, Bing unpacks boxes, wondering why he bothered to tote that Jell-O mold or toothpick holder or chipped juice glass across seven states. He knows why. Barbara made lime Jell-O in that mold every Easter, rested her wedding ring in that toothpick holder while she washed dishes, kept that juice glass beside her bed for three decades.

He lifts out her King James Bible and flips through dog-eared pages with verses underlined in ink, notes scribbled in margins. He runs his fingertip across her elegant cursive trying to imagine her hand holding a pen over the very spot where his hand now rests. He flips to the front looking for the chart where Barbara chronicled the momentous events of their lives.

Marriage: <u>October 22, 1948 – Bingham Edward Butler and Barbara Susan Lacy</u>.

Birth: <u>September 9, 1950 – Roger Bingham Butler</u>.

Birth: <u>January 12, 1952 – Susan Lacy Butler</u>.

Baptism: <u>Roger Butler – April 28, 1962</u>.

Baptism: <u>Susan Butler –   </u>.

Bing looks at the line where his daughter's baptism date should be. Of course it's not there, even if from Susie's twelfth birthday on Barbara tried to turn her daughter's attention toward making that outward sign. Reminded Susie every Sunday for three solid years about the day Pastor Manning lifted her purified brother out of the water. Until one Sunday dinner when Susie screeched her kitchen chair back and shouted, "Will you shut up? I don't even know if there is a god." Barbara sat there, stunned, fork trembling, peas bouncing onto the floor.

Barbara did shut up, but he remembers the day they stood at the living room window watching Susie teach the neighbor girl who lived in that HUD house how to ride a bike. Susie's bike. How their daughter cheered when that runny-nosed child wobbled down the street, fists clenching the handlebars with the nylon streamers fluttering. Bing and Barbara stood and watched as Susie gave that girl her bike. Said she didn't use it anymore—a lie.

"God knows our Susie's heart," Barbara had said, tears streaming.

Bing thinks of his wife as a true Christian, knowing he can't really say the same about himself. He went to church more for her than for God, and because that's what God-fearing people did on Sunday mornings. But Barbara never missed a midweek service, or Tuesday-morning Bible study. Countless times she buttoned her coat after supper to go sit with an ailing friend.

But that was Barbara, and wouldn't she shake her head if she knew Bing had stopped attending church after she died. Not all at once, but gradually, missing a few Sundays here and there when he just didn't feel like fighting with his tie. He hated sitting in that hard pew without her beside him to jab his ribs if his head started bobbing. Hated the fellowship afterwards, all those Black Widders fetching him cups of bitter coffee, plates of store-bought pastry.

Bing rests his palm on his dead wife's Bible. He ought to give it to Susie. Keep it in the family even if she doesn't believe in God. There's no one else to give it to. This last thought makes him look once more at his family history tallied in ink. Marriages. Births. Baptisms. Deaths. Only one death recorded in a shaky pen, and Bing still can't look at it head-on. Bing is once again moved by his wife's strength. Certainly he couldn't have catalogued this particular grief. He hasn't even had the courage to add Barbara's name to that sad, sad list.

MEXICANS

That night Bing dons his best jumpsuit and sits at the kitchen table appraising the polished cabinets, gleaming stove, a surprising tidiness given Susie's aversion to housework.

A clattering on the stairs and Bing stands as Susie enters, Brian on her heels.

"Will you slow down?" she says.

Brian charges to the refrigerator, yanks open the door, and starts chugging Gatorade straight out of a jug.

Susie looks at Bing. "You ready?" She eyes his getup for so long he looks down to see if he missed a tobacco stain.

"Something wrong?" he says, arms out for inspection.

"No. It's just that I thought, for tonight, you might—"

"Oh," Bing says. "I didn't know this was a fancy restaurant."

"It's not fancy."

"'Cause I can put on my Sunday suit if you want."

"You look fine."

Bing looks at his grandson for confirmation.

Brian shrugs. "Okay by me. You look like a paratrooper."

"You *would* like that," Susie says, slopping dog food in a bowl and setting it on the floor. "I understand you had a visitor today," she says to Bing.

He pictures those Chinaman slippers. "Yep."

"Ellen's a wonderful person," Susie says. "We're all just crazy about her."

"Not all of us," Brian mumbles.

Bing squints at Susie, suddenly suspicious she's trying to palm her old man off on the Widder next door.

"Not my cup of tea," Bing says, nipping any such designs in the bud.

"How do you mean?" Susie's face is scrunched as if she's trying to elicit a particular answer.

"I mean, I'm sure she's a fine woman who a lot of other men would go for, but she's not, well, your mother."

"Thank God for that," Brian says.

"Stop it," Susie mutters.

Glen enters, adjusting his tie. He, too, looks Bing up and down, but before his lips part Susie says, "Let's just go." She heads for the front door yelling upstairs, "Come on, Reenie!"

A slow *stomp-stomp-stomp* of descending footsteps. Bing sees her boots first, four-inch rubber heels, shafts laced up her doughy calves. Army fatigues cut off at the knees. Motorcycle jacket. Straight hair black as an oil slick. And her face, a sweet face, really, round and smooth, like Barbara's, except for the pancake makeup and thick charcoal ringing her eyes.

Bing wants to take a washcloth to her and see if there's any hint of the five-year-old girl he and Barbara watched when Susie and Glen went to Europe. What a handful she was. Stubborn about brushing her teeth and bedtime and dragging that freckle-faced dolly with her everywhere. But there were soft moments, like the day Bing set up the rotating sprinkler out front and watched her jump over the horizontal spray circling the yard, holding onto her sopping dolly for all it was worth. How she looked at him every time—every time—to make sure he saw how well she cleared it. He did see, and every time—every time—he'd nod and say, "Real good, honey. That's real good." How her face glowed from the praise.

It's not glowing now, her eyes boring into his. "What the hell are you looking at?"

"Reenie," Susie says.

Reenie brushes by, squatting in front of Frida on her pillow to glide her hand down the dog's back. Frida lifts her head and Reenie wraps her hand loosely around the dog's muzzle, gently pumping it like a hand. "You're a flea-bitten varmint with no reason to live," she coos. Frida's docked tail thumps.

Bing sits shotgun. As they pull away from the curb he looks at hills to his right. Not undulating peaks and valleys as he expected, more like a fuzzy green wall, but there's enough height to bring down that penned-in feeling. He doesn't realize he's popping his knuckles until Glen says, "Is my driving making you nervous?"

Glen drives like an old woman. Heavy on the brake. Two seconds too long at stop signs. Downtown is generally contained within a four-by-ten-block area, three- and five-story buildings hugging the sidewalks. A couple of ten-stories thrown in to add credibility. Old movie theaters with marquees flashing. Jewelry and sports goods and hardware stores. Night clubs designed for younger people, a Moose Lodge that looks more Bing's speed. A smattering of pedestrians. Yuppies jaywalking to a sushi bar. A pack of teens skateboarding in a parking lot. *I could be mayor of this*, Bing thinks, recalling Dillard's last omen. "I'd vote for you," his friend had promised, "—twice."

They stop at a red light and Bing says, "Not much to it."

On the corner, a gaunt woman sits on a bench reading a tabloid magazine, skirt hiked up her crossed thighs, a sandal dangling from her jittery foot. An old man walks over and stoops in front of her to tie his shoes. *Probably trying to peek up her skirt*, Bing thinks. *Dirty old man.* The man lopes off and heads into an alley. Seconds later the woman walks in that direction, too.

It's one of those Mexican chain restaurants they even have back in Houston. Prefab adobe, plastic timbers poking out the sides. A neon Chihuahua on the sign with a tail that wags.

Inside, the hostess smiles, mouth jammed with so many teeth Bing can't stop staring. "Dr. Babcock!" she says when she spots Glen.

"Hello, Tracy. You still owe me a paper," he says, collapsing the girl's grin.

"How many in your party?" she says.

Some party, Bing thinks, glancing over at his grandchildren skulking around the waiting area. Susie with her arms clamped across her chest. Only Glen looks truly happy to be here.

"Five," he says.

"Right this way." They file after her like a chain gang, piped-in mariachi music strumming overhead, tables and booths crammed full of eaters jabbering and laughing, silverware clanking. Bing can hear Dillard's jibe: *How many hillbillies does it take . . .*

It's a round table for six, and Bing hangs back as the family jockeys for seats. Glen sits first, Susie beside him tugging Brian's sleeve so he'll sit on her other side. Reenie plops beside her brother so Bing sits beside Glen, an empty chair between himself and his granddaughter. He wishes for a wider demilitarized zone.

"Enjoy your meal," Tracy says, doling out menus before racing away. A waiter boy appears with chips and salsa. When he leaves, Bing leans in for a chip at exactly the same time as Reenie. His hand jerks back. "You first."

A waitress scuffs over, scribbling on her ordering pad. Her nametag reads: Sunny. By the slouch of her shoulders and the flat pitch of her voice, Bing doubts there is anything sunny about her. Susie orders sodas and Michelob Lights. Everyone looks at Bing who says, "I'll have me a Michelob, too."

Sunny grunts and hurries off. Susie opens a menu and points out dishes Bing might enjoy. He's too distracted by Brian shooting straw covers at light fixtures, Reenie rolling pieces of napkin into balls to flick into the salsa.

Sunny returns with the drinks and sits down in the vacant seat beside Bing. "What do you all want?" Susie rattles everything off, Sunny writing furiously, punctuating the litany with, "Uh-huh, yeah, uh-huh." When Susie is finished, Sunny leaves without a nod or a smile.

"Not exactly what you'd call friendly," Bing says. A sudden image of Janey, his favorite waitress back home, flashing that gum-cracking smile. And oh, that sweet sashay. Sunny has no sashay at all.

"Shall we have a toast?" Glen says, holding up his beer. Nobody moves, so he urges, "Come on."

Brian hoists his soda. "What to?"

"To Grandpa Bing."

"Oh," Bing says, adding his bottle to the mix.

Susie brings hers up next.

"To new beginnings. And one big, happy family. Come on, Reenie," Glen says to his daughter who has not joined in the fun, if that's what this is.

"Reenie," Glen says. "You've hardly given your grandfather two syllables since he's been here."

"She gave me a little more than that," Bing blurts, surprising even himself at this shit-slippered nod.

"What's that?" Susie says. "What did Reenie give you?"

Reenie's cheeks puff out and she looks at Bing, eyes round.

Bing isn't inclined to squeal. "Reenie gave me her room."

Reenie's cheeks deflate.

Brian bolsters his right hand with his left. "My arm's getting tired."

Reenie pushes her drink to the middle of the table.

"Close enough," Glen says, clinking glasses.

Susie starts talking to Glen about tune-ups for the cars. Glen yanks a weekly planner from his shirt pocket, and Susie pulls its twin from her purse.

As Susie lists upcoming obligations, Brian's hand snakes toward her beer, fingers grazing the bottle, then incrementally drawing it to him. Bing looks at Susie and realizes her eyes aren't on her calendar, but on Brian's covert operation. She actually smiles as Brian slides the bottle from the table and turns away to take a big gulp. Reenie slips her hand under her armrest for her turn and just after the smooth transfer, Susie yells, "Hey, you two, that's enough." She grabs the bottle from Reenie.

Reenie slouches back in her chair, one arm drawn to her chest like she's holding an invisible something, a freckle-faced dolly, maybe, and suddenly Reenie is very much that five-year-old child who just cleared the sprinkler and is begging for someone to shout, *I see you, honey. I see.*

Bing hears a construction-worker catcall, over and over. Reenie pulls a cell phone from her pocket, flips it open, and says, "Help me."

Susie snaps a chip in two. "Junior."

Two servers approach with trays of food. "The plate is hot," one of them says, setting before Bing a cast-iron skillet loaded with refried beans and rice, a taco, a chalupa, and a dollop of the greenest guacamole he's ever seen. He tastes it, and it's tangy, like it spent too much time in a can.

Glen says, "Reenie, it's time to eat now. Say good-bye."

Reenie doesn't hang up, so Glen says it again, "Reenie, say good-bye."

Of course she doesn't, and Susie says, "Just, never mind."

They all dive in, fork tines screeching across plates, ice settling in water glasses, the chatter of distant families: husbands ordering for their wives in that syllable-expanding drawl, mothers pacifying babies. A nostalgic feeling washes over Bing, as if he's just settling into his favorite rocker, or slipping into a pair of broken-in boots.

"Bing!" Glen says, pulling Bing out of his reverie.

"What's that?" Bing says.

"Brian asked you a question."

"Oh!" he says, looking at his grandson.

"What did you do during the war?"

It's a glorious inquiry. "I was in the Navy. South Pacific."

"I know that," Brian says, "but what did you do?"

"I was a welder, son. And mechanic. Kept the fleet afloat."

"Cool," Brian says. "I bet those engines were something."

"They were," Bing says. "Humbling, too."

"Did you ever fire a torpedo?"

Bing sucks in a lungful to deliver his exploits, but Susie cuts him off, eyes flaring. "Grandpa doesn't want to go into all that."

"I wasn't asking about Roger," Brian says.

Susie grunts. "No war talk today."

"I don't mind," Bing says, lungs still at the ready.

Brian says, "But I just wanted to—"

Susie dings her fork against her beer bottle: *tink-tink-tink-tink*. "I know what you're up to, so you can stop it right now."

"What am I up to?" Brian asks.

Bing doesn't know what anyone is up to, but apparently Susie is raring to explain, and with a jolt she's rattling on about President Bush, and puppet master Cheney, and "Don't be so gullible, Brian!" Brian retorts with national security and weapons of mass destruction and protecting our interests—phrases Bing's been hearing from White House press conferences but never expected to spill from his grandson's mouth.

Bing's head is boggled since all he really wanted to say was that working on a ship engine was the closest thing to reverence he ever experienced, a kind of prayer. But Susie and Brian are far from that, waging their own war that's getting more and more explosive. People are beginning to stare. Glen tries to intercede, weave words into the few empty slots available: "Now—you—two—listen—" They don't listen and Glen's face just burns, but not as red as Susie's, not as veiny as Brian's. Reenie, however, sits perfectly poised wearing a grin that collapses only when she mutters into the phone before holding it up for Junior to listen.

Bing's heart rate increases along with the family's volume. Fighting is bad enough in the privacy of one's home, but in public. All he wants to do is get away from them and the rapt eyes of neighboring diners who might as well be at the circus. Bing is not on anyone's radar, so he eases his chair back, stands, and ambles off.

He bumps into Sunny, pencil gritted between her teeth.

"Where's the toilet?" he asks.

She points over her shoulder and grunts, "Aown na all," pencil in her teeth wobbling.

He follows her finger until he's knocked off course by a chorus of harried waiters yelling: "*HAPPY HAPPY BIRTHDAY! HAPPY BIRTHDAY TO YOU!*" at a little boy wearing a tourist sombrero, brim decorated with silver sequins and MEXICO spelled out in yarn. The boy's hands are cupped over his ears and his chin is puckered.

"'Scuse me, pardon me, sorry," Bing says, backing away, wanting to protect his own ears from the mean singing. He bumps his head against a parrot piñata. When he bats it away, he sees a hall and hopes it leads to the can.

What he finds is the kitchen, swinging door propped open by a five-gallon bucket of jalapeños. He turns to leave when he hears a familiar something that stops him. Inside, hair-netted and aproned, are half a dozen men, dark hair, dark skin, all speaking Spanish, glugging picante sauce from plastic jugs into bowl after bowl. Slopping spoonfuls of refried beans onto ceramic plates. Grilling onions and peppers, strips of chicken and steak. Smoke rising. Spatulas flying. Knives chopping.

Bing forgets where he is, how he got here. I-10? 610 Loop? FM 1960?—all Houston arteries, but no. *This can't be right. I moved. I'm gone.* One of the men tips his head back to laugh, and it makes Bing's eyes sting. *Damn onions.*

Behind him, in the dining room, another stanza of "*HAPPY HAPPY BIRTHDAY!*" threatens to yank him away from Texas for good. But he's not ready for that, so he'll just pause outside this door for a minute. Or two. Maybe three. That's all he needs, to just stand right there, close his eyes and listen to the melodic chatter, the full-throated vowels, the rhythmic rolling of Rs that will quiet his buzzing head, calm his thunking, thunking chest.

METH LABS

At home, Bing slips out back for his bedtime chaw. The porch looks out over a grassy rectangle penned in by a privacy fence. Flower beds run along the bottom where overgrown mums droop into the grass. Two Bradford pears shiver in the breeze. A window screeches open on the side of the house, up high. Bing leans over the railing, neck craned awkwardly as he peers up at a shadowy pair tipped out of the third floor window: Reenie and, presumably, Junior. It's difficult to make out his features, but he is a big fella. Bing feels like a snoop, but needs to find out what other pranks they have in store. Reenie strikes a match and holds it to a cigarette. Soon the smell of sulfur and something else, something burnt, but it's not tobacco. Bing sniffs and recognizes that sharp sting as the same one that wafted from beneath Susie's door decades back.

They're smoking the marijuana! He wonders if he should run and tell Susie but decides against it. *Don't make waves.* And besides, Susie may be their supplier.

Junior fans his hands in front of his face. "Why do you smoke that shit?"

"Because I like it."

"Your body is a temple, you know."

"A temple of *luv*," Reenie says. "Our anniversary is next week. Guess what I got you?"

Junior shrugs those meaty shoulders. "No idea."

Bing can only imagine what kinds of presents his grand-daughter might buy. Bag of razor blades. Semiautomatic weapons.

"What do you want?" Junior asks.

"You know."

Junior shakes his head. "We can't do that."

"But I am *so* ready."

"We promised your mom we wouldn't. And Ellen."

Wouldn't what? Bing wants to know. What is Reenie ready for? The word *sex* pops in his brain, but he doubts they waited more than two seconds for that.

"So what," Reenie says. "I'm nineteen. I can do anything I want."

"Anything but that."

Bing tries to envision what underworld scheme she has in mind, what other illegal paraphernalia she's got hidden up in that attic. A methamphetamine lab, maybe. Something that could get Bing arrested if the police showed up. Or worse, could explode, catch the whole house on fire with him trapped in the basement.

A sudden, smoldering image of himself trying to get out in all that smoke, coughing-gasping-gagging as he bumps his way upstairs, hand over his mouth, unable to see as he reaches the kitchen, the hall that leads to the front door, but the smoke is too thick and he goes down like a sack of bricks, tries to pull himself along those hardwood floors, all that flammable wood, inching along, overcome by exhaustion and fumes until he finally blacks out and succumbs.

When the firemen arrive and ax through the door, they will find him in a heap, clothes steaming. "So close," they will say, shaking their heads at the pitiable half a foot Bing just could not cross. Beside him, Frida, a deflated lump, front paws stretched out as she tried, unsuccessfully, to make it that last six inches, too.

DECOMMISSIONED

The following Sunday Bing heads upstairs hoping for pancakes and bacon. No such luck. He looks longingly at the empty coffee carafe. He'd just learned to make a decent pot back home, and now he figures he'll have to start over—if they even want him fooling with their small appliances. He's not in the mood for cereal, so he opens the cabinet under the sink to find not just one box of MoonPies, but two. A sticky note slapped on top reads: HELP YOURSELF. Bing spins around to see if he's being spied on, but no one is there.

He heads out front with his Skoal, amazed that he now lives in a houseful of people not the least bit sheepish about missing church. Bing feels a twinge of the same concern Barbara shouldered about who would introduce the grandchildren to Jesus.

On the porch swing, Bing watches Ellen Foley's front door open, and out she comes with a Tupperware container in one hand, Bible in the other. Bing hopes she doesn't see him in his pajamas and wild morning hair, isn't on her way over to deliver a Black Widder breakfast. But she turns the other way and starts walking down the street. Silver braid now coiled on top of her head. He scrutinizes that Tupperware, imagining honey buns inside, maybe fried apples.

A man jogs by her and waves. It's Glen puffing up to the house wearing the skimpiest shorts Bing's ever seen on a man, mesh tank top exposing a furry chest. Glen slows to a trot, grinds circles in the yard, and finally leans against the front of Bing's car to stretch his legs. The Olds looks so pitiful tucked up in the driveway like that.

Neglected. Hasn't been driven since Glen took the U-Haul back days ago.

"You a racer?" Bing says, trying not to stare at his son-in-law's ridiculous outfit, trying not to take offense that his automobile is being used as a leaning post.

"I run five miles a day," Glen huffs, sweat dripping off his chin.

"You in training for something?" Bing asks, figuring any man who would put his body through that must be out for a medal.

"Just trying to avoid a heart attack," Glen says, flicking a bug off of Bing's headlight. "You know something about that."

Bing considers his quadruple bypass. He wonders what he might have done as a younger man to avoid it. Certainly not run up and down the block with his manly equipment jangling around for all the world to see.

Glen starts picking at squished insects spackling Bing's bumper, his hood, a Monarch butterfly wedged in his grill. He grabs a stick to pry the wing loose, and Bing feels oddly possessive; those are his butterfly parts, after all. His bugs.

"How about I wash your car this morning?" Glen says.

"You don't have to do that," Bing says, wondering what kind of person would violate a man's automotive space so early in the day.

"It's no trouble. In fact I'll do it right now."

Bing opens his mouth, but Glen gallops down the driveway toward the back of the house.

Bing spies the morning paper wedged in the bushes. He'd better rescue it before his son-in-law decides to scrub it down, too. Glen comes back dragging a hose in one hand, bucket in the other. He starts spraying down the car and Bing backs up to avoid the cool mist.

"Easy, there," Bing says, alarmed at his son-in-law's rough rinsing.

"What's that?" Glen calls over the jetting stream.

Bing starts to shout but decides Glen is no longer listening. Bing inches up the steps, uncomfortable watching Glen bend and stretch, shorts riding up precariously.

Inside, Susie grades a stack of papers at the kitchen table, coffee mug, red pencils, eraser hunks scattered before her. She glances over her reading glasses as Bing enters.

"Morning," she says.

Bing points over his shoulder. "Glen's washing my car."

"He'll do that." She scribbles on one of those essays. "He's a little nutty about finding dirty dishes around the house, too."

"Noted." Bing pours himself coffee and hears footsteps thundering overhead, voices bickering, though he can't make out words. Reenie and Brian lobbing grenades at each other, probably over the same trivial crap Susie and Roger fought over: not refilling the toilet paper roll, using up the toothpaste. But it wasn't all trivial.

Bing is sucked back to that one blistering battle he stumbled into. Would have been much better if he'd walked past it. But he didn't. Just marched like a soldier straight into the living room where Susie huffed her onslaught rife with cuss words and pleas at Roger in his new military haircut; then at Bing, who kept tapping his watch, warning Roger that if he didn't leave soon he'd miss the transport. But Susie would not ease up with her antiwar blabberings, and finally her utterly impossible plan—didn't she see that? How ridiculous the idea was? Running south of the border like a yellow-bellied baboon? And Bing's veteran retorts that all began with: *No son of mine . . .*

Bing didn't walk past the skirmish then, but he can sidestep it now, a tactic he's been practicing for the last thirty years. He sits across from Susie, watching her eyes scan from left to right. Bing crooks his neck to read the paper's title: *Female Textile Workers in Appalachia.*

Susie scribbles notes in the margins about issues he knows nothing about to students who, however young, already have more education than Bing ever will. "Female Textile Workers in Appalachia," he says, to prove he can have an intelligent conversation.

"What's that?" Susie says, not looking up.

Bing nods at the paper. "Female Tex—"

"Oh. Yeah. Poor women."

Bing wants to ask: *Poor how?* but decides against it in case her answer is: *Because male textile workers make fifty cents more an hour.* Years ago Bing would have rebutted with something like: *But they might have five kids to support.* Today he doesn't say one word. He's curious about what other liberal stances she is force-feeding her students. If it's gotten her in trouble with her boss.

"You still like your job?"

"I love the students. Don't like the politics or the teaching load." Her head tips back to her work.

"Glen still like his job?"

Susie makes a face as if she just had a Band-Aid yanked from her knee. "More and more every day."

Bing wishes he could decode what that means.

Susie takes a deep breath and hunkers back over her papers.

"So when do you figure on retiring?"

A loud exhale. "No idea. Have to get the kids through college first. Of course it would have been a lot sooner if Reenie . . ."

Had taken that scholarship, Bing finishes, even if Susie cannot.

Susie takes off her glasses and looks fully at him. "Dad?"

"Yes," he says, leaning in.

"I have thirty-two papers to grade by tomorrow. Could we talk about this another time?"

"Oh," he says. "I don't mean to bother you."

"You're not bothering me, but, you know," she nods at the volume of papers.

"You have your work." He scrapes his chair back to stand.

"Thanks," Susie says, already sliding on her glasses. "And Dad, don't leave your chaw cans on the front porch. Draws ants."

"Oh. Sure. No problem." Bing walks to the basement steps, but before he heads down he holds up his coffee. "I'll bring the cup up when I'm done. Wouldn't want to upset Glen."

If Susie hears him, she doesn't let on.

Downstairs, Bing sits in his easy chair flipping TV channels where fifteen different flavors of televangelists thump Bibles, demanding repentance and a Visa card. When Bing can't take any more, he turns it off and listens to the unbelievable silence in this house— every bit as quiet as his house back home. Maybe more so. It's not even noon, and the day stretches out like a long empty hall. No windows to open, no doors. Certainly no doorbells. If Dillard were here . . . For the first time Bing looks at the phone on the end table and considers using it. He reaches over, hand hovering, wondering if he should yell upstairs to ask permission, to ask about long distance carriers or time zones. "Hell with it," he says, grabbing the phone, fingers dialing. It starts ringing, and Bing pictures miles and miles of black wire stretching from pole to pole across the country all the way to the avocado wall phone in Dillard's kitchen.

"Hello?"

"Dillard!"

"Bing! You old buzzard. You made it."

"Sure I did."

"Hot damn! Shorty and the boys owe me five bucks apiece. I *told* them you'd make it up there alive."

Bing tells him about the terrain he crossed, the crazy drivers, Mammoth Cave—not the getting lost part. But he doesn't want to talk about that. He wants to talk about Texas, about the weather down there, the new people who moved into his house. "They keeping up the yard?"

"Heck yeah," Dillard says. "That boy Alan—he's bigger than a John Deere."

"Isn't he though?"

"Been here a week and he's already cleared out all that dead brush in the back. Hauled off that pile of bricks and wood scraps."

"I was always meaning to do that." A sudden buzzing in Bing's ear.

"And his missus, Milly, or Tilly, painted up the shutters real nice, and the mailbox. And that boy has a riding lawn mower. Can you beat that? For a postage-stamp yard like yours? He cut his grass and mine yesterday in fifteen minutes and wouldn't take a dime, not even for gas."

"What'd he go and do a thing like that for?"

"Just being neighborly, he said. Probably because I'm old, but I don't care. Long as I get my lawn cut for free."

The buzzing in Bing's ear grows louder—and it's not from the phone. "Didn't run over Barbara's verbena, did he? Or her primrose."

"No, no. In fact the wife mulched everything up real good. Tore out all the weeds. Plugged up the holes with the sweetest red flowers you ever saw. Shoot, if I'd known they was moving in, I'd a kicked you out a long time ago."

Bing forces out a weak *ha-ha*, pinky reaming his ear to clear out the incessant *bzzzzz*.

"That boy's a doer, I tell you. He and six of his buddies tore off your old porch and already slapped on a new one."

"My porch?"

"Well that old thing was about to tip—"

"They tore off my porch?"

A thick pause until Dillard clears his throat. When he finally speaks, his words rush together. "That old porch of yours was a fine one, you bet. Lasted over fifty years. The one these boys nailed up won't last ten minutes. Count on it. Cheap lumber. Young people these days don't know a thing about craftsmanship. Not like you."

"That's right."

Another pause until Dillard says, "So what's it like up there? Bad as you thought?"

"It's all right."

"I bet you're not getting a minute's peace. A handy man like you around, they must be after you every second to put new washers in the faucets or unclog sinks."

Bing pictures Glen scrubbing down the Olds outside, Susie intently grading papers.

"And those kids are probably running all over top of you. Fighting over the last pork chop. Squeezing you off the sofa while you're trying to watch TV."

The kids battling away upstairs, completely oblivious to the old man now holed up in their basement, just trying to keep his head down.

NIPS, GOOKS, RAGHEADS

The next few weeks are filled with flimsy newspapers and dog walks, an accumulation of poop bags and spittoons. More Montel and Jenny Jones than Bing's ever watched in his life. Polite vegetarian suppers with Glen and Susie where more topics are avoided than discussed, which means they eat in a strained silence that usually ends with Glen pushing away from the table saying, "I'm going for a run," or "I left something at the office."

One morning, however, when the house should be empty, Bing hears a series of explosions upstairs. "Meth lab!" he yells, rushing up to the second floor, sniffing for smoke, about to head for the attic when he determines that the noise isn't coming from Reenie's room, but Brian's. Through the open door he sees his grandson hunched over a computer screen, fingers working joysticks and buttons, sounds of bombs detonating from the speakers.

"What'cha doing there?" Bing leans into the room, resisting the urge to ask, *Shouldn't you be in school?*

Brian nods toward his computer screen where two fighter planes are engaged in a dog fight. "You play?"

"Naw," Bing says, "but you go ahead."

Crazy sound effects of gun fire and engine roar fill the room. Bing inches forward to analyze the planes' silhouettes. He identifies the Iraqi enemy in a Russian MiG; the hero is in an F-14 Tomcat—*he's a Navy man.* The next thing Bing knows he's inside the F-14's animated cockpit, and Brian knows what every switch and button and light is for, the dizzying blur of analog numbers flashing on the screen. He trails the MiG with precision, though his opponent is cagey, full of quick maneuvers and dives. Brian stays on his tail, finally lining up his crosshairs to fire. *Direct hit!* Bing feels a rippling thrill in his gut when the plane explodes into a fiery ball that plunges into the desert below, a plume of black smoke swirling up.

But the game isn't over, and Brian skillfully sends MiGs and Mirages spiraling into sand dunes and smoking oil fields. With each fatality Brian shouts, "Die, raghead!" reminding Bing of his own war-time epithets: Krauts. Eye-Ties. Yella-bellied, slant-eyed, slope-headed Nips. Crude labels Barbara didn't like hearing any more than the Vietnam libels he dragged home from Dillard's: Dog-eatin, shit-burning, dinky dau, gooks.

Finally Brian rests his hands in his lap.

"That's a pretty high-tech game," Bing says.

"I've got to get better," Brian says, mostly to himself.

"You in some kind of tournament?"

"Not exactly," Brian says. "More like training."

"Training for what?"

Brian twists around in his chair and looks up, picks at a pimple on the side of his tender neck. "So how's it feel to be a war hero?"

"Oh, I wasn't a hero. But I knew a lot of men who were."

"I bet you did."

Without permission Bing lowers himself onto the end of Brian's bed. He rubs his knees as if he's wiping off layers of dust that have settled over his memories of the war, trying to polish them up before hoisting them to the surface.

"Spent most of my stint on floating dry docks in the Pacific—Admiral Nimitz's secret weapons. You know what a dry dock is?"

"Sure do," Brian says, chin jutting.

The focus in Brian's eyes, his alert body lingo, tells Bing it's all right to continue. He describes how dry docks were positioned in forward areas close enough to enemy territory and battles so crippled battleships could limp in or be towed. He tries to put words to the fierce sight of holes blown in their sides, hulls ripped off like a giant, cruel hand had reached down and gouged out indiscriminate chunks. How it was Bing's job—along with hundreds of others—to perform temporary patch-ups so the ships could make it to land-based dry docks for more permanent repairs before redeployment.

"Like a MASH unit for ships," Brian says. "You were like surgeons."

Bing snorts at this analogy, but he approves because the ships were like live things, and it was the mechanics' and welders' and electricians' duties to stop the bleeding, get the heart pumping, suture lacerations with torches and solder instead of needles and catgut.

"Dr. Bing," he says, laughing. The laughter is cut short because there were times when they found human remains amidst the twisted metal: a foot, an arm, a finger, and he would try to reconstruct the man from that one piece. Give him height and weight and hair color. A home in the States. A family. Bing looks at his own hand, his finger, wondering how a person might reconstruct him if they found just that thumb, that pinky.

"What'd you think about 9/11?" Brian asks.

Bing is sucked up half a century to a different kind of horror. "A terrible day for our country," he says, because that's what he's been saying since it happened. "Worse than Pearl Harbor, in my view. All those civilians. Cowardly act, if you ask me."

"I think so, too." Brian's eyes are aimed over Bing's shoulder. He turns to see a bulletin board on Brian's wall, four by five feet, at least. Bing stands for a better view of this 9/11 shrine: newspaper headlines and columns and photos of rescue workers, candlelight vigils and flags at half-staff. There's the charred field in Pennsylvania; the Pentagon with a ragged wound in one side; one of the Trade Center towers frozen in midattack, a jetliner plunged halfway into it. Beside it, the other tower, upper floors engulfed in smoke and flames, colored specks of something trickling down. Bing rubs his hand over it to clear off the specks, the dust, until he realizes it isn't dust at all, but people, stock brokers and law clerks and delivery men and cleaning ladies who just couldn't hold on any more, who could no longer suffer the heat, and he wonders what they were thinking as they plummeted, or if they were thinking at all.

"In all my life I never thought I'd see this," Bing whispers, his throat aching.

From behind him Brian says, "Somebody's got to do something."

Bing only nods, because he doesn't trust what might come out if he opens his mouth.

There is a hushed silence between them. A shared moment of reverence between grandfather and grandson who have both had their senses of security yanked out from beneath them—twice, Bing adds, for himself at least. Pearl Harbor and September 11th. But there were other losses that rattled his very core. He looks up at the ceiling wondering where God was in it all. Then he looks at his grandson, so young, wondering what cruelties await him.

TEX

A week later, as Susie prepares to go to work, she says, "The house-keeper is coming at eleven."

Bing chokes on his toast. "The what?"

"I have a cleaning service once a month."

"That must cost a pretty penny."

"Worth every cent. I sure don't have time, and even if I worked like a dog, I'd never keep it as spotless as Glen likes."

I'm not a dog, Bing hears Barbara's wounded voice. It was a Saturday morning, one of many Saturdays when Susie had to help vacuum and dust, change sheets, pick up Roger's room. Bing stood in the hall the day Susie finally ground her back molars and seethed, "From now on Roger can clean his own damn mess."

"But that's our job," Barbara had said, totally unflapped by the profanity. "Someday you'll have your own family to clean up after."

Boy didn't that send the Pledge can flying. "I'm not giving up my life for this." Susie jabbed a finger toward Bing. "Obeying that man's every command. He treats you like a dog, Mom. Like a stupid dog."

"Now hold on," Bing had said.

Susie stomped off too fast to endure the scolding, to even notice the pained expression her mean words had carved into her mother's face. Cheeks flushing, Barbara said to the plaster ceiling, "I'm proud of my house."

Bing walked up beside her. "You should be."

"I love what I do." Her head went down, and she whispered to the floor, "I'm not a dog."

"I hired a gal for your mother one time," Bing feels compelled to say now.

Susie pours coffee into a to-go cup. "You did?"

"When she sprained her ankle that time. Course you were already gone."

"She never told me that."

"She wouldn't. That girl quit after one day. Your mother wouldn't let her be. Just hobbled around after her all morning squawking, "The dishes don't go in the drying rack that way," and "Wash the whites first in case the colors streak up the machine." Nothing that child did pleased your mother."

"Doesn't surprise me one bit," Susie says, heading out.

Bing sits in the living room with his hands on his knees waiting for the cleaning girl. Frida is on her pillow, dreaming, lips fluttering. Bing pulls nail clippers from his pocket and snips off cuticles and hangnails, stands to dust the skin slivers from his belly. They float down and speckle the hardwood floor. "Shit," he says, pushing them around with his foot. He almost nudges them under the Oriental rug, but decides against it. *Give the maid something to sweep.*

There's a loud knocking, and when Bing opens the door it's the cleaning lady, all right, equipped with a mop and a bucket filled with spray cans and scrub brushes. The woman is older than Bing expected. Sixty, maybe, skin leathery as if she spent too much time in the sun. Peppered hair cut in a no-nonsense style. She looks at Bing's boots. "You must be Mr. Butler."

"That's me," he says, stepping aside.

She still won't look at his face. "I'm Aldine," she says as she passes. She slips off her jacket, and underneath she's wearing a white smock with *Antonio's Bakery* embroidered on the breast pocket.

"I'll take a coconut cream pie," Bing says.

Aldine peeks at him. "What?"

"Your shirt." Bing points at the red stitching but withdraws his hand when he realizes he's also pointing at her boob.

"Oh." She looks down. "I forgot." She peels off the smock and underneath is a yellow t-shirt that reads: *Old Maids*.

"You work two jobs?"

"Just finished over at the bakery."

"Aren't you tired?"

"No more than usual. This is nothing like doing twelve hours of piece work at Corbin's."

"Corbin's?"

"You know, where they make those fancy suits. I cut fabric for thirty-four years before the place shut down." She clucks her cheek. "Decent money, too."

Bing wonders why any woman her age has to work that hard. He feels suddenly guilty about the pile of nail clippings. He looks at the room through her eyes, opulent compared to where she must live. A trailer, maybe. One of those tar paper lean-tos he saw on the drive in.

"You want a cup of coffee?" he offers, immediately regretful since that may be inappropriate with the hired help. Plus he still hasn't figured out how to use the fancy Bunn machine. Maybe Aldine knows.

"I'd just as soon get started."

"Oh. Sure."

"I like to do the upstairs first." She heads toward the steps.

"Okay by me. I'll just—" but she's already halfway gone.

Bing can't relax knowing there's a strange woman in the house cleaning up after his daughter, her children. He can't imagine what Dillard would think. Bing paces from the kitchen to the living room, Frida's eyes following him back and forth, back and forth. He hears the scritch-scritch of toilets being scrubbed, smells the Sani-Flush even down in the kitchen. There goes the vacuum grinding from wood to carpet to wood. Mattresses creaking as beds are being made. *This is stupid*, he thinks as he stands there listening to a woman cleaning when he heard these very noises a million times back home. If Barbara got paid for all the house-work she did, he could have retired a wealthy man. He senses there is a flaw in that reasoning but doesn't bother to find it.

Instead he sits in the living room trying to read the *Lonesome Dove* novel Glen bought him. Aldine comes down with her fur-niture polish and rag. She starts spraying and wiping, and Bing watches her lift every pricey knickknack and bauble and swipe underneath. *That doodad could probably buy a month's worth of groceries.*

"This is the biggest house I ever lived in in my life." For some reason Bing wants her to know this.

"That right?"

"My old place back home wasn't nothin' but a shack."

"Your daughter has a lot of nice things." Aldine wipes a hunk of jade carved into a fish.

"A little royal for my blue-collar blood," Bing says, to commiserate. He waits for her to add something like: *But I wouldn't swap it for my granddaddy's cabin where we drink rain water and raise chickens.*

What she says is, "I'd move in here in a New York minute."

Bing's head jerks back.

"My husband liked that *Lonesome Dove* miniseries an awful lot. You see it?"

"Can't say as I did." Normally Bing wouldn't follow up, but something about this woman's predicament, her outlook, makes him ask, "What's your husband do?"

"He's on disability." She kneels to smooth out the fringe on one of those Oriental rugs. "Broke his neck in '74 and hasn't walked since."

Bing can't quite register what he just heard. She said it so matter of fact. "Coal mining accident?"

"Wayne worked for the railroad."

"I'm sorry," Bing says, waiting for her to look up so he can offer a heartfelt nod.

"These things happen." She's still lining up that fringe.

He knows these things happen, just like they happened to that kid in the Navy who got his leg all mangled. Or that foreman at the plant who got knocked in the head by an I-beam—didn't have the sense of a five-year-old after that. And Ralph Mason, Ralphie Boy, who welded too close to a buried gas tank and it blew up—just blew, leaving him nearly unrecognizable and missing both hands, but at least he was alive. That's what Bing told him in the hospital. "Least you're alive."

"Been better if I was dead," Ralph had said. "So Marge and the boys could get some insurance money." Bing had nodded. He understood that line of thinking, completely.

"Must be tough on you," he says to Aldine.

She pumps her shoulder. "That's life."

"Yeah, but it's a real pity—"

Aldine's head snaps up, and for the first time she looks at him full-faced. He has no problem decoding the fiery message in her eyes. *I don't need your pity, or want it.*

At noon, Bing leashes Frida up for her walk. They saunter down the block, and for once Bing doesn't urge. He's not anxious to get back to Aldine's furious cleaning, her sad-sad plight. He decides that today he'll expand his perimeters. He registers signposts and lawn ornaments to help him find his way back, taking rights and lefts into a neighborhood less tidy than Susie's with potholes in the street, dented cars lining the curbs. Houses with boarded-up windows, refrigerators on the front porch. *This*, he thinks, nodding at an Appalachian vision that finally lines up. *Now this.*

Frida paws a hardened pile of crap—obviously from a much larger dog. "In your dreams," Bing says. He hears a whir approaching and looks up to see two colored boys on bikes racing toward him on the sidewalk, nylon jackets ballooning out behind them. Bing clamps his hand over his wallet and steps into the street to avoid them. Frida snarls and snaps as they pass. Bing looks to see if some shop owner is in pursuit yelling, *Stop! Thieves!*

No one is there, so Bing moves on, hand still over his wallet as he works his way to the end of the block where he sees a nugget of heaven. A bar. Neon Budweiser sign flickering in the window. Green, striped awning announcing *Stew's Place*. Bing pictures a jar of pickled eggs on the counter. Bowls of pork rinds or peanuts. His throat gets achy, yearning for a cold one. Dog or no dog, it doesn't occur to Bing to go in. He is a slow mover. Back in Texas, Bing wouldn't set foot in a new restaurant until he circled it for weeks in his car, assessed the clientele, collected reviews from brave souls who had gone before.

The bar door opens, and a gangly man steps out and squints into the sky, a fringe of tidy bangs dusting his eyebrows. He jams his hands in his pockets, lopes off without looking, and bumps into Bing.

"'Scuse me," the man says, backing up a step. "Didn't see you there, buddy."

"No harm," Bing says.

The man looks down at Frida. "That's one old dog."

Bing nods, embarrassed to be tethered to a cocker spaniel. He always featured himself as a bluetick man.

"It's my daughter's dog." Bing decides to accelerate his fact finding and tips his chin toward the bar. "They got darts in there?" The man scratches his chin, and Bing reckons him to be in his thirties. *Wonder why he's not at work?*

"No darts," the man says. "They got cherry machines. And Keno. That's my game." The man pulls out a stack of folded Keno sheets. "Didn't collect shit today, but yesterday I won fifty bucks."

"That right." Bing tries not to let on that he knows very little about cherry machines or Keno. Drinking a beer or two is one thing, but gambling, well.

"And they got Regina in there."

"Regina?"

"Oooohhhh yeah. Reginaaaa. Do yourself a favor and go on in and have a look."

Bing looks down at Frida, relieved. "I can't. I've got the dog."

"Hell, Regina don't mind no dog. People's brought in dogs before. And cockatiels. One fella brought in a dang monkey, I swear to god. Meanest thing I ever seen in my life."

"Naw," Bing says. "A monkey?"

"You bet. So one dog ain't gonna throw her." He pushes up his flannel sleeve and looks at his watch. "Hell, I'm already late, what's another fifteen minutes. Come on in and I'll introduce you."

"That's all right. I don't really have—"

"It's no trouble," the man says, already opening the door, making kissy sounds so Frida will follow, which she does. Bing tries to hold her back as he fumbles for an excuse. But it's too late, he's already halfway through the door, stomach knotting.

"Just can't stay away, huh Ricky? Oh. Whose puppy dog?" A clicking of heels and it takes Bing's eyes a minute to adjust to the dimness so he can see the meaty blonde edging out from behind the bar.

Frida growls and Bing offers a warning. "She's not what you'd call friendly."

"Dogs love me," Regina says, at least he assumes she's Regina by the way Ricky ogles the cleavage spilling out as she leans over the dog. Bing steals a peek, too.

Of course Frida snaps, but Regina draws her hand back too quick. "You bitch," she says, smirking. "Gotta respect that." She looks up at Bing. "You want some water?"

"Water?" He wonders why any barmaid would offer him that.

"For your dog."

"Oh. I guess she could use a drink." Regardless of the hour, Bing decides he might as well imbibe, too. "I'll take a Lone Star."

"Don't carry that one," Regina says. "We got Corona."

Bing tugs his earlobe, the bristly hairs that need a good trimming, wondering what kind of establishment doesn't carry Lone Star until he remembers where he is. Where he isn't. "You got Pabst?"

"Sure thing," Regina says.

"A PBR man," Ricky says. "Make it two, baby doll."

Regina hands Bing a bowl, and he sets it on the floor where Frida begins lapping, water flying out the sides of her mouth. He imagines this is the first time she's been in a bar, and he feels guilty.

Ricky sits at the bar, so Bing sits, too, leaving one stool between them—the gentlemanly distance. A bell sounds to his left, a steady *ding-ding-ding* drawing Bing's attention to a shriveled woman in a jogging suit slumped before a slot machine. It's mesmerizing, and Bing stares at the rows of black bars and cherries. It's like trying not to look at those racy MTV girl videos he stumbles across from time to time. He leans in for a better view, looks for the infamous handle, *one-armed bandit*, wishing Dillard were here to see this. There is no handle; the woman presses a button, which sets the rows of bars and cherries spinning until they finally stop: single bar, cherries, double bar. "Shit," the woman says, before punching the button again.

"Here you go." Regina sets a bottle before Bing, another before Ricky.

Both men take long pulls from their beers. Ricky sets his down first, half empty. Bing takes two extra gulps to measure up.

"So where you from with that accent?" Ricky asks.

"Accent?"

"Yeah," Regina says. "You're not from around here, that's for sure."

Bing is astounded to discover that in these parts he's the one with the accent. "I'm from Texas."

"Texas." Ricky looks Bing up and down. "Where's your cowboy hat?" He snorts. "And giant silver belt buckle?"

"Not everybody in—"

"Your name Bubba?" Ricky slaps his thigh.

Regina rolls her eyes. "Ricky, leave the man alone."

Ricky polishes off his beer and slams the bottle down. "I bet you seen your share of illegals down there."

"One or two—million," Bing says, and this cracks Ricky up.

"That's a good one," he says. "Regina, bring this man another beer, on me."

Regina squints at Ricky who studies his knuckles.

"Much obliged," Bing says, finishing his beer in faster time than he's used to. Back home it took him forty minutes to nurse one and already his lips feel thick. He should get something in his belly since his breakfast is long gone. He looks around for a jar of Slim Jims or rack of Cheetos. All he sees is a movie theatre popcorn popper—no popcorn inside.

Regina sets two more bottles on the bar. "Keno?" she asks Ricky.

"Might as well."

Regina slaps a white form on the bar. "How about you?" she asks Bing.

"Naw," he says, embarrassed to admit that he doesn't know how to play. "Maybe later."

Ricky pulls a pencil from his shirt pocket and blackens in five numbers from the dozens available on the form. Regina feeds it into her cash register, and out spills a receipt. Bing waits for her to tell Ricky if he won, but they both turn toward a TV mounted on the wall behind the bar, words scrolling across the screen: *Game number 00024176 starts in six seconds! Five! Four! Three! Two! One!* A grid of numbers materializes and a cartoon ball bounces around before settling into the number twenty-three square.

"Got one!" Ricky says.

Bing feels a rush in his belly, and he watches another cartoon ball drop and bounce around until it finally lands on number three.

"Shit," Ricky says.

Bing is catching on. "It's a lot like bingo."

"Kinda like," Regina says.

Bing watches the game unfold, bursts of adrenalin surging as Ricky matches three more numbers. "Hot damn!" Ricky says, standing, fluttering his winning ticket at Bing, setting Frida barking. "You're my good luck charm," he says to Bing. "Regina, set this man up with a shot."

"Oh, no, I, uh—"

"A shot and a beer for my new best friend."

A new beer bottle sits before Bing, plus a shot of whiskey. He looks into the amber liquid trying to remember the last time he drank hard liquor. The Navy. His son's birth.

Ricky picks up the shot glass and presses it into Bing's hand. "Bottoms up."

Bing has to down it, has to, which he does like a pro, not a cough or gasp, clattering the glass on the bar when it's empty.

"Atta boy." Ricky slaps Bing's shoulder before pushing a new Keno form in his face. "Pick me out a few good ones."

"Naw," Bing says, measuring the warmth in his chest, his belly, as the alcohol seeps through his system. "I wouldn't feel right about that."

"No problem," Ricky says, aiming for his stool.

Bing's head droops forward, woozy, and he snaps it back in place, tries to focus on Regina behind the bar. He again admires the swell of her chest, her long fingers lighting a cigarette. Smoke slips out of her mouth and rises up in a rippling ribbon that bends when it hits the ceiling. Bing feels a tug on his wrist and looks down at the frayed loop dangling there, the leash that tethers him to Frida lying on her side on the floor. He watches her chest rising and falling, hears her soft snoring. Sirens wail beside him; the cherry machine lady yowls. She slides off her stool, hands in the air, fingers flapping as the machine lights flash to celebrate her three cherries in a row.

"Mister, you are good luck." She dances over to squeeze his knee. Frida growls, but the woman snaps her fingers and the dog halts. Up close, Bing can't stop looking at the woman's black hair, too black, extra thick and crooked. It's a wig, Bing decides, white wisps poking out from her temples.

"Way to go, Alice," Regina says. "You been in a slump too long."

"Amen to that," Alice says. "Set this man up with a beer."

Bing looks at the bottle and a half of Pabst still waiting on him. "Oh, no. I've got plenty."

"Another shot then," Alice says. "I insist."

Before Bing can protest there's a shot glass staring at him along with Alice, Regina, and Ricky.

The only thing Bing can do is drink it. This one doesn't go down as easy and his stomach clenches.

"Cash me out," Alice says. "Better quit while I'm ahead."

"I heard that." Regina leans over the bar to calculate the winnings.

"This is going to make Marty's day," Alice says as Regina piles crinkled tens and twenties in the old woman's palm. "Maybe I'll take him out for a steak dinner."

"Never took me out for no steak," Ricky says, eyeing the stack of bills in Alice's hand.

"You can buy your own damn meal." Alice shuffles out waving her winnings like a fan. "See you tomorrow," she calls over her shoulder. "You too, Tex."

"You bet," Bing says.

Regina clacks over to the jukebox and plunks in a handful of quarters. Soon a country-western gal warbles out a woeful tale about a whiskey-drinking lowlife who left her with a tarnished wedding band and a husband-shaped hole in her heart.

Bing looks at the golden ring on his finger. He remembers the day Barbara slid it there, how the brushed finish glinted in the sun streaming through the stained glass. The finish is now worn smooth by half a century of wear. Bing looks at his hand, and it seems far away, as if he could reach across the fifteen feet that separates him from the door and open it without leaving his barstool. The kink in his neck that he carried up from Texas is gone. He feels downright good. No joint pain. No toothache. He lets out a laugh.

"What," Ricky says, turning toward him.

"Nothing." Bing tries not to giggle.

Ricky leans over and stares into Bing's eyes. "You drunk?"

"No! I'm not drunk. Shoot." He turns away from Ricky and looks at the front window, Budweiser sign humming, the same hum as that electrical tower beside the plant back home. He grew so used to the constant buzzing in his ears that after he retired he kept listening for it, straining for it. He thinks he hears it now, and it must be true when he sees Dillard pull into the parking lot out front. Two-toned Ford pickup with a gun rack in the rear window.

"Dillard!" Bing says, elated to see his friend's truck. He stands too quickly and has to take a few extra steps to find firm ground. "Dillard!" he says again, anxious for his friend to get out of the truck and come inside for a game of darts, maybe order some nachos. See if the Rockets are playing on TV.

"Who you yammerin' about?" Ricky says.

"It's Dillard." Bing pokes his finger toward the truck, driver's door just now opening.

"It's Jake," Regina says.

"Jake?" Ricky hustles to his feet. "Shit." He twists his torso this way and that as he decides which way to go. "I'm not here!" he says, before sprinting toward the back, setting the kitchen door swinging.

"It's just Dillard." Bing's finger still jabs the air, but the figure closing the truck door, heading inside, is too sturdy. No bow-legged gait. No slumped left shoulder. The man pushing through the door is not Dillard at all, but a thick-necked, completely bald, brick wall of a man. Bing's knees buckle under the tremendous disappointment, and he has to grab the man's forearm to keep from falling.

"Easy there, old timer," the man says, looking at Bing, Regina.

"I'm all right," Bing says, trying to brush the man off even as he's holding on as if for dear life.

"You sure?"

"Sure I'm sure. I just gotta get home, that's all."

Bing takes one clumsy step toward the door, but Regina calls him back. "Now wait a minute. Who's gonna pay for all this?"

"Oh." Bing looks at the row of beers and shot glasses lined up, the kitchen door still gently swaying. "I got it." He tugs out his wallet and spills a few bills onto the counter. He heads for the door and realizes he's caught on something. He spins around to see what. Frida. "Oh," he says, yanking on the leash. "Come on, mutt."

"Come back soon, Tex," Regina calls after him.

"Will do," he says, pushing outside, stark sun smacking his face.

Frida zigzags up the block, jerking Bing past storefronts he doesn't remember passing before. He squints at signs over doors—the letters are blurred, doubled, and he cups his hand over one eye to unscramble them. He can't, so he peeks in windows at a beauty parlor where women in capes and curlers chatter like squirrels. In the laundromat, a mother slops clothes into a dryer, a toddler clinging to her legs. There's a five-and-dime with a gumball machine out front, the jumbo balls shiny and bright. Bing wants to see how much a piece of bubble gum costs these days, and he leans forward too far, bumping his head on the glass.

Frida drags Bing around corners until he doesn't know if he's heading toward Susie's house or away from it. Maybe he still has her address in his wallet. But who would he ask for help in his present state? He focuses on walking straight, putting one foot firmly in front of the other so he doesn't look like he's drunk. "I'm drunk!" he says, astounded.

A grumbly voice answers, "I been drunk for thirty years."

Bing spins to find the speaker. No one is there except a lump of garbage. Several lumps that move and Bing spots a grimy face gawking up at him. He scurries away, digging his fingernails into his palms to see just how much bite he can endure as a drunk man. Bing has enjoyed the faint numbness afforded by a couple of cold beers, but he's only found himself this irresponsibly drunk twice: V-J Day, and the night he and Dillard drove down to Gilley's to see what all that Urban Cowboy hubbub was about.

But that's it, two times, now three, and suddenly Bing can hear Barbara's sweet tittering the two times he saw her in an altered mind. The births of their children. The drugs the doctor administered made Barbara point and laugh at Bing's chin, too broken up to say what she found so entertaining. Bing didn't care; he was just relieved that she wouldn't have to endure the full agony of childbirth the way his mother had. He always felt his mother begrudged him for being such a big-headed baby.

Bing tallies the pain he's endured over his life—a heap more than a woman spends in labor, he figures. The responsibilities a man has to shoulder. Keeping food on the table whether the country's in a depression or recession or whatever they call it these days. Putting kids through college. Going to war. Fighting for one's country, one's flag, so the women and children can sleep soundly in their beds even if the soldiers can't sleep a wink, because they know that any minute a torpedo could be rushing at them under all that blue, blue water. Women know nothing about real fear, he decides, feeling suddenly entitled to the numbness those shots and beers bring. He has known real pressure, real fear.

Frida practically yanks his shoulder out of its socket bringing Bing back to the present: he's being dragged around this town that's barely a town, state that's barely a state, by a blind old dog. Bing's sole responsibility is to pick up her crap, and before it's all over someone will probably be cleaning up after him, too.

Bing's chest feels heavy and he has to stop, grab hold of a postal box on the corner and breathe, but his pulse does a trot when he sees a pack of girls heading for him, Reenie's age maybe, four or five of them in bleach-splattered jeans and flashing tennis shoes. A current of fear zings up Bing's back. *Since when was I ever afraid of a bunch of girls?* He recalls reading about those girl gangs back in Houston who flagged down cars, acting like they were in distress. When some unsuspecting Samaritan picked them up—usually male—they'd beat the crap out of him and steal his car. Or flat-out kill him. As the girls approach, Bing sees one of them put her hand in her purse. Probably going for a knife. Or a gun. *Stick 'em up!* Bing has to do something—run, duck into somebody's house if they answer his frantic pummeling—but he can't yank Frida away from whatever she's gnawing at over by the curb. He steels himself as the girls approach, tries to look firm but casual by slipping his hand in his pocket, jiggling his change— too vigorously, apparently, since as the girls walk by, one of them looks at the hand in Bing's pocket wildly pumping and screams, "Gross! Dirty old man."

Bing looks at her looking at his hand in his pants. "No!" he calls after them. "I'm just jiggling my change. See?" He draws out a fistful of silver and clanks it around in his palm. "See? I wasn't—"

The girls link arms and rush forward, one of them snarling over her shoulder, "Pervert. Get a life."

Bing's hand drops to his side, pennies and dimes clattering on the sidewalk, skittering into the street. He doesn't bother to collect them, just stands there looking at the receding girls, so young, so much life in front of them. *I have a life.* Bing looks from the girls to Frida, gacking up a candy wrapper, letting her nose guide her to even ranker treasures. She has no idea that her routing days are finite, that she'll be lucky to last another year. He doubts if

Frida remembers scrabbling up and down Susie's hardwood stairs, effortlessly jumping on couches and beds, chasing balls and sticks, the simplest canine pleasures she can no longer enjoy. But she doesn't know that. She's too busy peeling a wad of gum from the sidewalk, in her present mind the very feat she was bred for.

I had a life, Bing thinks, staggering backward into a wooden bench. He sits and props his elbows on his thighs, cups his face in his hands, feels a hardened scab of shaving cream on the back of his jaw. He picks it off and flings it toward his feet, shakes his head at the odd feeling in his gut, the hollow realization at what he has been reduced to: a drunken, dirty old man.

SEARCH AND RESCUE

A horn blast startles Bing. He looks up at a squat car in the street, taxi-cab yellow, passenger window buzzing down.

A woman's voice: "Bing? Is that you?"

Bing doesn't recognize the car or the voice, but Frida does and she strains at her leash. Bing harnesses Frida's momentum to help him stand. "Who's that?" He takes a step so clumsy he collapses to one knee, then leans forward to find Ellen Foley leaning across the passenger seat looking at him. "Ooooohhh," he says, trying to strain the wobble from his voice.

"Are you lost?"

"Heck no. I'm not lost. Just walking the dog here."

"I see." Ellen scans Bing's head, which keeps lolling forward. "Perhaps I'd better give you a ride home." She pops the passenger door as if it's already decided.

"No, thanks." But Frida hoists herself in one arthritic leg at a time and squeezes through the bucket seats to the rear. Bing follows, but the car is low and it's not easy to duck inside. He closes the door and fiddles with the seat belt, the metal tongue that won't fit in the slot.

"Let me," Ellen says, craning over to clip him in.

He holds his breath, but when Ellen finishes his manners kick in. "Much obliged."

Ellen's nostrils flare. "Lordy, Bing, where in the world have you been?"

Bing's cheeks burn as he tries to recall the name of the bar. "I don't know," he confesses. A ball of words tumbles from his mouth. "This fella bought me a drink, but they didn't have Lone Star, so I ordered a Pabst and too many shots. And the wig lady with the cherries. And of course Re-gin-aaaa—" Bing's hands fly up to his chest to indicate her endowment. "And she put on the jukebox and they didn't offer me a bowl of pretzels or nothing."

Ellen doesn't say one word, which is worse than a scolding, so Bing adds, "Frida went in first."

Ellen looks in the backseat at the dog. "She always was a bad influence."

Bing chuckles, relieved, and presses his back into the seat, shuffles his feet until he realizes he's mashing something around down there. He looks in the foot well, sees a Bible, and immediately scoops it up to swipe off his boot print. "Sorry about that," he says to Ellen, to God, guilt easing somewhat when he discovers that it's a knockoff translation, not the divinely inspired King James.

"No problem. I'm just coming from my women's Bible study."

That figures, Bing thinks, feeling omnipotently busted. "That's nice." He ought to add more, tell Ellen he truly is a God-fearing man, not one who typically drinks in the middle of the day. Certainly not one to get drunk. But Ellen doesn't appear to need an excuse. He looks at her hand on the gearshift, impressed by her smoothness, not a jerk, not a grind or stall.

He tried to teach Barbara how to drive their first car, a manual. She ground the gears until he swore he saw sparks. He gritted his teeth to keep from yelling, but yelled anyway because instead of listening to his instructions Barbara fiddled with the radio or yelled to passing neighbors, "Look at me! I'm driving!" He shouldn't have hollered, he knows, because even now he remembers how tiny her foot was on the clutch pedal. And her shoes were so pretty. Powder blue pumps with a flower on top. And her sheer-sheer stockings. Slender ankles that could make a drill sergeant weep.

Bing looks at Ellen's feet working the pedals. Not small, no, in black leather boots; he couldn't say small, but skillfully shifting from gas to clutch to brake. Her hand on the gearshift, not jerky or timid, but perfectly in tune with the car, and he knows she must be listening for the engine's whine, waiting for that perfect pitch when you know, you just know it's time to shift before the car starts to buck and rock. He hears it, the perfect pitch, and his left foot shoves in an invisible clutch, right hand grabs an imaginary stick shift at exactly the same moment Ellen does, and they do it together, upshift into third.

Bing watches the road, counts passing streets to see just how far off course he was. Not far, it appears, and when Ellen turns onto their street she says, "Uh-oh."

"What uh-oh?"

"Aldine's there."

"Aldine." Bing pictures that woman's disabled husband lying flat on his back.

"Why don't I pull around back to my garage?" Ellen says, driving past her house. She turns the corner and turns again into the alley, a gravelly mess that rattles Bing's teeth. Ellen pulls in front of a two-car garage and presses a box on her visor to raise the automatic door. "I'll fix you some coffee."

"Sounds grrrrrrreat," Bing says.

"Strong coffee," Ellen says, yanking up the parking brake.

Bing gets out and comes face-to-face with shelves and Peg-Boards full of tools, just loaded with them: all manner of screwdrivers, hammers, pliers, wrenches. Caulking guns. Levelers. Rows and rows of paint and varnish and wood stain and WD-40 and Gunk. He could stand there all day admiring the weed whacker and hedge clippers, and he wants to ask Ellen if her husband was handy, but it's apparent.

"Nice workshop." Bing scrapes over to the workbench, cuts and stains and penciled calculations marring the surface. He runs his hand over it, looks at the dirt on his fingertips, rubs his thumb around it to relish the gritty feel.

Ellen opens the door to her backyard. "You coming?"

"I miss this," he whispers.

Bing follows Ellen into her yard and again he stops short, not bowled over by tools, but by art. Large, looming art, scary art. Metal totem poles, sort of, littering the lawn—some twelve feet high, with sharp-edged arms reaching out every which way. Tin sheets bent and welded at odd angles. Bike tires and garbage can lids and stop signs attached in no particular order for no apparent reason—at least none that Bing can deduce.

Something glinting in the distance catches his eye, maybe six feet tall, that puts him in mind of those fertility goddesses he saw that time Barbara dragged him to the museum. Bing walks toward brushed-copper sheets welded into a gargantuan woman: thick, bent legs, knees pointing out; torso leaning forward, exaggerated breasts and belly succumbing to gravity; arms reaching up toward the sky, hands clasping a silver disk. Some of the angles are tricky, Bing notes, intricate, and he has to lean to discern the welding, figure out what filler Ellen used, what types of joint weld. Mostly corner and butt, and some root and groove face thrown in. Slot welds for nipples and kneecaps and the *O* of her mouth. He runs his hand over the seams, smooth and flawless, not a hint of slag, and he feels a twinge in his solar plexus.

"Better come on in," Ellen calls from her back porch. "And didn't you forget something?"

"Forget something?"

"Frida."

"Frida?"

"In the car."

Bing looks over his shoulder at the garage, pictures the car tucked inside. "Oh! I left the dog in the car. I'll get her."

"I should think," Ellen says, slipping inside her house.

Ellen slides a can of Folgers from the freezer, coffee filters from the top of the refrigerator, and starts measuring. Bing wipes his boots just inside the door, or tries to, but all he does is bunch up the rug as he waits for Ellen to ask him to sit. She doesn't, so he tamps down the braided fabric with his boot, gripping the counter to keep steady. He drops Frida's leash and she clicks over to a chipped cabinet by the stove and rakes her paw down it.

"Okay," Ellen says. "Don't get your panties in a bunch."

Bing cackles at the idea of Frida in a pair of lady's underwear. "Course you'd have to cut out a hole."

"What's that?"

"To poke her tail through." Bing stabs his finger in the air to demonstrate.

Ellen scrunches her forehead and opens the cabinet where a box of dog treats sits. She pulls out a biscuit and hands it to Frida who carries it toward the front of the house, leash dragging behind her like a snake.

"Frida!" Bing calls. Barbara didn't allow food anywhere but the kitchen.

"That's all right," Ellen says. "She likes to eat in the sun spot by the couch."

"You sure?" Bing imagines Barbara frantically vacuuming the pile of crumbs.

"I'm sure." Ellen turns back to the coffee.

Bing's body feels suddenly leaden. His chest starts to tip forward, so he makes himself say, "Mind if I sit?"

"Oh! Sit. Please. I'm so used to people just making themselves at home."

Bing lunges for the kitchen table, rustic and strong, not wobbling when he slaps both palms on it to keep from falling. He settles in a wide-bottomed chair with a plaid cushion, a pattern he hinted at for decades but Barbara considered too manly. Bing leans back, stretches his legs out fully and admires the table's surface, no dried flower arrangements or too-sweet candles cluttering it up. A smooth expanse for tinkering with a broken blender or rewiring a lamp.

He hears coffee tinkling into a carafe, inhales the thick aroma as he sizes up Ellen's kitchen. No frilly drapes. No pictures of piglets or ducklings or little girls in rain slickers. No framed embroidery of biblical sayings. These walls are paneled with barn wood, weathered and gray. Dozens of framed black-and-white photos crowd the walls: Afro-headed Black Panthers with their fists in the air. Braless hippie women swirling in patchwork skirts. Crinkled farm women and weary coal miners with pitiable faces that oddly comfort Bing.

"Maybe you should eat something," Ellen says. "How about a tuna salad sandwich?"

"It got sweet pickles in it?"

"Like there's any other kind."

Ellen eases four bread slices from a loaf, opens the refrigerator to drag out a covered bowl. Pulls a knife from the dish rack for slathering mayonnaise.

All this activity makes Bing's head droop, eyelids flutter and sag. He decides to lay his head down for just a minute, nestle his temple into the meaty part of his forearm and listen to the homey sounds that can only come from a kitchen: drawers opening, silverware clinking, plates sliding from cupboards, a toaster lever being depressed—the *tic-tic-tic* as the heating coils redden.

Ahhhh, Bing thinks, then *uh-oh* because the room starts to tip and sway. He pries open one eye to stop the motion, but he can't, so he thinks about his feet planted firmly on the floor, so weighted the room can't possibly spin, it just can't.

But it does and a wave of nausea washes over him. Bile and beer and whiskey gurgle up his throat. Bing swallows hard and tries to sit up, but all he can do is whirl with the spinning room, and soon he smells the Gulf of Mexico, briny fish air swirling together with sweet pickles and mayonnaise that makes his face pucker, his stomach clench and, ultimately, surrender. He clamps a hand over his mouth to keep the content from spilling, but it does anyway, a slick yellow slime that oozes between his fingers, streams down his wrist and onto his jumpsuit, the floor.

"Oh my," Ellen says, grabbing a washcloth to run under water. She comes at Bing, but he puts his hands up to stop her just as a second gush squirts out, this time coating his boots.

"I'm sorry," he says, head bobbing, hands out in supplication.

"It's okay." Ellen wipes his face, his hands, and he submits because the washcloth is so cool on his skin.

"Stand," she says.

Bing does. "I'm sorry, Barbara."

"It's okay. Let's just move you to the couch."

"Okay." Bing leans on his wife as she leads him to the front room, feet shuffling forward until they reach the couch where he sits and lets her take off the right boot, the left.

"Just lie down now," she says. Bing tips back, feels Barbara hovering as she settles a pillow under his head. She swings his legs up, and he bends his knees to accommodate because the couch isn't long enough for him to fully stretch out, but today, for some reason, it is, and he smiles at the sheer, small joy of it.

"I'm putting a wastebasket by your head."

"Fine," Bing says. "That's just fine."

Barbara draws the curtains to block out the afternoon light, but they don't block out the noise. The children outside, feet slapping the sidewalk as they run home from school. Roger in the front yard passing a football with the kid from up the street. "Go long!" Roger says. "Nice spiral!" the kid answers. Bing imagines the spiral, the football's perfect rotation as it sails through the air, higher and higher until it disappears into space, and Bing disappears right along with it.

Hot puffs of air tickle Bing's cheek. He tries to brush them away, but he can't, so he opens his eyes and not three inches away another eye peers back at him. Frida. Lying beside him on the couch, her head in the crook of his arm, nose angled up practically touching his chin. She stares at him, under-eye crusty from her weepy eye. Bing tries to move and she growls.

"Ah, shut up." He pulls his arm out from beneath her, but that small movement makes his pelvis ache. "I have to pee." Bing takes stock of his whereabouts. He's lying on a couch in someone's living room, and it's not Susie's. Orange afghan pulled up to his shoulders. He sits up, pressing his fingers against his temples to still his throbbing head, the squishy thump of pulse in his ears. His mouth is hot, bitter, tongue thick and tacky. He looks around the unfamiliar room. Green leather couch. Oversized yellow chair and ottoman. The coffee table is a square hunk of wood, an onyx chessboard set up with a game in progress. Weird concoctions dangle from the ceiling. Mobiles. Odd pieces of painted metal spinning and twirling in the breeze whishing in the side window. Art. He's looking at art and he remembers where he is. Ellen's.

Standing too quickly he wobbles, knocking over a trash can. As he stoops to right it, the afghan falls from him and he sees his stockinged feet, bare calves, bony knees. "What the—" He's standing in Ellen's living room in his boxer shorts and t-shirt. He scoops up the afghan—no easy feat with his pounding head—and drapes it around himself like a toga. "Oh, shit," he says when he looks at his watch. Susie is probably home wondering where the hell he is, where Frida is. The day's events rush back at Bing in reverse order: vomit and totem poles and garage tools and stick shifts and girl gangs and shot glasses and beer bottles lined up—dozens of them. The thought of all that swirling liquid makes his kidneys ache, reminding him of his pressing need. He shuffles forward, ear cocked as he listens for sounds, movement, anything to lead him to Ellen so he can ask where the facilities are. But he doesn't really want to see her in his present state, and it dawns on him that she's the one who peeled off his vomited-on jumpsuit.

Bing groans as he aims for a narrow door in the hall. He twists the glass knob, bladder already contracting at the thought of a porcelain bowl, but it's a closet, full of coats and sweaters, floor cluttered up with rubber boots and umbrellas. *Damn.* Bing closes the door and clenches his abdomen. He looks at the stairs and knows he has to go up. He pads up one step after another. "Hello?" he calls, not wanting to alarm Ellen, give her any scary ideas. No answer, so he quickens his ascent. Upstairs, he ducks his head into room after room until he finds the bathroom. He closes the door, settles in front of the john, and releases a stream.

"Ahhhhh," Bing says, impressed by the sheer volume. He looks around Ellen's bathroom. Bowl of crystals on the back of the commode. Stacks of magazines on the windowsill within easy reach: *Smithsonian, The Nation*. There's a photograph over the toilet of a woman standing on a beach at twilight, too dark to make out facial features, but she is definitely nude. Bing averts his eyes, but he's drawn back to the soft hint of moonlight on the woman's fleshy hip, her shoulder, the sag of her breasts. She's holding something in her hands, a length of hose, a coil of rope, a silver braid.

Ellen.

Gentle knocking from the other side of the door and Ellen's soft voice calls, "Bing?"

He flushes the toilet to drown out the sound of the healthy arc of urine still streaming.

"Yes!" he answers. He realizes he's still staring at Ellen's naked picture and he looks down, face flaming. "I'll be out in a sec!" he calls over the whirlpool swirling away in the bowl.

"Take your time. I just wanted to tell you that I washed your jumpsuit. I'll lay it on the bed for you, the first room on your right."

"Mighty kind," he says, wanting her to leave before the flush cycle ends.

"Okay then. I'll be downstairs."

Bing finishes, finally, and lathers his hands with soap, scrapes dried vomit from between his fingers. He fills a blue glass with cool water, aggressively gargles and spits, then he drinks and drinks and drinks.

Opening the door, he leans out and hears a teakettle whistling in the kitchen, so he figures it's safe. His jumpsuit is laid out in the master bedroom, an airy box with a king-size bed. No extra heart-shaped pillows thrown on. His clothes are still warm from the dryer, and Bing pulls them on and tugs up the zipper, the metal slider hot between his fingers. He's relieved that he wore a clean pair of drawers. A sudden image of Ellen pushing his passed-out body this way and that to undress him, grunting with effort. His boots are on the floor, newly shined, and he feels a re-newed spasm of shame. He sits on the bed to yank them on, gaze drifting over to a photo of a couple on the nightstand.

He listens for approaching footsteps and hearing none, picks up the picture to see if it's Ellen and her husband. Bing is curious about the sort of man who would marry a woman who welds, who would let her clutter up the backyard with those landfill monstrosities. Who would keep a naked picture of his wife in his bathroom for anyone to see. It's Ellen, all right, in a peach dress, tawny, upswept hair tucked under a floppy hat. She's gripping a bouquet of yellow roses, a tight bundle with a foot-long tangle of ribbons caught in midflutter.

She married late, Bing deduces, in the 1970s by the style of Ellen's dress and the husband's long hair. Another odd puzzle piece to add to this strange woman's life. And there he is, the groom, Ellen's height, maybe even a hair shorter, and just as narrow. Not surprised, Bing thinks, holding the picture up close to study the man's lean face. Most of it is in shadows, but Bing can make out a weak chin, dark hair blown back from a high forehead. There's something about the man's features, some soft thing, and his suit looks like a prom tux: powder blue with ruffles poking out of the vest and sleeves. Yellow rosebud pinned to his lapel. He and Ellen have their arms linked at the elbows as they exit what Bing assumes is a church, both looking out, up, smiling into their joint futures. *Don't look like man and wife*, Bing decides. He remembers his own exiting-the-church wedding picture. How Barbara clutched her cascading bouquet in one hand, folds of her gown in the other. Her head was bent down looking at her feet, trying to keep from getting tangled in the yards and yards of satin, trying not to scuff up her shoes. Their arms weren't looped, no, and Bing remembers cupping one hand on Barbara's elbow, the other on the small of her back as he guided her down the stone steps. It was he who had his head up, looking out into their futures. *As it should be*, he thinks, recalling the chain of command in their marriage that worked so well for so long.

But there's an odd twinge in Bing's gullet as he pictures Ellen and her husband walking so evenly out of the church. He can imagine the two of them sitting across from each other over that chessboard in the living room. Calculating their income taxes to-gether on that wide kitchen table. Mutually fretting over possible union strikes or layoffs—or whatever job fears Ellen's husband surely endured—the way Bing did so many times all by himself. He kept the precarious state of their finances from Barbara to keep her from worrying, because it was a man's duty to do the worrying for his family.

But, oh how comforting it would have been to have someone to agonize with when Roger's orders came through. Instead, Bing paced the length of his garage night after night, all alone. Sat in the backyard whittling a hunk of wood down to nothing just to keep his mind off the nightly war reports. Sometimes when he was out there he'd look up at the back of the house, at the rectangle of white light glowing from Roger's bedroom window. He knew Barbara was in there mending torn pants or darning socks, anything to keep her hands busy, her mind occupied, too. More than once he crept down the hall, peeked in that room, and found his wife on her knees, hands clasped in prayer for her son's safety. Maybe Bing should have been on his knees beside her, but it felt so private, so personal, he just backed quietly away. And besides, Barbara never asked him.

The words *I'm sorry* form in Bing's brain, but he isn't sure if it's his voice or his wife's.

Downstairs, Bing moseys into the kitchen where Ellen pulls a pan of yellow cupcakes from the oven. Frida lies patiently on the linoleum. Bing clears his throat and Ellen turns, an endearing smudge of flour on her chin.

"How do you feel?"

Bing looks at the smudge, the barn wood walls, the black-and-white photo of weary coal miners. "Like I ought to know better," he says, unable to meet the somber stares of those hardworking men.

"These things happen," Ellen says.

"Not to me." Bing points at a conspicuously well-scrubbed portion of the floor. "I'm real sorry about—"

"No problem, Bing."

Bing's head perks up at the sound of his name ringing out of her mouth like a clock chime. He hasn't heard it spoken aloud in a while, and his ear lingers over the resonating *iinnngggg*.

"Would you like that coffee now? Or I just made a pot of tea."

Bing looks at her tea cup on the counter, tendrils of steam swirling out. He wonders if this woman genuinely wants his company after the trouble he's put her through. "I expect Susie's about to have a conniption wondering where I am."

"I took the liberty of calling."

"What did you say to her?" Bing's middle finger thumps his thigh.

"I told her you were helping me fix my washer."

Bing's finger stops thumping. "Your washer broke?"

"Nope."

Bing's mouth unfurls into a kind of grin that hasn't sliced his face in years.

"Have some tea," Ellen says. It isn't a suggestion, so Bing dutifully sits as Ellen fills another cup and sets it on the table. He accepts the cream and sugar and watches Ellen scrape pink frosting from a bowl and slather it on cupcakes. She holds one out to him. "You up for this?"

Bing rubs his belly, assessing. "Sure," he says, accepting the gift. He swirls his fingertip through creamy icing and lets it dissolve on his tongue. *Nothing better*, he thinks, wondering how many times Ellen's husband sat in this very spot eating baked goods straight from the oven. He probably helped her make them, or at least offered to wash up after. Something Glen would do—if he even eats sweets.

Bing thinks about his daughter and son-in-law next door, their skimpy cuisine and aloof children. He has no desire to go back, and he realizes that, regardless of how he got into this kitchen, he feels oddly relaxed, calmer than he's felt since he left Texas, maybe even long before that.

A scalding gush surges beneath his skin as if he'd just been caught gossiping about his wife.

"P.J. loved cupcakes, too," Ellen says.

"That right?" Bing assumes that's the husband, relieved to be thinking about someone else's spouse. Just two people mourning their losses. He wants to ask about P.J., an intrigue that startles him. He's never been one to pry, but for some reason, with Ellen, a woman who's seen him in his boxers, he figures it would be all right.

"I saw your wedding picture upstairs," he says, a bold opener.

Ellen's hand hesitates over a cupcake, and Bing thinks he has upset her. He doesn't know how long she's been a widow.

"You make a nice couple," he offers, words he heard Barbara use a hundred times as they worked their way through wedding receiving lines.

"We thought so."

"You have kids?"

Ellen looks at the row of African violets on the windowsill over the sink. "No. No children."

"I'm sorry." Bing assumes a medical condition, female trouble, maybe. A flash of Ellen's fleshy hip from that picture on the bathroom wall upstairs makes his right foot twitch. "Course you married late."

"What? Oh, yes, I guess we did. Though we'd been together since college."

Why'd you wait so long? is what he wants to ask. "What'd your husband do?" is what he says, a safe question, he figures, safer than reproductive issues.

"P.J. was a nurse."

"A *nurse*?" he says, so obviously bowled over he tries to rectify. "He was ahead of his time."

Ellen plunks her frosting knife in the sink. "That's true."

"He in the war?" Bing asks, more neutral territory.

It's a simple question, but he watches Ellen pick up her tea cup and take a sip, study a spot on the ceiling for so long Bing looks up to see what she's ogling. When she brings her gaze back down, she looks directly at him, and he knows she's sizing him up. But for what? What if P.J. was 4-F, or a deserter, or wounded—maybe that's why they couldn't have children. He wants to take the question back, let Ellen off this troublesome hook. As he tries to figure out how to retreat he watches her eyebrows draw together, lips purse. Finally she says, "I think you've been through enough for one day."

She sends him home with a plate of cupcakes, which he is not inclined to share. He hides them in his sock drawer—all but one, which he wraps in a napkin and tucks under the kitchen sink with his own scrawled note: *Enjoy.* By breakfast the next day it is gone.

WELDER'S BURN

Two days later Ellen raps on Bing's door and invites him over for lunch, chicken 'n' dumplings. He accepts, Frida heading the parade as chaperone. The following day it's grilled cheese; the day after that tuna melts. The three of them tumble into a pattern, except Wednesdays—Ellen's Bible study—and Bing begins to wake up downright chipper even though he still has to grind through empty mornings, tedious late afternoons, and tense suppers.

But at least now he has the sweet reverie of a rib-sticking meal and the chance to swap stories about growing up during the Depression, about trolley cars and horse-drawn vegetable carts, Uncle Miltie and Tokyo Rose. Bing is surprised that West Virginia struggled through the same highs and lows, advances and retreats as the rest of the country at the very same time—not on a twenty-year delay as he always believed. They had immigrants and robber barons; the WPA and CCC; coal mining, yes, but also steel industry and glass works and chemical plants; race riots and Vietnam War protests.

They talk about welding, of course, for hours and hours. Ellen leads Bing out back through her sculpture maze. She mercifully doesn't linger as they wend their way past what Bing considers a regrettable use of good metal, yet he admires her soldering skills, her finesse. She opens the door to that well-stocked garage, to her separate workshop in the back. A sacred space with all the welders' trappings Bing recognizes and jewelry-making paraphernalia he does not. And there it is, her torch, a sweet little Mig, a Miller, no less, a top-of-the-line brand he coveted for years but could never afford. And beside it her visor, nice and dark, ten or eleven minimum because you need a darker shade with a Mig. Bing is not a bit jealous. Not one speck, though he might be if this was one of his buddies back home.

One afternoon Ellen serves pound cake in the living room. Bing settles on the couch, Frida beside him, and eyes that chessboard set up on the coffee table, onyx rooks and bishops caught in midstrategy. "Are you ever going to finish this game?"

Ellen sits in a chair opposite Bing and looks at the board between them. "No," she says, a remote look in her eyes.

Bing regrets the inquiry because she was playing with her husband, no doubt—a spousal topic they have both neatly avoided these past weeks. He figures Ellen hasn't yet had the heart to dismantle the game because her husband's fingers touched that pawn, that queen. "I'm sorry. I didn't mean—"

"It's okay," Ellen says. "P.J. was a lousy chess player. Had the attention span of a fruit fly." Ellen picks up a knight, her first move since P.J. died, Bing guesses, and buffs it against her corduroy slacks. "You play?" she asks, voice tinged with a challenge. A hopeful one at that.

Bing studies Ellen's face, the cocked eyebrow, direct gaze: a worthy opponent. He doesn't answer, just swivels the board toward him, "White on the right," and starts realigning his troops. "Queen on her color," he says as a reminder because it's been a long time. He wonders if the rules have changed since his Navy days, or the smattering of games he played over the years with Barbara's brother at otherwise intolerable family reunions.

"You do!" Ellen's hands clap together like a schoolgirl's.

"Don't look so surprised."

"Doesn't surprise me one bit." She leans forward to line up her regiment.

"Don't tell Susie," Bing says. "Wouldn't want to burst her bubble."

"What bubble?"

"She thinks I'm just a backwoods checkers man, though I am particularly skilled at that, too."

"Your secret is safe with me."

The kings' pawns come out, and in less than three minutes Ellen has defeated Bing with a four-move checkmate.

"What?" Bing says, replaying the skirmish in his mind.

"I'm sorry. I tend to show off. Another reason P.J. didn't like to play."

"That's okay. That's okay," Bing says, already resetting the board. "Now I know what tricks you've got up your sleeve."

"Not all of them."

Soon they are deep into game two, and as the rust flakes off Bing realizes, *This is fun.* He watches Ellen's face between moves as she plots and schemes, especially when he baffles her with preemptive strikes. She's cunning, too, and he soon discovers her affection for hostage taking and invisible attacks, making him dust off ruthless countermaneuvers and affronts that he would use on any man.

A noise in the kitchen, the back door opening, and someone yells, "Frida!"

Bing bolts upright as if he's been caught necking in the parlor.

"It's all right," Ellen says. "It's just Reenie."

"Reenie!" Bing says—even worse than he thought—ogling the front door, the stairs, the closet.

"Where's my baby?" Reenie calls.

Frida eases from the couch, scut thumping, and clicks forward as Reenie clods into the room. She drops to her knees and scratches Frida's shoulder blades. "Are you begging from the neighbors again?"

"No!" Bing says. "I was invited."

Reenie looks up, sees Bing, and her lips snarl. She looks over at Ellen as if to say, *What the hell is he doing here?*

"Your grandfather and I were just playing chess."

"Chess?" Reenie says, with the exact same look Bing would expect Susie to don if she discovered this hoity-toity game in his repertoire.

"He's quite good, actually," Ellen adds.

Reenie stands and looks at her boots. "Yeah. Well. I just came to get the dog. So, come on, Frida."

Ellen stands and holds out a hand. "Wait a minute. While you're here, why don't you go upstairs and take a look at the—"

"No!" Reenie holds out her own halting hand. "I can look at it later."

Bing looks from Ellen to Reenie wondering what the heck *it* is.

"Suit yourself," Ellen says. "But it's coming along beautifully."

"Thanks," Reenie mutters, already bolting to the back door, Frida bringing up the rear.

Bing reckons he should head out as well, but he looks at the chessboard, torn.

"It's not going anywhere," Ellen says.

Bing nods, still eyeing the preempted match.

"Don't worry. I won't touch a thing."

"Better not." Bing taps his temple. "I've got it all up here."

But the following day Ellen appears at Bing's door wearing overalls and butter-colored work boots. "I have to go to the junkyard. Want to come along?"

"Heck, yeah," Bing says, already envisioning a kind of scrap heap heaven. He hasn't been to a junkyard since he and Dillard scrounged lot after lot for an authentic taillight for that '57 Chevy Dillard spent twenty years restoring. Bing anticipates the sweet smells of motor oil and brake fluid, disintegrating rubber and oxidized metal: the universal odors of junkyards.

Ellen's tires crunch through the gravel lot across the street from the yard. Bing cranes in awe at corrugated sheets fencing it in—an entire city block worth—and he gets out even before Ellen cricks up the brake.

Inside, Bing is welcomed not only by the rich smells he remembers, but by a cinder-block building, part office, part three-stall garage, mechanics inside unhitching wrecked cars from tow trucks. The sign over the office reads: *Plymale's Salvage and Scrap.* The office door chimes open and out steps a hulk of a man, early twenties, a mop of dark hair framing his face. His hands jammed into dungarees riding so low half of them are crumpled around his steel-toed boots.

"Afternoon, Ms. Foley," he says.

"Nice to see you, Junior. You've no doubt met Reenie's grandpa."

"Mr. Butler?" Junior says at the exact moment Bing blurts, "Junior?"

Junior thrusts out his hand. "It's a pleasure to finally meet you, sir."

Bing is wary. The boy was smoking dope with his grand-daughter, or an accomplice to it, anyway. The three silver hoops dangling from each earlobe are also regrettable, even if one has a Jesus fish attached. Junior's grip swallows Bing's hand whole, like a snug baseball mitt, yet a surprisingly gentle grip—a man who knows his own strength.

"Welcome to paradise," Junior says, ushering him in.

"This your business?" he asks.

"Me and my dad's," Junior says. "He made me partner last year, and I'll take over when he retires."

Junior's line of work immediately endears him to Bing. The warmth grows as he takes the grand tour: car after mashed car, pickups, even a few big rig cabs. There's a section for motorcycles and lawn mowers. Aisles devoted to doorless refrigerators, stoves, and trash compactors. A row of carports protecting goods salvaged from condemned houses: claw-footed bathtubs, fireplace mantles, paint-peeled doors, stained-glass windows, pedestal sinks, bins of glass doorknobs, *hot* and *cold* porcelain handles, brass hardware. The entire back fence displays hubcaps crowded together like a wall of mirrors glinting in the sun.

The lot is crowded with customers, too. Not only underweight, pimple-faced, grease-monkey boys, but whole tribes of moms and dads and tousle-haired children poking around for usable tire rims and fenders and grills, boat motors and pontoon covers. Yuppies looking for original door bells and light fixtures and gas valves for renovating houses.

"Must make a good living," Bing says.

Junior tugs one of those earrings. "Decent."

"More than just decent," Ellen says.

Junior hangs his head, and Bing appreciates the financial modesty.

Ellen loops her arm through Junior's. "So what have you got for me today?"

"Oh, Ms. Foley, just you wait and see."

"Goodie-goodie," Ellen says, that little girl again practically bouncing.

Junior leads them to one of the automotive bays. Leaning against the side wall is a cast-iron gate webbed with elaborate swirls and circles.

"It's fabulous." Ellen tips it forward to stand upright, kneeling to caress the bent curves and angles. The scripted gold M in the middle. "I can use this," she says, eyes drawing inward as if she's already sculpting in there.

Junior leaves them to cluck and fawn, and search for even more treasure.

Hours and hours later, when they finally pull out of the gravel lot, Ellen's trunk is heavily weighted. "That Junior," Ellen says. "Always tucking away some jewel just for me."

"Got manners, too," Bing says. "Don't see that much these days. More than I can say about Reenie. Don't know what in the world he sees in that girl."

A thick pause and Bing realizes he may have opined too much. "I mean—"

Ellen repositions her hands on the steering wheel. "It's okay. I know what you mean. But she's a darling girl, really, underneath it all. Just as bright and warm—"

"Warm?" Bing recalls that shit-filled slipper.

"Yes, and funny. I don't expect you to take my word for it. She's just going through a rough patch right now."

"Been sliding through that rough patch for six or seven years now."

"Be patient, Bing. She'll take to you eventually. Just don't crowd her."

"Hard to crowd a person you never see."

Back at Ellen's, she won't let Bing leave without a plate of brownies. "It's an offering," she says, a puzzling remark.

Bing steps from Ellen's porch and hears an engine revving. Brian's Camaro is parked behind the Olds in Susie's driveway. Bing looks at the patch of overgrown grass underneath his car—an unmowable swatch that's probably driving Glen nuts. Brian is bent under the Camaro's hood, and Junior, still in his work clothes, hovers behind him. Reenie sits cross-legged on Bing's trunk tapping a screwdriver against his paint job.

As he nears he debates whether to tell her to stop and suffer the derogatory arrow she will undoubtedly fling. Or maybe it will be the screwdriver. But as soon as she sees him, she hops down and says, "Brownies!" Brian's head pops up, and he and Junior aim for Bing, swiping their hands down their jeans, leaving grimy streaks. Reenie gets there first, and Bing sways backward as she peels off the plastic wrap. He looks down at the crown of her head, the double cowlick, hair dyed unmercifully black except for the roots, which betray her ancestry. It's Barbara's original color, exactly.

"Much obliged," Junior says.

"Thanks," Brian says.

Now Bing understands Ellen's offering. He twists around to see if she is watching this beneficent moment she orchestrated. But she isn't there.

Junior points at the Camaro. "Brian says you could probably help us figure out what's wrong with this piece of crap."

"He does?" Bing squints at his grandson.

Brian juts his chin toward the car, an invitation. Bing accepts and sets the food on the grass, never mind Frida, who noses over.

"What'cha got there?" Bing says.

"Seventy-seven Z28," Brian says, voice firm with pride.

Bing leans under the hood to inspect the engine, so polished it looks like it just came off the line. "Real nice," he says, poking at hoses and belts, distributor cap. "Don't see those much anymore," he says about the four-barrel carb. "How's she been acting?"

"Idles rough and stalls out when I hit the gas," Brian says. "I looked at the fuel pump and put in a new filter."

"And checked the timing," Junior adds.

"None of that worked?"

"Nope," says Brian.

"Your gas mixture might be too rich," Bing says. "Could be the choke on the carb."

Brian nods. "Could be."

"Frida!" Reenie races to the dog, who is mashing a brownie between her molars, brown clumps tumbling out of her mouth. Reenie nudges the dog aside. "Chocolate's not good for you." She scoops up the plate and balances it on her palm like a waitress.

"Did Uncle Roger have a car?" Brian asks.

"Uncle Roger?" Bing says, wondering how his grandson even knows about Bing's uncle, his mother's brother whose greatest feats were being shot in the buttocks in World War I and brewing potato beer during prohibition.

"Maybe a '65 Mustang," Brian says. "Or a Corvair."

"Corvair?" Bing says, stumped. "They didn't have those back then. Been lucky to get his hands on a Model T."

"What are you talking about?" Brian says. "He would have started driving in, what, the sixties?"

"My Uncle Roger died in 1958."

"I'm talking about *my* Uncle Roger."

"*Your* Uncle Roger?"

"Your son, Grandpa. Roger."

"My son," Bing says. Words he hasn't spoken in years. How had he forgotten that Roger would be Brian's uncle? And Reenie's. Bing's forever eighteen-year-old son, an uncle to these two. He looks at Reenie sitting back on the trunk, gnawing at her fingernail, bored stiff. At nineteen, she's already breathed through more days than Roger. Bing looks back at Brian, seventeen, nearly reaching that calamitous age.

"Roger didn't have a car," Bing says, voice so brittle it's as if he dragged it up from the very day he taught Roger how to change oil in the Studebaker. The car Roger took his driver's test in. He was timid behind the wheel, too cautious. Bing remembers the night Barbara made Roger pose in front of the car in his too-small prom tux, true torture. Bing can see that bashful smile even now; as he had steadied the camera, Barbara yelled in his ear, "Take the picture. Quick-quick."

And the day Bing sat behind the wheel of that same car, Roger beside him in his khakis, green duffle stowed in the trunk. Patent leather shoes shined to a high gloss. How Barbara wanted to go, pleaded to go, but Bing said no. *This is a father's job*, driving his son to the airport just as Bing's father had driven him to the train station twenty-odd years earlier. There were things that needed to be said, especially after Susie's antiwar tirade in the living room. Enough to rattle a man's courage, didn't she know that? Leaving Bing to counter with jargon like *stiff upper lip* and *make your country proud* and *a man's gotta do what a man's gotta do.*

Roger needed to say things, too, but Bing will not, will not let those Studebaker words surface, resurface, after so many years, though he can still feel his son's cold-cold grip, fingers wrapped so tightly around his father's wrist that Bing's hand went completely numb.

"Wonder what he would have thought about Iraq," Brian says.

"What?" Bing says.

"I bet he'd join up in a heartbeat. Show Saddam what real weapons of mass destruction can do."

"Don't be stupid, Brian," Reenie says. "Uncle Roger was drafted."

"He would have joined anyway, wouldn't he, Grandpa?"

Reenie and Brian look at Bing, who doesn't know the answer to that. Or maybe he does, so he looks up in the trees and notices that the leaves have changed. "When did that happen?" He looks at sweet gums and sugar maples, leaves deep red, brilliant orange, flaming yellow, and behind him that fuzzy green wall. It's no longer green but a curtain of splotchy colors. Rich and warm as a crazy quilt, one of his mother's quilts, and he feels her wrapping him in it right now. *Got to keep you warm*, she says, and his hair feels wet, skin waxy and cold. So cold because he just had to go out and see the first snow of his life, a freak of nature in Houston. How white the flakes were, big as quarters, and he stayed out there for hours without a jacket, no gloves, until his fingers turned purple, but he didn't care, because he needed to catch another snowflake on his tongue. "Just one more," he says. "Please."

"What's he talking about?" Reenie says, her voice garbled, underwater.

Junior lays his hand on Bing's shoulder. "Mr. Butler."

"What?" Bing looks at Junior's meaty hand, how weighty it feels after all those snowflakes, practically pushing him into the earth.

"You and Ms. Foley find everything you need today?" Junior's eyes bore into Bing's as if he's trying to reach in and grab his soul from the bottom of a deep pit.

"Today?" Bing's pupils dilate back into focus.

"At the yard. Ms. Foley find everything she need?"

"Oh! Yeah. The gate. She picked up a couple of hood ornaments and some copper tubing."

Brian claps crumbs from his hands. "She's been needing a good tubing her whole life."

"Stop it," Reenie says, screwdriver clanking.

Bing doesn't get it, so he pushes on. "And a piece of tail pipe."

Brian snorts. "Piece of tail. She would like that."

"Shut up," Reenie says.

Bing looks from Reenie to Brian to Junior, rewinding the conversation to find the offending barb. He can't, so he looks back at Ellen's house. A light goes on in an upstairs window, and Bing tries to figure out which room it is. The master bedroom, he decides, imagining Ellen putting away folded shirts, balled up socks, stacks of white cotton handkerchiefs.

"Wonder if she still has her husband's clothes," Bing says, though he meant to think it.

"Husband!" Brian snorts. "Probably wears the old dyke's stuff."

"Shut the hell up!" Reenie says, screwdriver clunking madly. Even Bing can see the volley of dings she's pounding into his trunk.

"Stupid lesbo makes me wanna puke," Brian says.

Reenie jumps off that trunk so fast, screwdriver arced over her shoulder ready to plunge into her brother. Junior grabs her by the waist and whips her aside like a cardboard cutout of herself. He wrenches the tool from her and flings it into the grass like a dart.

"Settle down, Reenie," Junior says. "He's just trying to rile you up. He doesn't mean it."

Mean what? Bing wants to ask.

"The hell I don't," Brian says. "I never wanted to live next door to a bunch of lesbians."

"Lesbians?" Bing says, a word that's never slid from his mouth.

"All their bull dyke friends coming over for bull dyke parties."

Reenie struggles under Junior's grip. "What's she ever done to you? Huh? Why the hell do you eat her food if she makes you so sick?"

"Ellen's not a lesbian," Bing says.

"Then I won't eat her butch food," Brian says. He walks to the plate of brownies, picks it up like a Frisbee, and flings it toward Ellen's house. It sails perfectly level with the horizon, hits the brick porch and shatters, brown chunks and ceramic shards spilling into the azaleas.

"Asshole!" Reenie yells.

Susie bangs out the front door. "What's going on out here?"

Bing appraises the scene from his daughter's eyes: Junior's arms strapped around Reenie, whose claws reach toward her brother. Brian standing with his hands on his hips, scowling. Frida wobbling her way to mounds of brown something in Ellen's azaleas.

Reenie wrangles out of Junior's grip, and she looks at her brother, eyes narrowed. "Nothing. Nothing's going on out here."

Bing shakes his head at the absurdity of it all. He holds his hands out, palms up, and says, "Ellen's not a, a—" he has to whisper the word, "lesbian."

Susie looks from Reenie, to Brian, who looks at his feet. She exhales and grips Bing's forearm, offering preemptive support. "Well, Dad. I've been trying to figure out how to tell you."

Bing slumps in silence at the kitchen table. Supper has been over for twenty minutes, and he remembers pushing something beige around the plate with his fork.

Lesbian, he thinks, still hit and run over by the revelation, the word bouncing around his brain, his mouth, tip of his tongue flicking that incomprehensible *L*. For three weeks he's been eating lunch nearly every day with a lesbian. Played chess with a lesbian. Went to the junkyard with a lesbian. How could he not know? But how could he, really, when the only homosexuals he ever saw were when the Houston news covered the gay pride parade down on Westheimer? Most of the footage was of men in sequined dresses and platinum wigs. Giant fake boobs.

Course there were some lady golfers he and Dillard used to speculate about. And plenty of gay women tennis pros with their broad shoulders and muscular legs: Billie Jean King. Martina Navratilova. Still, they didn't really distress Bing since he only brushed up against them through the television. Maybe the sports page. Bing remembers all those women welders who descended on the Gulf Coast during World War II. They came by car, train, bus to work in the shipyards because all the men were off fighting. Bing always wondered about those gals. Shouldn't he have wondered about Ellen? Shouldn't he have known by the manly decor in her house, the sturdy kitchen table, those butter-colored work boots? Bing recalls mashing a Bible around the footwell of Ellen's car, her weekly study group. *What the hell kind of Christian is she?* And that wedding picture of Ellen and her, what? Groom? No. But not a wife, either. No wonder they looked so even, so equal, walking out of that church.

Bing stands and shakes his head. It was wrong of him to doubt that he and Barbara's marriage should have been anything other than what it was. He needs a chaw, bad, so he heads out back, those two Bradford pears shedding their orange-purple leaves. Bing packs his lip and sits on a soda fountain chair with its vinyl cushion no bigger than a toilet seat, wire back biting his spine. Above his head, half a dozen metal cylinders dangle from the porch roof, all timidly clinking in the breeze. It is a soothing sound, calming.

Bing is neither soothed nor calmed.

"What the hell have I done?" Bing whispers about relocating to Huntington where he's living next to a lesbian. Stuck in a house filled with crystal and jade and housekeepers and meth labs and a granddaughter who hangs out of windows. Susie and Glen too caught up in their own frazzled lives to care about drug-addicted, school-skipping children, never mind the old man in the basement. If Bing was back home right now, he'd be sitting on his wobbly front porch in his squeaky metal rocker, annoying, yes, but at least the bottom was wide enough to accommodate his behind. Cushion mildewed and cracking, but more agreeable than this unforgiving tailbone breaker. He could spit in the shrubs if he wanted. Never had to worry about getting scolded for leaving his spittoons out—not since Barbara died, anyway. Certainly never had to worry about exploding attics.

But there no longer is a wobbly porch back home. Yanked off by the new owners before Bing's road dust even settled. He doubts he'd recognize the old place. Maybe it's filled with jade fish and marble tabletops, too. Marijuana plants mixed in with Barbara's verbena.

Something sits on Bing's chest, not an elephant, exactly, not the weight of a heart attack, but enough to stifle his breathing as he realizes that for the first time in his life he is unmoored. No doormat to set his boots on. Not back in Texas. Certainly not here. No one in this town, this state, this planet to draw back the curtains to watch and wait for him to pull into the driveway. No one to throw open the door and say, *Welcome home!* A sinking, sinking feeling in his very core as Bing realizes what he has lost, what he will probably never find again.

He closes his eyes and tries to focus on the wind chimes, the melodic clinks and pings. But the persistent weight and the falling sensation inside, so deep inside that Bing can't catch himself.

He sees it before he hears it, even with his eyes shut, the bright, blinding light that lassos him and yanks him back up into his body. He opens his eyes and there, to his right, over the top of the privacy fence, is a halo of brilliant light, whiter than the sun. Like a strobe light flashing and flaring, making the Bradford trees shudder. He stands and leans toward Ellen's backyard so he can hear, he hopes he can still hear, and how elated he is when he finally detects a noise that calms his very soul: the sound of eggs frying, whites sputtering and slapping in the grease. But it's not eggs, Bing knows, it's a welder's torch, Ellen's sweet little Mig, the flame set just right when it sounds like frying eggs.

Bing closes his eyes out of habit, protecting himself from welder's flash. He's had his share already which is why his vision is shot. Particularly after that last bad case when his eyes looked like raw hamburger, felt like someone was grinding palms full of sand into them. He tried all the remedies: staring into a glass of milk, or a light bulb. Laying a slice of potato over each eye. He hopes Ellen is wearing a leather cape, something to protect her arms, keep them from looking like Bing's: a pockmarked mess. He worries about her visor—if she pulled it down snugly. He has an urge to go to the fence and shout over, ask her if she is working on galvanized metal, if she drank a glass of buttermilk beforehand to keep the vapors from giving her sour stomach.

But he doesn't, and he reminds himself that, at her age, she must know all of this, too. Still, he would like to know what she's working on. Even if it's one of those god-awful art monstrosities, or if she's already working on that gate. He could go over there right now, maybe borrow some gear so he could stand beside her and offer advice. But no. Ellen doesn't need his advice. After gliding his hand over the sweet welds in her sculptures, Bing knows Ellen could probably show him a thing or two. For the first time in his life he wouldn't mind that. Learning a thing or two from a woman.

Barbara wouldn't mind either, he feels sure. Him striking up a friendship with a member of the opposite sex. *You wouldn't mind, would you?* He can hear Dillard snorting even now.

But there's that thing about Ellen, that horrible thing, and these gleaming possibilities are chipped off like hardened globs of slag.

COVERT OPERATIONS

The next morning after the family scatters, Bing sprinkles jock-itch powder in his boots, puts salt in his coffee. He doesn't know how to get the day going now that his routine is kaput. At noon, Frida whimpers, but Bing doesn't dare walk her out front. Instead he leads her to the backyard where she delivers her litany, looking at him forlornly. "Sorry," Bing mutters, "but I don't want to see that woman."

An hour later the phone rings. Bing edges toward it and waits for the answering machine to kick on because he knows who it is. "Bing. Lunch is ready. I just made the most beautiful sweet potato pie." So much eagerness over a stupid thing like that. But it's not stupid, not to Bing, who sucks his tongue at the memory of sweetness, hints of butter and brown sugar. *Wonder if she adds pecans.* "Shoot," Bing says over the sadness of it all, the loss. Fifteen minutes later the phone rings again. This time the message is, "Guess you're not home."

That evening as Bing watches the news Glen comes down holding a Tupperware box. "This was on the front porch." The note slapped on the lid reads: *Bing: Missed you today. —E.*

After Glen leaves, Bing eats the cold wedge imagining Ellen's hands mashing the tubers, sprinkling in sugar and vanilla or whatever goes into it. The clumpy goo stuck between her fingers, imbedded in the geometric shapes in her wedding band, the rings she made for herself and her hus—

A lump catches in his throat and Bing has to stand to pummel his sternum. "Goddamn lying woman!"

Susie calls from the top of the stairs, "You okay down there, Dad?"

"Yep!" Bing garbles. "Never better!"

For days Bing refuses to pick up Ellen's calls, even when the message is, "Rook to king four." A conniving move, though just days ago he would have considered it subtle. He will not leave the house and risk facing her. But he can't keep away from the front window, hoping to find a plate of pot roast on the porch swing, oatmeal cookies on the rocker. Wanting the phone to ring so he can ignore it and reveal his anger through the back door since he can't do it head-on.

Once, however, while he's peeking out he sees her heading his way. He backs into the dining room, out of view, heart pounding at her rapid tapping on the storm door. Frida barks and Bing says, "Shhhhhh."

Through the door Ellen scolds, "Oh, hush. Bing! Haven't seen you in a few days. Are you all right in there? Bing?"

Bing pictures her leaning close to the glass, cupping her hands around her eyes, scanning to see if he is slumped there somewhere, the victim of stroke. If he had fallen, Ellen would probably break the glass to get inside, never mind the mess, the expense, and call 911.

So *un*like Barbara, when he had his heart attack. She flailed her hands and wailed before she had the presence to call an ambulance, by which time her voice was so screechy Bing marveled that the dispatcher could make out their address. He slumped on the cold kitchen floor, his head in Barbara's lap as she tried and tried to flatten his cowlick before the paramedics arrived, the hot tears dripping off her chin, splattering Bing's ashen forehead.

Bing feels like he's losing Barbara all over again, especially when Ellen bleats, "Just wanted to make sure you were all right, friend!"

That night Susie brings home KFC.

"Where's Glen?" Bing asks.

"Late meeting," she says, voice hard-edged.

Brian tumbles into the kitchen. "What smells good?" He grins at the bucket, the tubs of side dishes, before loading up a plate. "Thanks, Mom," he slurs as he heads back to his room.

Susie clasps her chest. "Did he say thank you?"

"Yes indeed." Bing piles his own plate.

Susie pulls in her chair, and they both dive in, manners be damned as they suck fat from their fingertips and let the spent chicken bones fall where they may.

"Good eatin'," Bing says.

"And how," Susie says, which would have been enough. But. "How's Ellen?"

Bing swallows hard, wanting to swallow this subject too. "Haven't seen her."

"The answering machine has racked up a lot of her messages."

"Hadn't noticed." Bing wonders why his daughter would want to ruin a perfectly decent meal.

With her fork, Susie plows a trench in her potatoes. "Don't you think you owe her an explanation?"

A hot wave rushes through Bing. He's the one who deserves an explanation.

"You two were getting to be good buddies."

Bing studies the milk ring by his plate. "You should have told me."

"I know. But nothing's changed. She's still the same person—"

"She's not the same." Bing stands, crumbs tumbling from his jumpsuit to the floor. "Nothing is the same." He shakes his head. His daughter stares at him, face round and uncomprehending. Can't she see that a person's got to stand for something, for decency and morals, even if the world around him is going to hell?

"You can't just leave her hanging, Dad."

Bing's chin goes down because she doesn't understand anything. All he can do is aim for the basement, his bunker in this world that he does not agree with, and that apparently doesn't agree with him.

As he makes his way down Susie mumbles, "Coward."

It's tiring, this avoidance, this self-imposed house arrest. And boring. One morning, however, Bing hears a sweet sound: a toilet running on the second floor. He feels like an intruder as he enters the bathroom, then heaves a sigh, because instead of finding gallons of water gushing on the tile floor, all he has to do is jiggle the handle to resettle the flapper.

He starts to head back downstairs but decides to do a little reconnaissance, find out what keeps these people so busy they don't have time for him. He leans inside the master bedroom and can tell which side of the bed is Glen's—the one that looks as if it wasn't slept in. Susie's side is a disheveled mess: blankets twisted, pillow scrunched and pounded as if she were boxing someone's ears in her sleep, a student's perhaps, or Reenie's. Maybe Bing's. He spots Susie's sweatpants and t-shirt bunched up on the floor, Glen's pajamas folded over a chair back. Bing wonders again how this marriage functions. Sure, they share leftist leanings and foot-long academic words, but it's the day-to-day getting along that really matters: towels left on the bathroom floor; missing toothpaste caps; constantly having one's glass hauled to the sink when there was still one good swig left. It would be better if Bing heard them fighting, because it would mean there's still a spark there. But Glen and Susie clock through their separate days, separate lives, suffering a kind of strained silence, not the comfortable quiet that settled around Bing and Barbara over the years. It's a different kind of hush altogether.

He clicks his cheek, turns around, and sees Reenie's attic door partially open. Though his heart jigs, he feels it's his duty to find out if there is a meth lab up there that could blow a hole through the roof. He is a hero, he tells himself, trying to keep his daughter and son-in-law safe. Bing opens the door and steps into the box stairwell, painted black, a foreboding of much darker things to come: pentagrams and caged rats and cat skulls. He climbs, slowly, wishing someone were here with him. Dillard. Even the dog would do. But he must do this alone. *I am not a coward.* He reaches the halfway point where the stairs turn a sharp corner for the last six steps, five, four, and it's brighter than he expected, thankfully, natural light from the windows pouring in. He won't have to flail blindly through cobwebs and stuffed ravens for a pull string to the bare bulb dangling from the rafters. Finally he plants his feet on the attic floor and looks around at his granddaughter's room, stunned.

Not scary at all! No swooping bats or fiberglass insulation or tar seeping through roof beams. It's an open space completely finished with drywall, lemon paint coating the walls. White ceiling fan and hardwood floors dotted with rugs. Bing shuffles around, flinching at every creaky board, but he can't stop gawking at the four-poster bed, completely made, a lop-eared bunny nestled between the pillows.

There is evidence of Reenie's darker side: photos of painted-up rock stars taped to the walls; a coat tree draped with her motorcycle jacket and bandoleers, but also a straw hat with baby's breath around the rim. Slapped on her vanity mirror are stickers that shout: *Defy Authority!* and *Bite Me!* but also *I ♥ my Cocker Spaniel* and *Jesus was a Feminist.*

Bing frets over the two columns of numbers that should tally up to his granddaughter, but don't. Add to the mix a jewelry box crammed with a studded dog collar and a strand of pearls. Is that Barbara's cameo pin? *It is!* A gushy ball forms in his stomach.

Suddenly he can see Barbara's taste in the lacy curtains, doilies beneath table lamps, figurines of little girls holding kittens.

Bing spies a bookcase. Ten minutes ago he would have imagined shelves crammed with manuals on pipe bombs or poison cocktails. He kneels and runs his fingers along book spines: calculus, physics, zoology. But also books devoted to domestic affairs: cookbooks, cross-stitch samplers, laundry-stain remedies, *Bride* magazine. *Bride?* A wedding planner and catalogues of china patterns and flatware and invitations.

Strings of information unravel from the mental knot Bing's been worrying over since he overheard Reenie and Junior hanging out of that very window. "You know what I want," she had said. "I am so ready." Junior's stall, "We promised your mom we wouldn't."

Reenie wants to get married.

"I'll be jiggered," Bing says, flabbergasted.

A car door slams outside. Bing moves to the front window and squints at Susie getting out of her car, someone walking toward her on the sidewalk, arm raised in greeting. Ellen. Bing takes a step backward, yet can't resist leaning forward to get her in his sights. There she is. Wearing those overalls and butter boots and lugging—what is that—a muffler?

Been to the junkyard.

Ellen holds up the muffler as if it's a sailfish she spent hours reeling in. Bing pictures her scavenging through the junkyard without him—getting on with her life. She and Susie yak a bit, hands flapping, until Ellen points at the house sending Bing back a step further. Susie holds her hands out in supplication. Ellen's head flops down as she listens and nods at whatever difficult news Susie is delivering. Bing knows what news, and he feels an itching beneath his skin. Not anger, no. Whatever it is builds and only heightens when Susie leans forward and hugs Ellen, patting her shoulder, her braid. Ellen hugs her back, not killing the messenger, and she actually kisses Susie's cheek before turning to walk back to her house, muffler dragging desolately behind.

Bing pummels down the stairs, Susie's accusation banging around his skull: *coward.*

Four days later Bing decides he is *not* a coward, and to prove it he takes Frida for her noon walk. Out front, he tries to yank her away from Ellen's house, but the dog will have none of that. Bing flips up his collar against the November chill and reminds himself that it's only fourteen steps across Ellen's sidewalk, her driveway, and he will be free to ignore any attempt at communication, will be able to blame poor hearing. But his hearing isn't poor today because there's the sound of Ellen's front door opening, that galling creak he promised to WD-40 but never had the chance. He only has a few more paces to go, though it looks like a mile, and he feels her eyes boring into the back of his neck.

"Bing."

He quickens his gait because he can't bear to look at her, refuses to endure what he's sure will be an angry barrage lined with language so foul neighbors will pour from their houses.

"Bing!" she yells this time, but he will not stop. "I should have told you. I was just waiting for the right time."

Bing's left foot hesitates, but he forces it forward and marches on.

"That's just a part of who I am," Ellen says. "Just one part."

Bing wants to look back, but he can't. He gazes up into trees, barren now, black branches clattering together like bones in the bitter wind, making a woeful, woeful sound.

ALLIES

Saturday afternoon Bing lopes out back and chokes on his Skoal because Susie and Reenie are raking leaves together, a mother-daughter snapshot he never expected to see. He's captivated by their efficiency: Susie raking, Reenie holding open the leaf bag, tamping it down between loads. They aren't talking, and there's a comfort in their silence. The *scritch-scritch* of the rake, the dry crunch of leaves, the distant cawing of crows. A kind of bliss.

Still, Bing wonders what Susie and Reenie might debate if they opened their mouths: global warming, the Taliban. They could do it, he knows, shoot the breeze about alternative fuels and fundamentalist regimes.

Bing recalls odd dashes of lace and studded dog collars in Reenie's room, that puzzling blend of smarts, Dark Princess, and housewife. He imagines that she goes to her parents for intellectual matters, to Junior for all things carnal, but who does she rely on for domestic advice? Who would she show her soft underbelly to? Not Susie, who suffered none of that, not now, not eons ago whenever Barbara tried to talk about Lady Gillettes or training bras or freezer burn—topics that sent Bing scrounging for something to hammer.

There's a thump in his chest for Reenie who lost more than a grandmother when Barbara died. She lost a coconspirator in housekeeping. He feels drawn to his grandchild, and he steps from the porch and into the grass to offer, what? Even he doesn't know, but it feels like something Barbara would want him to do.

"What'cha doing there?" Bing asks.

Reenie looks at him as if he's an idiot. "Raking leaves."

"Course. Sure. I mean . . ." Bing doesn't know what he means, so more words gallop forward. "Nice day for it."

"How do you like your first West Virginia fall?" Susie asks.

Bing's head bobbles up and down. "I like it," he says, and he does. Crisp air almost void of moisture—a pleasant bonus. "Don't miss Texas humidity." It feels like a back stab.

"Wait'll you see snow!" Reenie says, her gusto astonishing.

"You like snow?" Bing asks.

Reenie immediately forces her glee back into whatever pocket she's been hauling it around in. "It's okay."

"You wait, Dad," Susie says. "She'll be the first one making snow angels."

"Will not."

"Will *too*." Susie nudges her daughter with her shoulder.

Reenie nudges her mother right back. "Will *not*."

More jostling and bumping and Bing is alarmed until he realizes they are *playing*. Bing laughs, an emotive hiccup he's kept buttoned in his own pocket. It feels good, the stutter in his chest, the wind scraping his adenoids.

Until he shuts it all down, all of it, the scrapbook moment, the snow angels, the laughter, with one sentence. "You know Barbara and I got married when she was just eighteen."

It's like that game of freeze tag the kids played years ago. Susie and Reenie have both been tagged, and they stand there, frozen, if only for a second, waiting for the game to resume.

Susie shakes it off first. "What?"

Reenie's eyelids flutter, but when she again looks at Bing her eyes are full of, what is that, gratitude?

Susie looks at her daughter. "Did you put him up to this?"

The gratitude dissolves when Reenie plants a fist on her hip. "No."

Susie aims herself at Bing. "Did she put you up to this?"

Bing doesn't have a chance to answer because Reenie repeats, "I said *no!*"

Susie opens her mouth, but all that comes out are grunts. She throws down her rake and stomps to the house calling over her shoulder, "Just finish the stupid leaves."

Reenie stands there, mouth crimped. She looks down at the leaves, or through them, head almost imperceptibly shaking.

Bing feels it's his duty to proffer words of apology or commiseration, but he stays put until Reenie picks up the rake and starts pulling leaves into a sloppy pile. Bing bends to open the bag, offer support in the only way he knows how.

"I'll do it," Reenie says, not angry, just resigned.

Bing backs quietly away. The scritch of the rake, the rustle of leaves, the cawing of crows no longer blissful.

Hours later, in the basement, Bing sits in his recliner watching Frida heap his dirty laundry into a mound with her paws and plop on top like a queen. But her reign is short-lived; both of their heads perk up at the wafting allure of frying meat. Bing looks at Frida, Frida looks at Bing, and they grunt to their feet.

Reenie stands at the kitchen counter peeling an onion. Bing spies cans of tomato sauce and paste. A green pepper. Spice jars and garlic bulbs. A steaming pot of water on the stove. Glorious box of spaghetti beside it.

This time Bing measures his words instead of blurting some evident blather like *What are you making?* "What's the occasion?"

He's not surprised when she doesn't turn to face him; he's hoping to get any answer at all. "Mom and Dad went to some dumb faculty thing."

"That so?" Bing says, stung because Susie didn't bother to tell him—punishment for his morning gaffe.

Reenie dices that onion like she knows what she's doing.

"You look like you know what you're doing," Bing says.

Frida paws at Reenie's foot. She picks a hamburger glob out of the frying pan, blows on it, and slides it into the dog's mouth. Then she dices the bell pepper, scoops up handfuls to toss in with the meat, stirs it with a wooden spoon. She adds pinches of this and smidgeons of that and finally looks over her shoulder at the wall clock. "He's late."

"Brian?" Bing asks, still hovering.

"Junior. He was supposed to help me with this." Reenie looks at Bing, really looks at him. He suspects that he's in for a delayed blasting for fueling the mother-daughter feud. He grips a chair back, but what she says is, "Would you open those?" She nods at the alert unit of tomato cans lined up. Bing understands that this is about more than just opening cans.

"I can't do much in the kitchen, but I can do that." He looks around for the can opener.

"It's over there." She points to a contraption hooked underneath a cabinet.

He bundles the cans together in his arms. It takes him a minute to figure out the opener, but he's whirring off lids in no time, delivering the cans back to the chef.

"You can start on the salad if you want," Reenie says. "Veggies are in the fridge."

"Okay," Bing says, pushing up his sleeves because this is a real assignment. He finds the ingredients, and when he twists back around, Reenie has set up his station: cutting board, paring knife, carrot scraper, salad bowl.

A sudden image of Grandma Lottie's butcher block table barricaded behind a wall of unpacked boxes in the basement. Now Bing knows who it belongs to. Not Susie, who would probably pile it up with stacks of dusty books or student papers. Reenie would use it, he knows, and he watches her fold tomato sauce into the meat, swirl it around, dab her tongue on the spoon.

Make a nice wedding gift, he decides, words he won't dare utter aloud—even if Susie isn't home.

Bing starts on the carrots, scraping, slicing. He wants to get this right, and the knife feels so good in his hand, the stoic resistance of the carrot, the satisfying snap at the end when the knife cleaves through. It's like a duet, his *chop-chop* blending with Reenie's pattering and stirring, and he regrets that he never cooked with Barbara. He could have sliced a million radishes or potatoes or okra for her, opened thousands of cans instead of just unscrewing the occasional jar. He never offered, of course, *woman's work*, and he can already imagine the ribbing he would earn from Dillard. Besides, Barbara never asked, and even if she did, he imagines she would have quibbled over the angle of his carrot disks, the width of the celery.

But Reenie hasn't looked over his shoulder, hasn't critiqued his form, and it reminds him of his welding days when a crew went out. Each man had a specific section, a task, and you had to rely on their skill and attention to safety the way they relied on yours. Reenie is relying on Bing, and it feels good to once again be trusted, empowered, even if it's only with a garden salad.

"Sorry I'm late." Junior comes in with a plastic grocery sack weighing down his hand. He sets the bag on the table with a thud. "Mr. Butler." He offers Bing a respectful bow.

"Get the bread?" Reenie asks.

Junior pulls a loaf from the sack.

"And the—"

Bing already knows what she's looking for, can see the red wine peeking out of the bag. He wonders what's stalling her and then remembers her age, or *under*age.

"Won't bother me," Bing says. "If you're old enough to vote, you're old enough to drink." He remembers the rancor he felt when he couldn't offer his son a legal farewell toast before sending him off to fight for his country. If there was ever a time when a man needed to be numbed, it was during war.

Bing wipes his hands on a dish towel and holds out the paring knife for Junior to take over his job.

"You finish," Reenie says. "Junior can set the table."

Bing's eyes well up. What shocks him even more is that Junior sets three places, and after supper is ready and they scooch in their chairs, Junior bows his head and prays. Nothing fancy, just a few syllables waved over the food. Bing looks over at Reenie expecting her mother's grimace, but Reenie's eyes are closed and at the end she even dots the prayer with an amen.

It's the best meal Bing's had in this house, and salad never tasted better—stringy celery, field greens, and all. Junior and Reenie yammer on about professors and burning CDs and what Junior found in that wrecked van he towed into the lot. Bing doesn't mind being the proverbial fly, but Junior eventually asks him about his early days with Barbara. Bing downs a slug of wine before weaving tales about her botched laundry and crispy eggs. He confesses to the free Arthur Murray dance lesson—just the one—and how he butchered Barbara's bangs that time.

The dessert—the sweetest finale of all—comes *after* the chocolate pie, when Reenie says, "Next Saturday we'll all make stuffed peppers."

What a glorious thought. That night and the next Bing dreams about ground chuck. During the week he flits through the house. Hardly thinks about Ellen. Doesn't feel *as* ruffled when Aldine comes to clean, though he makes sure his toilet is flushed and his dirty underwear is buried.

Susie must note the lift in Bing's heel, the extra wave in his pompadour, because she comes to the basement one night with two mugs of coffee. "What's got you feeling so peppy?"

Bing sits up in his recliner. "Stuffed peppers."

Susie sits across from him. "Doesn't take much."

"You know what else I've been mulling over?"

"What's that?"

"Your mother's corn pudding. You think Reenie would like that?"

"Reenie?"

"She's probably never had it, and that's just not right."

Susie nods, a peculiar look in her eyes. "Yeah, I heard about your cooking extravaganza."

There's that look again, and if Bing had to name it, he might call it jealousy.

"You can help, too," he says, not wanting to stoke the furnace. "In fact, you can help me find Barbara's recipe file." He juts his thumb toward the back wall. "It's in one of those boxes."

Susie slurps her coffee, and Bing worries that he has offended her academic credentials by suggesting such a trivial chore.

She pumps her shoulders. "I can do that."

Bing grins. They both stand and saunter to the last of the box-es Bing has resisted unpacking because it would make the move too permanent.

WAR CRIMES

Bing and Susie ease onto the floor, opening boxes, scattering hunting clothes and Christmas doodads around the carpet. Eventually Bing notes that each time he draws out a bag of emergency candles or dainty bars of soap it's punctuated by a sniff, not his, but Susie's. Now her head is bent over the satin pillowcase Barbara slept on so her hairdo wouldn't get mussed. Tears drip, fat splats that turn the pink weave brown. "Mom's pillowcase," she says, as if Bing didn't know that, as if he hadn't slept beside it for decades. Susie buries her face in the fabric. "I miss her."

Do you? Bing wants to ask, because aside from the obligatory grief she expressed at the funeral, he never knew how Susie felt deep down about her mother's death—or her life.

But these tears are authentic, and Susie rocks forward and back, forward and back, until she's that little girl who just found the neighbor's cat dead by the side of the road. Bing looks away, wondering if he should leave, let her cry in peace. Or maybe reach out a hand and pat her shoulder the way Barbara probably would have.

He almost does. Almost.

When Bing looks back up, he sees the grapefruit-sized globe in Susie's grip, a tin bank of the world that Roger earned by saving Mallo Cup cards or Bazooka wrappers. Susie shakes the planet, probably hoping for wheat pennies, but there are no coins inside. Her face crumbles into that teenage grimace she wore for months after she heard the terrible news. Not from Barbara. Not from Bing. From a truant neighbor boy who had no business holding such potent words in his mouth. But he did, and Bing later learned how the kid saw the military vehicle from his tree house and jumped down in awe. How he trailed the uniformed man as he marched to the front porch and rang the bell, hid in the bushes as Barbara opened the door and collapsed to one knee even before those dark words spilled like a hex from the soldier's mouth. And the boy, the little boy with such big news, scrambled from the bushes and ran to the corner to wait for the school bus so that when its doors hissed open he could dart inside and tell Susie the horrible thing that would shadow them the rest of their lives.

How sad Bing felt for her, being told such private news in public, having to drop her textbooks and scramble home where Bing already was, having rushed from work in his own blind haze. How Barbara tried to console her, but Susie pushed her mother's arms away and ran to her father—not for comfort—but to pound his chest, his arms, though he couldn't feel a thing.

"It's your fault!" she had said, eyes pinched shut just as they are now. "He never would have gone if not for you!" There were other wounding phrases. So many cutting words he can't remember, because he got stuck on her first condemnation. Had uttered that very indictment to himself twenty minutes before Susie arrived home and a million times after: *It's my fault. It's all my fault.*

After that he couldn't look at her.

Can't look at her now, but Susie won't meet his eyes either. She stands abruptly, cheeks splotchy. "I'll help you with all of this later." She turns and rushes up the steps away from her father, from the man, Bing imagines, she still blames for casting such a wicked, wicked spell.

When she is gone Bing looks at Roger's picture over the mantle. Such a mild face. Bing tries not to conjure the look of terror that might have twisted there during Roger's last hour, last minute, last second of life. When he knew he was in real trouble. If he knew. Bing's only hope, from the minute he heard, was that it happened so unexpectedly, so quickly, that Roger never saw it coming, never knew what hit him, never had to experience that sense of impending death—no matter how brief. But maybe his whole tour was like that: the imminent knowing, the waiting. The only crushing question was *When?*

Bing looks at the bits and pieces of his life scattered across the floor. Goods he wants to scoop back into boxes, forget the packing tape, and shove into some truck, any truck no matter its destination, and get the hell out of here. But he can't, he knows, and the only thing he can do is keep searching for Barbara's recipe file. He knows how stupid it is, how silly and irrelevant in light of such pain, but it's the only balm of value he knows to offer to his daughter, to this family.

He sifts through box after box until it's well after midnight, one, two in the morning. Bing doesn't care. He's on a mission. Doesn't even stop to pee. He deserves this discomfort, plus the crick in his neck, the ache in his back.

And then he finds it. The tiny wooden box with brass hinges. Before he opens it he holds it to his nose to smell the sweet musk of age. He lifts the lid and jammed inside are hundreds of yellowed, dog-eared, food-stained index cards, a lifetime of dishes

Barbara collected from church dinners and baby showers and ladies' magazines. Recipes clipped and transcribed in Barbara's neat pen. He flips through the alphabetized stack: Alamo tamales; au gratin potatoes; banana upside-down cake (a disaster, as he recalls); beer bread (a triumph); carrot cake; candied apricots; *corn pudding!* There it is: the sweet combination of whole corn and eggs and cream, as hearty and wholesome a dish as frankfurters and beans, macaroni and cheese, comfort food that Bing hopes to God will bring comfort, if only for a minute, if only for a taste.

Bing tries to stand with the wooden box in one hand, corn recipe in the other, but his knees grind, and when he reaches for something to steady himself nothing is there. He refuses to let go of the hard-won swag, and as his arms flail, the cards fly out of the box and hundreds of ivory slips flutter down as he crashes into now-empty boxes and unforgiving, disheveled piles of junk. When the last card settles Bing doesn't think about his bruised palms, scraped knees, torn jumpsuit. He can envision the tizzy Barbara would be in if she saw her collection scattered like leaves. He kneels to gather them in, pluck them from where they landed among what he now considers absurd debris.

He draws in handfuls of cards, cramming them back in the box, leave the sorting for later, until he feels an odd texture in the mix: a newspaper clipping folded up, probably a recipe Barbara never got around to copying. It's brittle in his fingers and he lets it flap open. It's an obituary from the *Houston Post*. *Where'd she get this?* It was the rival *Chronicle* that landed on Bing's porch every morning. He holds it up to scrutinize the man's face.

Before he reads the name, he knows who it is, the faded print only confirming: Charles Winston Morgan. Not even Chuck. Charles, always. Bing collapses onto his bum, the paper rattling in his hands, wondering why Barbara kept this, *hid* this in the one place she probably never imagined Bing would find it.

"Son of a bitch," Bing says, not about Barbara, never about Barbara, but about Charles, the man—the boy, really, Barbara was dating before Bing snatched her away. How she broke his heart, Charles claimed, broke it clean in two when she picked a muscle-armed Navy man over him: a brain-logged, pencil-necked, milquetoast—at least that's what Bing called him. Charles wasn't too timid to call Barbara after Bing shipped out, and at least once a month even after they were married. Barbara swore they were *just friends*, but Bing knew the kinds of delirious urges that could pump into a man's skull, his loins—learned that lesson when he bunked with hundreds of hormone-torqued sailors—himself included. So the last time *Chuck* called, Bing yanked the phone from his wife's grip, pulled the cord from the wall, and hollered, "No more!"

Now here he is again, Charles, no longer a milquetoast, wearing a dapper suit, with a fleshed-out face and a foot-long obituary crammed full of accomplishments. Bing has to read it, has to read something to avoid the thought trying to push its way in—the idea that Barbara had been pining for Charles all those years, had wondered where he was, how his life played out. Why else would she have saved the man's obituary in such an intimate place? Bing reads about Charles's World War II service—*so he joined up after all, and he was a fly boy.* His advanced degrees. His rise to CEO of Stillwater Oil in Houston. He'd been there all along? How did Bing not know this? Probably had a home in River Oaks, he decides, anxious about what Barbara made of it all when *she* read this weighty list of successes.

A tableau forms in Bing's head of Barbara sitting in their squat living room with her knitting needles clacking, daydreaming about a three-story house with a gardener and chauffeur; shopping sprees at the Galleria; weekly pedicures; luxuries Bing's salary could never afford. Ever. Extravagances she deserved and that Charles would have happily lavished.

Bing has to stop and calculate how many years Barbara might have lived with those regrets. Four years, he figures, between this obituary and her own. That's a long time to not measure up. Bing reads on, looking for survivors: the pampered wife, silver-spoon children, trust-fund grandbabies. But there are none. Had Charles loved Barbara that much? He must have, and Bing hates to imagine how he would have felt if her coin had tossed the other way. If he never had her for fifty-two years, four months, five days.

He feels an odd sympathy for Charles, for his rich life that was ultimately so poor he had to fill it with petroleum and the antique car club. Beck Museum Ball Committee. Charter member of the Bellaire Bridge Club along with his devoted friend and bridge partner for over fifty years, Barbara Lacy Butler.

Barbara Lacy Butler.

What? Bing scans it again to convince himself that he read it wrong, but he didn't and he knows there can't be two Barbara Lacy Butlers in the entire world. But Barbara stopped talking to

Charles, ended that *friend*ship a lifetime ago. And besides, she didn't even play bridge. *Did she?*

Bing collapses onto the pile of junk. He lies there, numb, staring at drop-ceiling tiles; uneven wallpaper; a crooked American Gothic print; and he doesn't move, and he doesn't move. Not even when blue dawn filters in, especially when probing light begins to invade, because he knows it will make all of this—whatever the hell this is—real.

RETREAT

Something wet dabs Bing's cheek, then a blast of hot breath, the stench of rotting teeth. Frida. Bing opens his eyes as the dog nudges him. He pushes her off, leans up on one elbow, glasses cockeyed. Frida paws at his knee, whimpering.

It takes Bing three tries to stand because his body feels as if it's one of those sand-bottomed, inflatable clowns the kids used to punch-punch-*punch!* Finally he stands, his footing wobbly as he crunches over pumpkin salt-and-pepper shakers, wicker napkin holders, a hodgepodge of recipe cards, those goddamn recipe cards. He spots Barbara's wooden box and kicks it against the baseboard, the impact breaking a hinge.

Bing reaches for the back of his recliner, feeling the obituary scrunched in his hand. He rubs his eyes, the gritty salt that he must grind and grind as he walks to his room to put the obituary, *where?* Some private place, the Safeway sack in his nightstand drawer, containing Barbara's executed will, his unexecuted one, Susie's birth certificate, Roger's Vietnam letters. Bing opens the drawer to tug out the sack and shove the paper into the mix, but he can't defile these sacred documents with this scandalous one. So he rips the obituary into pieces which he flushes down the commode, a swirl of letters glugging down the pipes.

Bing leans forward in the shower, hands high against the ceramic tiles—a man being frisked—the hot spray pulsing down on his head.

He studies his feet, the fungal toenails, water pooling in the drain clogged with soap scum and pubic hairs and snot, wondering if his whole life was a lie.

He scans the years for clues. Those late-night phone calls from ailing friends. *Just being a good Christian*, he always thought, and the inverted guilt because he never offered to go with her. Not once. All those Bible studies and visits to church shut-ins. *Ha!* What did all those good-bye pecks mean? Bing in his rocker, or lying in bed, sitting at the kitchen table and Barbara's head tipping down to plant her lips on the top of his head. *I won't be long!* she always promised, and she never was, *was she?*

Bridge partners. *Right.* How she probably couldn't wait to tear across town, Charles panting at his picture window, throwing open the door as her car—*Bing's* car— pulled up to the stately house. *No wonder she wanted to learn to drive.* It's not seventy-year-old Barbara he pictures, not sixty or fifty, but Barbara in her late thirties and forties—at her voluptuous peak—when childbirth and slowing metabolism had fleshed out her bones, given her those hips, those glorious hips, and a swell in her inner thighs that drove him wild.

Probably drove Charles wild, too.

Bing's stomach lurches at the image of Barbara's legs, arms twined around another man's body. Bing punches the tiles, cracking one in two, grout crumbling, knuckle bleeding. He wonders, *God no*, if it was Charles she pictured all those nights when she and Bing made love. Her eyelids fluttering as she imagined those lips on her collar bone, hands massaging her spine, were not his at all, but Charles's. And after, after, when she and Bing spooned, his face nestled in the nape of her neck, right arm strapped around her waist, pulling her to him, belly to back. How he never slept better. Never. Especially when she stroked his forearms with her fingernails, back and forth, back and forth.

But as the now-cold shower water beats down on his head, he no longer knows whose arm she stroked in her mind, who she whispered *I love you* to.

Bing doesn't shave, doesn't even comb his hair, just towels off, tugs on clean boxers and jumpsuit, and trudges through heaps of still-scattered junk—detouring around Frida who has curled up on wadded newspapers and bubble wrap—to collapse into his recliner because he doesn't have the wherewithal to stand. He clicks on the TV, a once-soothing diversion that no longer diverts, because on top of the TV sits Barbara's framed cross-stitch, *Bless this Box*, dragged all the way from Texas. He spies all the other loving tributes he situated around this room to remind himself of his home, his wife, so she would never be too far from his thoughts. Maybe Charles's home was also punctuated with porcelain roses and teddy bears and egg baskets. Maybe Barbara had her own side in Charles's bedroom closet, a walk-in closet, no doubt, crowded with Lord and Taylor dresses she could only don when she was with him. Did she claim a couple of his dresser drawers, too? Have a satin-covered pillow on his king-sized bed?

"Supper's ready!" Glen hollers from the top of the stairs.

Supper? How did Bing miss all the preamble? The feet shuffling overhead, cabinets opening and closing, the can opener growling. He puts a hand on his belly, but even that slight pressure makes him gag.

"Not hungry!" he yells back up.

"What?" Glen's voice is more shocked than inquiring.

"I had a big lunch." Even the lie makes him want to puke. He looks over at the junk mounds cluttering his floor, sees Roger's globe, and he imagines his daughter has lost her appetite, too. But Frida, well, she deserves to eat so Bing calls to her, "Your hog slop is ready," the putrid words tangling in his throat. Frida lifts her head, looks toward the stairs. "Go on up," but Frida curls into a ball and closes her eyes.

Bing can't shake an unbearable vision. Barbara's first cancer surgery, when Charles was still alive. Bing stepping out to the vending machines for coffee, two coffees, because he left Susie sitting in the visitor's chair holding her mother's hand, droning on about Reenie and Brian. Bing and Susie understood that Barbara probably couldn't hear one word, was so heavily medicated, thankfully, she wouldn't have to endure the pain. On his way back he picked up the pace as the heat of the scalding coffee seeped through the paper cups, burning his palms. Two doors away, a man dashed out of Barbara's room and raced down the hall. Bing remembers the man's blue-and-white seersucker jacket, how the man's head bent down, hands to his face, how his shoulders shook and shook and shook. Back in the room he found Susie, no longer in the visitor's chair, but leaning against the wall, arms crossed over her chest as the tears poured, just poured. "Who was that?" he asked. Susie didn't look at him. "Nobody," she said. "He was in the wrong room."

It was Charles. Bing begins to realize the far-reaching implications of Barbara's double life. Susie probably knew, likely encouraged her mother to find happiness with another man because she couldn't possibly be happy with Bing, the man responsible for so much pain. Her father, the uneducated, blue-collar dolt who was far too simpleminded to ever suspect that his wife could be capable of such a thing. *He'll never know, Mother*, Susie probably said. *You deserve to be happy.*

Saturday morning someone pads downstairs, waking Bing from a tormented sleep. He tries to lift his neck but a bundle of stick-pins jabs the base of his skull. He swivels his recliner toward the blurry figure: Susie heading to the laundry room lugging a clothes basket. Soon the sounds of fabric tumbling onto the floor, shirts and towels and jeans being yanked out and sorted. The grind of the washer knob, water spilling into the drum, the liquid rush muffled when Susie piles in clothes. The lid closing with a clang.

Bing wants to rub his neck, tries to lift his arm, but he feels a searing flash from his right hand to his elbow. He looks down at the purple welt on his middle knuckle, a blood-crusted gash, earned from bashing the shower tiles.

Susie tiptoes out and starts heading upstairs, but she glances at Bing. "I didn't know you were awake."

"I am now," he says, voice phlegmy.

Susie takes a good look at him, and what a sight she must see: two-day beard, wild hair, neck pinched sideways, bruised hand. He wants her to step closer so he can get a good look at her, too, see if he can calculate just how much of her mother's secret she was in on, or just what the secret was. See if there is a gratified smirk there: *You deserve this, old man.*

But there is no smirk, and Bing can tell that Susie is trying to spit something out, is measuring words. What she finally says is, "I won't be home for supper tonight. I'm going out with the girls."

"The girls?"

"Just blowing off steam."

Bing nods. He knows something about needing to blow off steam. "What about Glen?"

Susie nibbles her lip, wrestling with those words again. "He's got his own thing." She really gnaws at that lip. "But I guess you and Reenie will do all right by those stuffed peppers."

Bing's stomach shudders. "I don't think I'm up for stuffed peppers today."

"You're not? What's wrong?"

"Indigestion. Better tell Reenie she'll have to fly solo on this one. Of course, Junior will help out."

Susie looks as if she's not buying it but, like her father, she doesn't probe, just stands there until she points to the junk heap on the floor. "Sorry I left you with all this to deal with."

Does she know exactly what he was left to deal with?

She takes a step toward the heap, nudges a snow globe with little cowboy boots and oil derricks swirling around inside. Beside it, Barbara's mangled recipe box. Susie's eyebrows draw together, and Bing watches her scan the scattered recipe cards. She leans down to pick one up, but thinks better of it.

"Did you find Mom's corn—"

"No!" Bing's chest thunks because he's not ready to talk about it, say it out loud, give it a name.

Susie waves a hand over the mound, and Bing wishes for a magic wand that could make it all vanish. "I can help you put all this away now if you like."

Bing looks at the jumbled mess. So much wasted time and packing tape. The backbreaking labor as he and Dillard loaded box after box into the U-Haul. Bing had no idea what all he was loading, what he would drag halfway across the country.

"I didn't know," he says.

Susie's head juts forward. "Didn't know what?"

"I didn't know . . . it would be so much work. Don't know why I bothered to haul all this trash up here."

"It's not trash."

Bing swivels completely around to face the imposing pile. "Ought to get a backhoe in here and haul it over to Junior's junkyard."

"It's *not trash!*" Susie repeats, bending to scoop up Roger's bank, the recipe box, the snow globe.

Bing's jaw hangs open. Susie cradles the treasures, looking as if she needs for him to say something, offer something, *ask* something. Or maybe she's wrestling with her own inner question: *Does he know?* Perhaps she's been struggling to bring everything to light, too. Maybe this secret she's been harboring for so many years is a burden she needs to cast off. Bing looks at his daughter looking at him, both trying to read each other, he guesses, to see who knows what. The snag of it pinched between their fingers, a loose thread ready to be tugged and unraveled. He knows it, and he knows that the moment is slipping away when Susie breaks eye contact and lets out a sigh.

"Okay then," she says, turning toward the stairs.

Bing's right fingers knock against the chair arm and it hurts, that sore knuckle, but he persists, because his daughter is hoisting her right foot up one step, left foot up the next as she begins her ascent. "I'll be upstairs."

God dammit, just ask her!

But he can't, because he's afraid that the knowing might cleave him in two.

RECONNAISSANCE

That evening Bing hears clattering in the kitchen. He swipes his hand across his oily forehead, then limps to the bathroom, runs a wash-rag over his haggard face, his hair sticking out as though it has been electrified. *I need a haircut.* He tries to pat it down with water, run a comb through the cowlicks, but they will not be tamed.

He heads back to his den, which smells moldy and rotten, won-dering what else he unleashed from those boxes. He just can't stay down here another minute, so he shoves on his boots, never mind socks or clean underwear or changing his wrinkled jumpsuit.

Bing hovers at the top of the stairs watching Reenie hand peppers to Junior, who plunks them into a pot of boiling water. "And don't forget to stir the hamburger," she says.

Like a married couple already. Even more married when Reenie holds up one of Susie's mud-colored plates. "Do you like these?" as if Junior has an opinion on that.

"Not really," Junior says. Bing expects that to be the end of it. "I like the green ones we saw at Macy's."

Reenie says, "I could live with those."

An image of Barbara's first tight kitchen in their garage apartment, Barbara frying sausage while Bing read the paper at that wobbly table. She couldn't turn around without rattling his sports section. Not like this couple who will soon have their own cramped starter kitchen, Bing figures, with Junior at the stove stirring ground beef, setting the table after a full day at the junkyard. No newspaper reverie for him, but he seems to like this collaboration and Bing is reminded again of everything his marriage was not. No real solidarity, not over cooking, or china patterns, or burying a son. Bing groans under the weight of that realization.

Reenie turns around. "It's alive!"

Junior points to the boiling peppers. "We could use an extra set of hands."

Bing is not yet ready for domestic bliss. "I was just on my way out to—" *What? Grab a chaw?* That wouldn't take him far enough away from this functioning couple that nearly breaks his heart. "Get a haircut," he says. "Can you recommend a good barber?" He looks at Junior's unruly mane and figures the answer is *No,* but Junior blurts, "Frank's Barbershop on Fourth." Before Bing can even file the name away Junior rattles off directions: "Take a left on First Street, drive six blocks, a right on Fourth, sixteen blocks to Hal Greer Boulevard. It's on the left, can't miss it, but if you get lost, just ask anybody."

"I won't get lost," Bing says, but he already is.

"Maybe you should go with him," Reenie says, nodding.

"What?" Junior eyes those boiling peppers.

"No," Bing says, "I'll find it. How hard can it be in a town this size?"

"He doesn't mind," Reenie says.

"Really," Bing says, "I can find it. I navigated a city of four million people for nearly eighty years, didn't I?"

"You did!" Junior says, and with that the men have won.

Bing plucks his keys from the table by the front door and heads out, hoping the Olds will start. She revs right up as if she's been waiting to be taken for a spin.

Bing remembers the front part of Junior's directions: *left on First*. He heads toward town, down under a viaduct, train clattering overhead, and back up, where he's confronted by an odd angle of Huntington—all sewer grates and basement windows—as if he's peeking up her sad, sad skirt. Bing settles into his seat, the distraction of driving already pulling him out of his head, that muddy hole he's been laboring in. He imagines easing into a vinyl chair; a white-coated barber flapping a sheet over Bing's torso. Massaging his scalp with some citrusy tonic. Snipping his ear hairs. Bing might spring for a shave. Hot towel hugging his face, softening his skin, his whiskers. Slather of Barbasol that always makes him sneeze.

A horn blast and Bing jerks in his seat, surprised to find himself stopped at a red light in a right-turn lane. Cars stacked up behind him urge him to accelerate, which he does, earning him another shrill honk from the cabbie Bing pulls out in front of. He's on a one-way street with four lanes, cars zipping along so fast Bing has to zip, too, or be run over.

He finds himself in the middle of the university, a blur of red brick and glass, college students bolting into traffic, darting between cars, not even looking, coming within inches of lead-footed drivers who will not slow down, making it impossible for Bing to slow down, either.

Thankfully there's a red light up ahead and Bing can breathe as he stops and waits for pedestrians to cross. A humped-over woman dragging a cart of groceries. A hard-hatted laborer lugging one of those minicoolers that replaced the silver lunch pail a few years back. A little Asian girl running ahead of a blonde woman chasing after her: "Wait, Courtney! Hold Mommy's hand!"

Those names don't match up. *Must be adopted*, Bing decides, picturing an orphanage crowded with black-haired, slant-eyed babies. Through a two-way mirror, dozens of childless, American couples clap their cheeks and point: *That one! I'll take that one!* Bing always wondered about couples who adopted children from another race, raised other people's babies.

Bing careens back into that hole he's been digging in his mind to scoop even deeper, darker loads. Perhaps his children, Roger, Susie, might not be his children at all. Maybe Bing's been raising another man's babies: agonizing over polio vaccines and dental bills; keeping food in their bellies and clothes on their backs; sending a boy off to war; writing checks for tuition and hippy weddings. And that would mean Reenie and Brian aren't his grandchildren either. Bing turned on the lawn sprinkler for some-one else's baby girl. Maybe he's no kin to anyone up here in West Virginia. Uprooted his life for strangers. Has nothing in common, no shared ancestry, no lineage forward or back. Bing feels like a disconnected dot on the planet.

Bing peels out leaving two black strips before the light changes. He mashes the pedal, wants to push it through the floor, feel the rough road burn through the bottom of his boot, so he can suffer something other than this thing exploding in his

head-chest-gut. He crosses lanes and lanes of traffic without looking, hears horns and screeches, but he doesn't care. He takes a left
turn too fast, radials squealing, tire iron in the trunk clanking,
and he imagines his Olds is regretting this joy ride after all. He
steals turn after turn, left, right, bumping over curbs, knocking
over orange traffic cones, ka-thunking over potholes as he tries to
outrun this feeling of isolation and panic that's stalking him.

Then he sees it. That stupid neon dog with the pointed ears
and red sombrero, glowing tail wagging like a metronome: the
Mexican restaurant Glen dragged the whole family to. Bing aims
for it because he has to land somewhere. He rattles over the parking lot speed bumps, ignoring open parking slots in the front,
opting for the back where there are no lined spaces at all. He
grinds to a halt beside the dumpster, facing the rear of the fake
adobe structure, jams the car into park, and the Olds actually
sighs when he finally cuts the engine.

Bing squeezes the steering wheel hoping some of the tormented thoughts flooding his mind will funnel down his arms,
his fingertips, and seep into the hard plastic and steel. But they
don't, and now his brain crackles with *what ifs*, his heart thumping too fast. Bing can't pull his eyes into focus, so he forces them
to settle on things he understands: speedometer, radio knob,
windshield wiper, hood ornament, and beyond it the back of that
pink restaurant: plastic milk crates stacked six high against the
wall; a heap of bulging trash bags that haven't yet made it to the
dumpster. Half a dozen crows peck at the trash bags, yanking out
tortilla chips and wadded napkins with their sharp beaks.

A screen door opens and the birds take flight as one of those Mexican cooks comes out, hairnet snug on his head, smeared white apron tied around his waist. He pulls a crate from the stack, plunks it on the ground, and sits down. He fumbles for a pack of cigarettes in his shirt pocket and lights one up, inhales deeply, and blows the smoke up into the sky. A gray sky, Bing notes, low bank of clouds obscuring the sun, though he finds the fuzzy glow where it would push through if it could.

Bing's gaze drops to the floodwall at his right, more hard gray slicing his view in two. On this side, pitted parking lots and gravel and train tracks. On the other side, across the river into Ohio, he thinks, the tops of hills in the distance. Black tree branches bare now, most of the leaves having blown off when Bing wasn't looking, but a few still hold on for dear life, like Bing.

He looks down the floodwall and sees an opening where the gates would slide in place if it ever came to that. A hint of brown Ohio River roiling past. Beyond it, up high, a green bridge spans the murky water, clamping the two states together, silhouettes of SUVs and big rigs and Beetles zipping across, ants on a high wire. Bing wants to be up there too, and hear grated metal humming under his tires, feel the vibration in his seat, his teeth. He always hated bridges and overpasses, dreaded crossing them, especially in slow traffic with the possibility of getting stuck at the very top, like being trapped on a Ferris wheel. But today he wouldn't mind being stopped up there. Wouldn't mind shifting the Olds in park, engine idling as he cranes his neck this way and that to see what Huntington really looks like.

Mayor Bing, Dillard had said, and Bing pictures himself on that bridge, getting out of the car. Walking to the railing to scan Huntington's skyline, her main arteries, this very floodwall, that courthouse dome, from an omnipotent perspective. It wouldn't take much for him to hoist his right leg over the railing, then the left leg, to stand on the narrow ledge, hands gripping the cold metal rail as he teeters, the wind blustering his uncut hair—*doesn't matter now*—billowing his jumpsuit, swaying him back and forth as his constituents gather on the riverbank and point to him, cheer him on: *Mayor Bing! Mayor Bing!* Encouraging him with their hand-painted signs and white Styrofoam hats and noisemakers. He would scan the crowd for familiar faces, but there will be none, not anymore. So he imagines bending toward the mob goading Bing to *Jump! Jump!* Make this ultimate sacrifice that will once and for all appease whatever spiteful god that has brought him to this, has peppered Bing's life with so much pain. What can a mayor do but succumb to the masses' pleasure, to the god's demand? So he holds his arms up like a big band leader, Glenn Miller, Artie Shaw, waiting for one sturdy gust to lift him like a kite, and he will hang on the wind for a second, two, three, before spiraling like a downed P-38 Lightning toward the river below, the waves clapping, parting, eager to claim him.

The cold, stinging shock as he hits water feet first and darts down through the murk, hands flapping overhead as he sinks to the bottom, jumpsuit swishing around his body. Deeper and deeper, past algae and tangled fishing line and tree limbs. The sudden jolt as his heavy boots plunge into the gushy floor, mud filling his boots, anchoring him down as his pant legs rise up, catfish and gar or whatever live in these waters nibbling at his ankles, his poor, sockless ankles.

He will bobble there, his big lungful of air expanding his chest, bubbles trickling from his mouth rising up to the surface, and he will look up through the brackish water, see a radiance on the water's surface, maybe even a shadow of the green bridge now dotted with people, his cheering supporters tossing their Styrofoam hats into the water, along with red carnations and white ribbons all floating on the surface, an homage to Bing, their hero. They will urge him to let go, *let go* of that lungful of air keeping him alive. *Exhale!* they will cry. *Complete the sacrifice that will set you free.*

A melodic sound sucks Bing out of the Ohio's depths, skims him across the waves and over the shoreline where he can breathe in fresh air even as his body sails over railroad tracks and pitted parking lots toward a dumpster behind a tacky Mexican restaurant, and beside it a late-model Olds where Bing is jammed back into the driver's seat, his fingers still gripping the steering wheel, his jumpsuit dry. All of this to the accompaniment of that sweet, sweet familiar sound, finally something familiar. Bing rolls down his window for the full orchestral suite of six, no, seven Mexican cooks now sitting in a circle, plastic crates as seats, all smoking and flicking ashes into the center where a campfire would be if they were out on the range. He cranes his ear to take it in, the language he can't decipher, but he remembers eating meal after meal back home to this sound that became even more vital than the food: families arguing and flirting and nagging and pouting in that lullaby chatter that spilled from their tables, crossed the floor, and ultimately captivated Bing.

AWOL

Bing is bouncing, rather the Olds is, up-down, up-down, shock absorbers creaking. Before anything registers—fear, anger—Bing checks the rearview mirror. A lanky figure is pumping the fender like it's a railroad handcar. Beyond him is another fellow, short and stocky, denim shirt with the arms cut off, healed-over cigarette burns—*or bullet wounds?*—scattered across his forearms.

Bing opens his mouth to cuss or scream, but the thug punishing his car leaps forward and pokes his head in Bing's open window, practically headbutting him. The man laughs, sour beer breath fumigating the car. "Tex!" he says. "How ya been there, buddy?"

Bing scours the man's face. *Who are you?* Nobody he recognizes— *or does he?*—but the fringe of tidy bangs looks vaguely familiar. The man must read Bing's confusion. He looks over his shoulder at the other thug who says, "Hurry it up, Ricky."

"Sure thing, Johnny Ray. You bet." Ricky turns back around to Bing. "You got that money you owe me?"

"Do I know—"

"From Stew's Place. Remember? You were in with your dog, and I loaned you a few bucks for Keno and all those shots. Boy, maybe you need to slow down on the whiskey. You were getting pretty sloppy there at the end."

"Oh." Bing's hand flies to his face burning from shame as he recalls fragmented pieces of that day: This fella, the jackpot lady,

Regin*aaaa*, and Ellen. Ellen. He doesn't recollect anything about borrowing money. It's possible, because he remembers shot after shot, beers, a whole chorus line of empties lined up on the bar.

"Had to pay for your cab, too," Ricky says.

"I walked home." That staggered stroll firmly entrenched.

Ricky lets out a staccato laugh. "Well, you left before it got there, but I still had to pay the driver for his troubles. Couldn't stick Regina with that, could I? Probably come right outta her paycheck."

Bing makes an oath to never touch another drop. "How much do I owe you?"

Ricky's eyelids snap open. "How much ya got?"

Bing takes out his wallet and thumbs through crinkled bills. "Thirty-two dollars."

Ricky groans but reaches in and snatches the money. "We'll consider it a down payment." He folds the bills and starts to slip them in his shirt pocket, but a beefy hand reaches over Ricky's shoulder and yanks them out first.

"That all he got?" Johnny Ray grumbles.

"Yeah." Ricky turns back to Bing. "I'll knock off another twenty if you give us a ride to the dog track."

"Dog track?"

"Come on, Johnny Ray. He says he'll give us a lift."

Bing swallows hard. "Now wait—"

But Ricky is already sliding across Bing's hood, opening the passenger door, and hopping in.

Johnny Ray gets in the back. Bing looks in the rearview at the man's meaty neck, mashed nose probably broken in a prison brawl. He starts the engine but no longer feels his heart beating in his chest. "How far is it?"

Ricky slaps the bench seat between them. "Not but a few miles. Take ten minutes to get there. Fifteen tops."

Bing lurches forward, eyeing that circle of Mexicans all standing to crush out cigarettes, retie aprons, adjust hairnets.

"Buncha wetbacks," Ricky says. He punches Bing's thigh. "Iddn't that right, Tex?"

Bing rubs his tender leg. "Right." As he drives past the cooks he looks over at one in particular, less than two feet away, standing with his arms crossed over his chest, watching the Olds, watching Bing. Their eyes meet, and Bing tries to translate the man's crinkled brow, his shaking head, his parting caution, "No vaya con ellos."

"Watch where you're going," Ricky says.

Bing doesn't want to break eye contact, because as long as he's staring into those dark pupils he's linked to something, someone he understands. But he has to look forward to veer around one of those plastic crates and aim for the street. He feels like he's back in that dark hole in his mind, only this time he's got two strangers digging a tunnel off to the side, a cave. Mammoth Cave. Where he's got nothing to hold onto, nothing holding him back, not anymore. No red *X* marking a grave in Texas. No daughter and son-in-law in West Virginia. No Reenie or Brian. Nobody to report to at all. "Which way?" he asks, resigned.

Ricky reaches under his shirt to scratch his armpit. "Make a left." He pulls his fingers back out for a sniff. "We just have to make one stop first."

Ricky's foot batters the floor mat as he rattles off directions. Bing slows for a red light, looks to his left, and sees Frank's Barbershop. "I knew I could find it!"

Ricky's foot stops thumping. "Say what?"

Bing nods toward the barber pole. "I was going for a trim."

Ricky looks at Bing's gaunt face, electric hair, rumpled jump-suit. "You do look like hell. Almost didn't recognize you." He slaps Bing's shoulder. "But it's a good thing I did, right buddy?"

"Damn lucky for you," Johnny Ray growls. "And this better be for real."

Ricky clears his throat. "Just take Hal Greer all the way out."

"Out to where?" Bing says.

"My cousin's place. It's just off Route 10."

Bing sees a pay phone beside that spinning barber pole. Fear returns, or maybe it's reason, and he wants to jump out, shove in change, and call Susie to tell her that he may be in real trouble here, but the light turns green and his foot presses the gas, because that's what it's been trained to do for over sixty years.

Bing passes a strip of public housing; a patchwork hospital that looks like it's been added onto half a dozen times; a drive-in hot dog stand with a giant root beer mug spinning on top. He sees signs for I-64 and recognizes the grade school he passed when he first drove in. "A million years ago."

"What's that?" Ricky says.

"I passed that school when I first moved here."

"Why the hell'd you leave Texas, anyway?" Ricky says. "You got people up here?"

Bing wiggles around in his seat. He doesn't know the answer to either of those questions. Not anymore. "Naw," he finally says, because kin or not, he won't drag Susie's family along for this joyless ride. "Just liked the mountains."

"Yeah, right," Johnny Ray says, their eyes connecting for a frightening second in the rearview.

Bing pulls his eyes away and looks ahead at the I-64 overpass looming, the on-ramp. He wants to swerve onto it and squeal off into the sunset. Or jam the gas pedal so hard they launch into orbit, the Olds an Apollo rocket, Bing at the controls pressing a red button that will jettison the rear end with Johnny Ray inside, leaving that hulking goon floating aimlessly in space.

But Bing drives under the overpass as instructed. He squints at approaching hills on each side, the narrowing road winding deeper and deeper into shadow, leaving city lights behind. He watches for road signs, squiggly lines indicating crazy *S* curves ahead, and they *are* crazy. Bing is used to straight stretches, nothing but miles and miles of it down in Texas. Dependable horizon always in view. He could steer with one fingertip on the wheel. *Couldn't do that here.* He's taking these curves too fast, no faster than the truck behind him bearing down, trying to push him out of the way, but Bing's passengers don't seem a bit flustered. In fact, it looks as if Ricky's right foot is punching his own accelerator over there, wanting the car to speed up, maybe even blast off.

Minutes of thick silence pass: ten, fifteen, twenty, until Ricky grips his knees and says, "Take a right up ahead."

Bing grinds the brake. The tailgating truck honks as Bing juts his head forward to look for a street sign or some indication that there is a turnoff to the right.

"Right here! Right here!" Ricky points to a rutted road, scraggly weeds poking up between two mud-hardened tracks. Bing swerves and the Olds' front end tips down into the lane, car teetering. Bing imagines his grill eating a mouthful of earth. The tires bump along in the grooves, whitewalls scuffing the edges, weeds scraping the oil pan. He looks to the left, low brambles leading to trees at the base of the hill. In the last bit of blue light he can just make out an animal grazing at the tree line, a horse, probably. Bing adjusts his glasses and widens his eyes to see what kind of horse it is. But it's not a horse.

"That's a buck," he says, amazed at the size of the thing. Twice as big as the ones he and Dillard used to track.

Ricky says, "Damn, Johnny Ray. That's an eight-pointer. Where's my rifle when I need it?"

"Where's my .45?" Johnny Ray says, sounding like he'd use it.

The brambles give way to a decent-sized garden surrounded by wooden poles with pie tins and wind-inflated plastic grocery sacks tied to the tops, all that silver and white fluttering, warding off birds and other critters. Most of the garden has shriveled to crisp vines and stalks, but Bing spots dashes of orange and yellow in the dirt: lopsided pumpkins and butternut squash. They pass a leaning tobacco barn; a rabbit hutch; a rusty, corrugated shed. Beyond them the lane ends at a house, a white frame job with a front porch, potted mums dangling from the rafters. Yellow light glowing from inside.

"This your cousin's place?" Bing asks, relieved.

"Naw," Ricky says. "It's up the road a piece."

"What road?" Bing says. He doesn't see any more road, yet Ricky points to an even narrower path. Bing stops. "I can't get through that."

"Shoot. I've taken bigger cars than this up there."

"I don't think—"

"Just go," Johnny Ray commands.

That tremor in Ricky's foot bubbles up his leg, his torso, carbonating his voice. "You can make it."

Bing plows in. He had already given up on his oil pan. Now he has doubts about the paint as they part through briars and nettle that snag his side mirrors. They rock along, Bing's head shaking, wondering how any sane driver could take this road. *Do they even own cars up these hollers? Get mail? Newspaper delivery?* Finally the Olds bursts out into a clearing. A dog starts barking, two dogs, maybe three, and there's the gray silhouette of a low, long, drooping shanty. A banged-up truck and two four-wheelers are pulled up by the steps. Bing parks behind them just as a snarling black something jumps up on his window: a vision of sharp teeth, red gums, and massive paws.

"Shut up, Rambo!" Ricky shouts into Bing's ear.

Rambo doesn't shut up, just keeps growling, streaking up Bing's window with saliva and fog and muddy paw prints. Johnny Ray flings open his door, whacking Rambo's hindquarter. The dog yelps, tucks tail, and scrambles underneath the house.

Ricky gets out and gallops over to open Bing's door. "Hurry it up."

Bing doesn't want to hurry it up. He wants to shove the car in reverse and squeal out of here, leave Ricky and Johnny Ray in the dust, but he knows he no longer has the speed or agility to carry out such a plan.

He cuts the engine and gets out, two docile mutts weaving between the men, bumping into their legs, streaking their pants with dirt and slobber and stink as they work their way past stacks of bald tires, overturned metal lawn chairs, a broken birdbath. To his right, a dog pen crowded with three more whimpering hounds clawing at the chain-link, wanting to run free with the rest of the pack. To his left, a car engine dangles from a tree limb; a cinderblock-propped Trans Am beneath it. Beyond it, a decoy deer leans against hay bales, a tattered bull's-eye taped to its flank. Bing stumbles up the dubious steps to the house.

"Watch it," Johnny Ray scolds.

The porch is stacked with firewood, a garbage can heaped with empty beer and soda cans, a soiled box spring where the loose dogs obviously sleep. There's a stew pot filled with leafy water, a bucket of dog food crawling with bugs, and a heap of un-namable something covered with a blue tarp that's weighted down with toolboxes and rocks, reminding Bing of his own tarpless heap in Susie's basement.

Ricky raises his hand to knock, but before he does, a voice bellows from inside: "Who is it?" The drapes covering the picture window are tugged open a crack by a pair of fingers. Ricky's chest rises and falls before he lets loose that staccato laugh. "It's me, Leonard! Open up!"

Grumbling from within and someone yells, "Who the hell is that?"

"It's Ricky!" Ricky says, popping his knuckles.

Footsteps clomp forward. The door opens an inch, then all the way, and Bing is struck by the stinging reek of cat piss and kerosene and bacon grease.

"How you doin' there, Cuz?" Ricky says.

Cuz must be Leonard. Bing sees the family resemblance: long and lanky except for a cantaloupe-sized belly. Beyond him, three men sit at a kitchen table in the corner, alert eyes on the action at the door.

Leonard says, "You got that money you owe me, Ricky?"

Johnny Ray bulldozes between Bing and Ricky to stand nose to nose with Leonard. "He's gotta settle up with me first."

The three men at the table bolt upright, one of them reaching for something tucked under his shirt.

Ricky pumps his hands in the air up and down, fingers splayed, trying to press the men back into their seats. "It's okay! Everything's okay!" Ricky says. "Johnny Ray's a friend of mine. A business associate. We got a proposition to make."

The man at the table wearing a Peterbilt cap leans forward to get a better look. "That you, Johnny Ray?"

Johnny Ray says, "Yeah."

"He's okay," Peterbilt says to Leonard.

Everyone looks at Leonard who studies Johnny Ray before nodding toward Bing. "Who's this?"

"That's Tex," Ricky says. "He won't cause no trouble, will you, Tex?"

Six pairs of scary eyes bead down on Bing and his fingers start trembling. "I'm just giving them a lift."

Leonard scratches his chin, looks beyond the porch as if he's checking for headlights. "Better come in."

One of the men at the table says, "Don't let those dogs in!"

Another says, "And lock the goddamn door!"

Leonard, Johnny Ray, and Ricky head for the kitchen table and all the men sit. Bing hangs back. Whatever the hell they're up to, he wants no part of it. He doesn't know if he should just hover in a corner somewhere, or sit. He glances around the living room, dark wood paneling dotted with black-and-white family photos; an American flag thumbtacked to the wall; that painting of Jesus with the Vandyke beard. There's a gun cabinet loaded with an impressive assortment of rifles. A Zenith TV console—the same model Bing bought about thirty years back. There are two couches set side by side: one plaid, one floral, both stained and coated in animal hair, the bottom halves used as scratching posts.

Something pokes out from beneath the floral couch then pulls back under. Bing leans over. Out it comes again, an orange cat's paw, then two, and a black third one—*two cats*—batting something around, some squirming thing Bing realizes is a field mouse, skinny tail whipping as it tries to escape. The orange cat mashes both paws on the mouse's gray body. It squeals before being pulled back underneath the couch.

Bing hears a loud crack away to his left. He looks toward the sound, down the longest, darkest hall he's ever seen. A shape rushes from the shadows, a wild figure, a girl Reenie's age, maybe a little older, in skintight jeans and a sweatshirt. She's running toward him with her arms flailing. Bing stumbles backward, falls onto one of the sofas. The girl takes no notice, just gallops to the kitchen table. "Why, Leonard? Why?"

Leonard pushes out of his seat. "I told you to stay back there, Drema!" He runs after her, and she squeals, though it's a lot louder than that field mouse. Bing tries to blend in with the upholstery, flushing as pink in the cheeks, as green around the gills as those tapestry bouquets. Especially when Drema scoops a coffee mug from the top of the Zenith and flings it at Leonard, a direct hit in the center of his forehead. This sends him scrabbling backward, hand to his face. *Good shot!* Bing thinks, admiring her aim, wondering if any of the rifles in that gun case are hers, hoping she doesn't turn her eye on him.

The men at the table cackle, hands slapping thighs, and Leonard's face burns red. He launches himself at Drema, whose mouth opens but no sound comes out. Her eyes fling left, right, finally landing on the front door. She makes a mad lunge, arms stretching toward that tarnished knob. She's within inches when Leonard grabs her around the waist and yanks her back so hard Bing hears the air pressing out of her lungs.

Drema writhes and twists. "No!" She tries to latch onto any fixed thing, knocking over a lamp, a stack of *Hustler* magazines, as Leonard drags her kicking and scratching back down the hall, opens a door, and tosses her inside like a sack of meal. "Now stay in there!" He slams the door, fumbling with a lock at the top.

Leonard tugs down his t-shirt and shakes his hair off his face as he ambles back down the hall to the kitchen, his bruised forehead already swelling. "Now, where were we?" He sits and scrapes in his chair.

The men pull in close to the table and lean in to discuss business. Bing does not want to listen, doesn't want any sideline involvement, so he looks away from them, eyes resting on those wide-open *Hustlers* covered with pictures of wide-open women. He drags his eyes away and tries not to think about the tumbling *whomp-whomp-whomp* he feels beneath his seat, two cats, one mouse, so he focuses on Drema, Leonard's child bride or girlfriend. His daughter or sister. A girl he kidnapped from a truck stop. All distinct possibilities. He imagines what she's doing on the other side of the door. Lighting the drapes on fire. Slitting her wrists.

"I wanna see it first," Johnny Ray says.

"Fair enough," says Leonard, standing, about ready to fetch whatever *it* is, but he spots Bing on the couch and pauses. "Hey, Pops. Why don't you go say hello to my old man. He could use the company."

"Old man?"

Leonard points down the hall. "My dad. He's back in his room all the way at the end."

Bing does not want to go down the hall, past that scary locked door, but he knows he has no choice. "All right." Bing stands, brushing down his pant legs, sending cat hairs flying. He works his way into the darkness, looking over his shoulder at Leonard who says, "Go on. He don't bite. Much." Gross laughter from the kitchen table again, so Bing figures he better press on or be tackled and dragged off just like Drema.

He marches bravely forward, eyes adjusting to the dimness, running one finger along the paneled wall to steady his gait. A swatch of light streams from beneath Drema's door. Leonard is back in the kitchen, so Bing pauses, head tipped to catch her broken sobs and hiccups. "Why?" she wails, over and over. "Why?" He sees the hook-and-eye latch that's keeping her there, trapping her, and he wants to undo it, let her dart down the hall and out the front door to freedom. He raises a finger toward it.

"Fucker!" she yells. "I see you out there!"

Bing wonders if this is a see-through trick door, but before he can step back, something crashes against it, glass shattering from inside: a mirror, a vase. "Get away!"

Bing steps quickly down the hall, passing more closed doors that may also hold locked-up women. He doesn't pause to investigate, just pushes on toward a flickering light—*a light at the end of the tunnel*—a TV.

Bing doesn't want to barge into the man's bedroom, so he stands outside and clears his throat, making his presence known, waiting for the *Who is it?* that will serve as an invitation. He doesn't get one, so he leans in and a wave of hot air whooshes across his face. A kerosene heater in the middle of the room sits dangerously close to heaps of clothes, stacks of dirty dishes. There are two dressers—*they like things in pairs up here*—and a pine rocker draped with dungarees and work shirts, sturdy boots shoved underneath.

Jammed in the corner is a full-size bed, and on it seven cats ringed around the skeletal form lying there, so skinny and frail Bing has to walk in a few steps and bend over to make sure it really is a person, not just blankets scrunched up. But it's a man, all right. Completely bald, plastic tubing hooked under his nose, draped over his ears, running down the side of the bed where it's connected to an oxygen tank, flame-shaped decal warning: FLAMMABLE. Bing looks at that kerosene heater again, the scent stinging his nose.

Bing peers into the man's face to see if he is sleeping, or dead, because his eyes are open and fixed toward the base of his bed at the portable TV sitting on top of a stack of dark, probably broken, progressively larger and older TVs.

"Water," the man's phlegmy voice grumbles.

Bing leans in. "What's that?"

The man raises a quaking hand toward an empty glass on the table beside him.

"Oh! Sure thing." Bing picks up the glass, ring after gray ring etched along the inside indicating where various water levels had been. He heads back into the hall, but he doesn't dare go to the kitchen where they are scheming God knows what. There must be a bathroom behind one of these doors, these scary doors.

The first door is locked, but the second one opens and Bing sees a hint of sink and tub. He feels for the wall switch to turn on the light, and the room is a sight. The floor is linoleum in theory, corners curled up, patches worn down exposing wooden slats. There's a crack in the floor by the claw-footed tub, one hind leg poking through the wood making the entire cast-iron basin list to starboard. Bing doesn't want to think about what disgusting things are clumped up inside the toilet.

Bing spins toward the pedestal sink, porcelain bowl streaked with rust and hawk, grimy ceramic *H* and *C* handles. He tugs his sleeve over his fingers to turn on the spigot, hears the pipes creak and glug until water sputters out. He holds the glass underneath to catch the spray, and it takes its sweet time to fill, the contents cloudy with foam on top.

Bing heads back with his offering, such as it is. The old man has propped himself up and turned on a bedside light. He's down to three cats. Bing looks around the floor, but they are not mixed in with the visible mess. *Probably under the bed eating mice.* He holds out the water and the man takes it in his jittery grip. He jiggles a yellow capsule in his palm and prepares to swallow it with that frothy water.

Bing looks away to offer the man some pill-taking privacy, eyes settling on a dusty photo over the bed. A bride and groom cutting a wedding cake, the groom in World War II uniform—*is that a Bronze Star?*—the bride in a print dress with an orchid corsage. The groom is a lot thinner now, lying here in the bed, loose wedding ring looping around the now-bony finger. He's a widower, Bing can tell. Bing can always tell. He looks back up at the bride wondering if she hoarded a secret as calamitous as the one Barbara kept so close to her chest.

"Thanks." The man hands back the glass. Bing sets it on a book, not just any book, a Bible: a well-read one by the looks of the cracked spine, crumpled leather edges, thumbed-up pages. A week ago Bing would have moved that glass to a less sacred spot. Today he leaves it right there.

"Who are you again?" the man asks.

"I'm Bing."

The man offers his hand and Bing takes it, the feeble grip, waxy fingers cold even in this stoked room. "Odell."

Bing nods and Odell points to the rocker. "Better set down," he says, as if he's used to strangers being sent back here to bide their time. Bing has to move a stack of folded undershirts to sit. Both he and Odell face the TV.

"You a friend of Leonard's?" Odell asks.

"No," Bing says, eyes forward. "I just drove Ricky out here."

Odell shakes his head. "You ought not be hanging around that boy. Leonard neither. Nothing but trouble, and I hate to say it 'cause they are blood. But it's the God's-honest truth. I'd watch my wallet if I was you, too."

Bing puts his hand on his wallet, already emptied.

A fuzzy newscast begins, a picture of George W. and Colin Powell with a question over their heads: WAR IMMINENT? Bing is surprised to see this news out here, that map of Iraq now filling the screen. This hollow seems too deep, too disconnected from the world outside to be involved in such matters. Apparently it's not, because the next footage is of a West Virginia armory filling up with troops of activated reserves. Wives hug husbands good-bye; children hug daddies. The men are just kids, really. Eighteen. Nineteen. Twenty. Same age as Bing when he served.

Odell points toward the TV. "My little Maggie got called up last spring."

"Your who?"

"My granddaughter. Maggie. Yanked her right outta Marshall, and you know she waddn't counting on that."

"Uh-huh." Bing still isn't comfortable with the idea of women on the front lines.

"Only joined up to get her college paid for. Couldn't afford it no other way."

"That's a fact," Bing says, newly appreciative of Glen's and Susie's upper-middle-class bank accounts.

"If it was my grandson, I'd a told him to just suck it up. Gotta do what a man's gotta do, you know?"

"I do." Bing does know that, remembers sitting in the Studebaker and uttering that very phrase to his son back in 1968.

"But my little Magpie, well . . . she's just a mite of a thing, and now she's over in Afghanistan."

Bing thinks about Reenie, maybe not a mite of a thing, but he's thankful she'll never have to hump artillery through the desert looking for some terrorist in a cave.

Odell spins that ring on his finger. "You wouldn't have a smoke, would you?"

Bing looks at the heater, the flammable oxygen. "Nope." He pulls his Skoal from his pocket. "Will this do?"

"Yes, sir." Odell holds out his hand. Bing twists the lid off first, unwilling to watch this war hero struggle to pull off a cardboard cap. Odell reaches his fingers in for a goodly pinch and rams it in his mouth.

"Hits the spot." He nods at the Skoal. "Join me?"

Bing does and as soon as he packs his lip he realizes he doesn't have a spit can handy. Odell must be mulling over the same dilemma, because his eyes skim the junk on his bedside table, finally resting on a Campbell's Soup can that's been recommissioned as a pencil holder. Odell spills out the pens and pencils and hands the spittoon to Bing. He points down toward the floor by his bed. "Hand me that thing-a-ma-jigger."

Bing cranes over and sees a portable plastic urinal, identical to the one the hospital gave him after his prostate surgery. He hesitates to pick it up.

"It's never been used," Odell says. "I might as well spit in it."

Bing hands Odell the urinal, and they just sit there, spitting, watching the sportscaster, followed by the weather, the national news. They don't talk, and it settles into a comfortable silence, much like Bing had with Dillard. Those missing cats slink out from their hiding places and leap on the bed to snuggle up to Odell. A Siamese jumps onto Bing's lap uninvited. Bing makes room and lets the cat knead his thighs before curling into a lump.

"What are you two yakking about?" It's Ricky leaning against the door frame.

"Nothin'," Odell says. "We waddn't talkin' about nothing."

"I bet." Ricky looks at Bing. "Don't you believe a word Odie says. He's full of piss and vinegar. Ain't that right, Uncle?"

"Whatever you say."

Ricky jerks his head toward the hall. "Come on, Tex. We're about finished up out here." Ricky lopes back down the hall.

Bing sets the Siamese on the floor and stands, though he wouldn't mind sitting back here awhile longer. For the first time the two men really look at each other. Bing feels he is staring into himself, or at least a version of himself that he could easily be.

Outside, a scuttling of paws on the porch. Rambo snarls but spots Johnny Ray and bolts under the house. The other dogs tangle up in the men's legs as they try to navigate the steps—no easy feat in this pitch dark now, no streetlights, no porch lights to help Bing make his way to the Olds, no flat horizon to let him get his bearings. He feels walled in on all sides by imposing hills he can't see but can feel pressing down, pressing him into the earth. It must be how coal miners feel when they tunnel into the shaft, this suffocating blackness. But no, it's probably worse down there. Much worse.

"Can't see a thing," he confesses, but that's not exactly true. When he looks up, he spots stars that haven't pulsed this bright since his Navy days when he floated out in the Pacific with no city lights to taint the view. Giant dots of light, hundreds of them. Thousands. Now he can make out the ridgelines where jagged darkness ends and stars begin. "There's the North Star," Bing says, orienting himself, a navigation point he hasn't looked for in years because he didn't think he needed any orienting.

Ricky nudges past Bing and holds out his hand. "Better let me drive, Tex. Gets kinda tricky out here after dark."

Bing is not inclined to turn over his keys. "Naw. I can—"

"Don't worry. I have my license. Somewhere."

Bing understands, again, that he has no choice, so he fumbles in his pockets and pulls out the jumble of car keys and house keys and the key to his locker at the plant that he never turned in. He holds them over Ricky's palm, but his fingers won't unclasp.

Ricky yanks them out, leaving Bing standing there as Ricky opens the door and claims the driver's seat. Johnny Ray gets in the passenger side as the engine revs. Bing figures he better hop in or be left out here under the stars.

Ricky punches the gas and Bing bumps back into the seat. He cranes around to look at the house, the dim glow from Odell's room all the way at the end. Bing holds up his fingers in a parting salute before twisting around to stare at the back of Ricky's head.

Ricky turns on the radio and twists the knob to find head-banging noise that would delight Reenie. Bing immediately regrets the comparison. He doesn't want to link Reenie with

Ricky, or Johnny Ray, or that wild girl locked up back there. Even if Reenie isn't really his granddaughter, Bing wants to keep her tucked safely in that three-story, air-freshened, maid-cleaned house, with a hard-working boyfriend, and a college education that won't demand combat duty in return.

Ricky rumbles through briars, over that dirt lane before pulling out onto the main road, tires pealing, cutting turns so sharply Bing has to grip the bench seat. Thankfully, they even out on a straight patch by the interstate overpass. Bing sighs, stomach settling, until Ricky barrels up the eastbound on-ramp and speeds past a sign that reads: *Charleston 47 Miles*.

"Where we going again?" Bing asks, because it feels as if he's traveled through another time zone, another country, since he sat parked behind that Mexican restaurant and agreed to give these boys a lift, if agreed is the right word.

"Dog track," Ricky says. "Just settle in, Tex. Won't take but a minute."

SCARED DOGS

It takes a lot longer than a minute, Ricky edging through traffic. Bing doesn't want to know what number his speedometer needle is tagging, the Olds a vibrating bucket. Ricky is a fidgety mess. Fiddling with the windshield wipers, hazard lights, cruise control, seat adjustments, like he's a fifteen-year-old behind the wheel for the first time.

Dog track. Bing is going to a dog track, and he wishes Dillard were here with him. Or Odell, who could probably offer more insight. He has visions of a dirt lot cleared out of the woods, a mob of scary men like Johnny Ray and Leonard gathered around a mud track, throwing crumpled fives and tens over the rickety wooden fence at wild dogs with numbers spray painted on their sides. Probably a cockfighting ring off to the side, maybe a makeshift stand selling moonshine. Bing steels himself, as much as he is able to muster nerve at this point.

Johnny Ray sits there like a boulder. Doesn't even respond as Ricky tries to chat him up. "I knew you'd like this deal. It's a sweet one for sure. Can't lose. You got a method for picking dogs up here? I like the ones that take a dump right before the race. Lighter on their feet. You know it's gonna be crowded as hell tonight, right? Giving away a pair of Beemers *plus* that million-dollar jackpot. Bring out every leisure suit and wrinkled prune in the tri-state."

Finally Bing spots a road sign: *Greyhound Racing*. In the distance, stretched out on a flat piece of earth gouged out of a hillside, the thing itself, looking more like a mall than a gambling mecca.

Baseball-field-quality lights flooding the enterprise. Blacktopped parking lot loaded with cars.

Ricky follows two lanes of taillights aiming for the track. Not only beat-up trucks, but polished sedans and station wagons. A Lexus and a Mercedes. Beside them, an old man in a Buick looks over, cigar wagging in his mouth. Bing can only imagine the sight his Olds must be. *I owe you*, he offers, patting the seat. They crest the hill and head down toward the track, the road lined with lights, an airport runway guiding them in. An unexpected gush of relief oozes through Bing; nothing bad can happen under this much illumination. It's like going to an Astros game. Bing feels a surprising gurgle in his belly, a yearning for vendor nachos and cheese, soft pretzel crusted with salt.

They park in the *W* section and Bing gets out. The Olds is a mess: whitewalls streaked with dirt, weeds tangled around the bumper, wheel wells clumped with mud, a medley of fine scratches running from stem to stern. He points to the offense. "You think rubbing compound will take those out?" But Ricky and Johnny Ray are yards ahead swaggering toward the entrance, swallowed up by the throng of gamblers hustling to get inside.

"Hey! Wait!" Bing hotfoots after them. "Ricky!"

Ricky looks back, then dives into the swarm. Bing picks up the pace, looking over his shoulder so he can remember where he's parked, passing a row of motor homes and tour buses with license plates from Kentucky and Ohio.

Closer in, the layout loses that stadium feel; it's more like a four-star hotel with water fountains, a carport topped with three glass pyramids. Bing bumps into a sign for valet parking, the attendant taking keys from a buxom woman with platinum hair, Lincoln Town Car behind her. "Don't drive too fast. And don't change the radio!" she warns, as her gaggle of clucking hens gets out, clutching metallic purses to their chests. *Black Widders spending their dead husbands' pensions.* One of them gives Bing the once-over, lips pinched in disapproval. He tries to smooth his errant cowlick, brush off cat and dog hairs. Both efforts are fruitless, so he walks away and through the glass doors where a wall of sound assaults his eardrums. He looks up into crystal chandeliers trying to name the clamor, or at least separate it into recognizable parts: dings and hums and harp strings. On top of it all, one sustained note that might come from a church organ, a breathy *ahhhhhhhhh* that sighs on and on. But of course, this is no church.

The momentum of the crowd pushes Bing through the foyer, past a statue of a court jester and two BMW convertibles—one red, one black—cordoned off by velvet ropes. There are rows and rows of slot machines, hundreds of them, and now Bing understands the dings, the techno trills, the coins clinking into metal trays. There's not much overhead light, but the one-armed bandits offer colorful radiance. Plus there's a hovering artificial tree draped with Spanish moss and twinkling lights. He pushes forward, passing men and woman hunched over those machines, mostly middle-aged or older: *Leisure suits and wrinkled prunes.* Bing decides that they are not *un*like himself—at least when he is cleaned up—solid citizens in velour jogging suits, neat slacks, and Banlon shirts. Looking pretty much like the people who lined his church pews back home. Bing spots black people, too, a few Asians, plus packs of college-aged boys whooping it up, professional couples in suits. They press the lighted buttons that spin the wheels, rotating 7s, or fruit, or bars, the outcome earning cusswords or cheers, depending.

He bumbles into an alcove with pay phones lining the walls. He should call Susie. He thrusts his hand in his pocket where there is no change, but what exactly would he tell her anyway? That he's spent the last hours in the company of ruffians? That he needs for her to come and help him find his car keys? He can already envision the look on her face and all future apprehensive looks whenever he might want to go to the bank, or the post office, or just for a drive. No. He's come this far, and it's almost over. Despite recent events, being in Leonard's scary house, having his car hijacked, Bing no longer feels like he's in real danger. He doesn't need any help. All he needs are his keys and he will be home free, if he can still consider it home.

He pushes forward with new vim, passing a wrought iron fence that segregates a restaurant called the French Quarter, meant to look like an outdoor café: linen-covered tables with china and wine glasses, upscale patrons eating thick steaks. Black-tied waiters grinding pepper, uncorking wine. Bing puts his hand on his empty wallet. He still has plastic but doubts that frowning hostess would welcome him in his present state. Still, the hunger gnaws, overriding his concern for keys. He passes another artificial tree draped with lights and Mardi Gras beads.

He finds a concession stand that looks more his speed. Styrofoam cups and plastic forks. Neon menu above the counter offering Philly cheese steak and BBQ and cheeseburgers. No nachos or pretzels, but at least there's no stern hostess grading his attire. Bing queues up, inching forward, eavesdropping on the girl in front of him talking on a cell phone. She's a big white girl, maybe two hundred pounds. "I told the shit it was his baby, and I ain't heard a word from him since!"

Bing orders BBQ, picturing shredded brisket, heavy bread to sop up the juice. When the server girl hands it over, he lifts the puckered hamburger bun to appraise ground meat in tomato sauce, dollop of coleslaw in the middle crowned with a limp pickle. "I ordered the BBQ?"

The server looks at him. "That's what'cha got."

Bing studies the disappointment. "Oh." He backs away, shoulders stooped.

Like the fare, the patrons here are closer to Bing's ilk. Blue-collar couples wearing ball caps and practical shoes. There's a foursome at a table beside him, two married couples maybe fifteen years younger than Bing, the wives huddled together, laughing, munching Fritos out of snack-size bags. The men lean back in their chairs grunting at each other, toothpicks jutting. Bing can't make out the words, but he guesses they are discussing what he and Dillard might have back then: adjusting to retirement, keeping up with home repairs, the annoying aches that come with age. Bing realizes that could be Dillard and him over there with Barbara and Tootie. Grabbing a bite after a round of mini golf, or playing bingo, or going to that cakewalk where Dillard won a whole pie.

Bing looks at his empty plate, the goop on his fingers, shocked that he ate that whole whatever-it-was without tasting one bite, too caught up in nostalgia. Wallowing in the comfortable memories surfacing at last. Recollections of the good times they all had. *And they were good, dammit.*

The foursome stands, the men adjusting their belts, the women gathering empty plates and cups to dump into the trash, and they begin to walk away.

Bing opens his mouth to say *Wait!* because he wants to hold them there awhile longer so he can pretend, but the word won't come and he watches Barbara and Tootie loop arms and march forward, giggling. Dillard and the man who could be Bing walk a few paces behind, hands in their pockets, one eye on the casino action, the other guarding the wives.

Bing follows to see what new memories they make. Trying not to be conspicuous, looking at his shoes when he thinks they might turn around. They pause in front of that French Quarter café, bending to read the menu posted under glass out front to see what they missed out on. A lot, Bing guesses, walking right up behind them.

"Look at the price of that filet mignon," Tootie says.

Barbara says, "Can you imagine."

The men joke about how many hamburgers that would buy, and Tootie says, "Glenda, the woman at that table has on your same blouse."

Glenda's eyes follow Tootie's finger, and so do Bing's, assessing the woman just on the other side of the railing, not six feet away. He looks from her, to Glenda, the twin violet blouses, clusters of yellow rosebuds tossed here and there. "She does!" Glenda says. "Bet she didn't get hers at Value City for $7.98."

The women laugh and press on, followed by the men, but this time Bing does not tag along. He's captivated by the new Barbara sitting there in her pricey blouse, eating expensive something, trout amandine, maybe, dabbing the corners of her mouth with a cloth napkin. The man sitting too closely beside her is not wearing a seersucker jacket, but he might as well be as he leans in and utters words Bing cannot hear, probably something like, *Bing could never afford this place. Let me spoil you rotten, Barbara. You deserve it.*

Bing's fingers curl into fists. He wants to grab Charles by the throat and yank him out of his seat. Drag him away from Barbara, out under that carport, and beat the tar out of him. Hold his head under one of those fountains until his body goes limp.

"Is there something you need?" It's the hostess, standing with her arms crossed over her chest.

Bing points to Charles. "That son-of-a-bitch is out with my wife!"

The hostess's eyelids flare as she looks at the couple. "You must be mistaken. That's Dr. and Mrs. Connelly."

"So he's a *doctor* now, is he?" Bing shouts at Barbara, making the couple look at him, the man leaning forward to inspect Bing's face. "Keep your hands off my wife!"

Barbara's hands fly to her cheeks. Charles stands and throws his napkin on the floor, but Bing doesn't care; his eyes are latched onto his wife.

"How could you?" he yells. "How could you," he says again, softer, the words tumbling out like a plea.

Barbara looks at him as if he has lost his mind.

"Do I have to call security?" the hostess asks. Over her shoulder Bing sees one of the male bartenders already sprinting over.

"No," Bing says, not worried about security or bruising bartenders. What disturbs him is the look on Barbara's face, that frightened furrow in her brow, and she is undoubtedly frightened—of *him*. He opens his mouth, but that burly bartender grips his arm and yanks him away. "Let's go."

Bing looks over his shoulder at Barbara, at Charles sitting back down beside her, clamping his possessive arm around her shoulder, the sour look on his face, and the relief on Barbara's as she watches Bing being hustled off. What a pitiful sight he must be.

Bing can barely keep up with the bartender's stride. "Are you going to leave those people alone or do I have to take you outside?"

"No," Bing says. His escort's grip tightens. "I mean *yes*. I'm going to leave them alone. I only wanted to . . . I only needed to . . . I'm just looking for the dog races. Do they even have dog races here?"

"Yes," the bartender says. "This way."

He drags Bing through the crowd, curious eyes following the humiliating expulsion, into a hallway that connects to another casino. The bartender stops in front of the security guard sitting on a stool at the entrance working a crossword puzzle. He points to Bing's face and says to the guard, "Don't let him back in here."

The guard looks up at them both. "No problem."

The bartender nods to the back corner of the room. Bold letters painted high on the wall read: *Greyhound Racing*, a gigantic red arrow pointing down. "Races are downstairs," he says. "Now get lost."

The guard taps his temple with the end of a pencil. "I never forget a face."

Bing understands the warning and he heads into the room, cutting through less noise but more smoke, passing even more slot machines. The atmosphere here is stark, low ceilings, cinderblock walls, no Mardi Gras flavor at all. The clientele is stark, too. Clothes not from fancy stores, not even from Sears. More like Goodwill or the Salvation Army. Big hairdos and metallic purses replaced by scraggly ponytails and missing teeth—on both sexes. It's sadder in here, as if the people know they're going to lose, are expecting it and are absolutely resigned, but still can't stop because maybe, just maybe. Miraculously a machine starts flashing, sirens wailing. The lucky winner jumps up, a scrawny black woman, arms flailing as she yells, "Thank you, Jesus! Thank you, Lord!"

Bing has to stop and look at this woman in a worn t-shirt that reads *God is My Co-pilot*. He starts laughing, a real guffaw, and the woman looks at him and cackles too. But he's not laughing with her; he's laughing at her, this silly woman jumping up and down, offering gratitude to a deity who had nothing to do with her jackpot, probably has nothing to do with anything at all. *Stupid idiot.*

Bing is blasted back thirty years to his kitchen table, Susie pushing her chair back so hard it tipped over as she announced to the world: *I don't even know if there is a god.*

The woman continues to yodel, "Thank you, Lord! Thank you, Jesus!" Bing shoves past her. He's never seen anything so witless in his life. For so many years, just like these losers sliding nickels into cruel machines, he slid in and out of church pews expecting a jackpot of salvation at the end of it all. *What a fool. What a stupid, stupid fool.*

Bing stomps forward into a man waiting in one of many lines leading to a wall of bank teller windows. "Watch it, buddy," the man says. Bing doesn't even offer a *'Scuse me.* He just cuts through the lines, picking up bits and pieces of what these people are saying to the tellers. *Two dollars to win on Number Eight. Two on One to place.* Bing heads for the colossal arrow painted on the wall and the wide carpeted ramp beneath it. As he starts down, two little boys run toward him, the one in front wearing a Spiderman costume with built-in muscles, the other lagging behind, hindered by a beach towel pinned around his neck.

A man trudging up the ramp says, "Watch where you're going, boys!" But he's not watching either, too busy scribbling in the magazine he's holding up to his face.

The boys veer before they reach Bing and press their faces to a glass wall, heels bouncing as they point to a row of dogs. "I like that one! Pick that one, Daddy."

Bing goes over to see these live racing greyhounds presented like a police lineup, wearing colorful vests with numbers on both sides. The animals held in check by handlers, boys in their teens and twenties. They are as skinny as their charges, and Bing's never seen a dog's waist that narrow. He could wrap both hands around one and his thumbs would overlap. The dogs tug against their handlers' leads, panting beneath the muzzles, chests pumping, ears flattened back so far they are almost nonexistent, nervous eyes flitting, whites showing. Some bury their heads behind the handlers' legs.

Spiderman continues to bounce as his father assesses the dogs. Bing sidles over to get a closer look at the magazine in the dad's hand, a racing program.

"I like that one, Daddy," Spiderman says.

The other boy says, "Me, too! And he's lucky Seven!"

"So he is," the dad says. "Should we bet on him?"

"Yes!"

A crackling voice bleats over the intercom: "Five minutes to post. Please place your bets. Don't get shut out!"

Dad heads up the ramp. The two boys turn to follow, but the littlest one looks up at Bing and says, "We're going to win the trifecta!"

Bing says, "Well, that's just fine."

The boys fly off, and Bing marvels that they speak this gambling language so fluently. He wonders if their mother knows they are here, if this is the father's weekend visitation and instead of taking them roller-skating or to the zoo, he drags his impressionable youngsters to the track. *Don't tell Mommy.*

Dogs and handlers stampede through a glass door that leads outside. Bing follows down the ramp, through his own glass doors into the chilled evening air. He watches the dogs through a chain-link fence as they sniff the path leading to the track, bumping their muzzles against the dirt, trying to smell each other, too, as they aim for a yellowed patch of grass. Bing can see why it's yellow since most of the dogs squat to take a collective piss before the race; some do indeed hunker down to shit, as Ricky had said.

This is no makeshift dirt affair. The course reminds Bing of the Kentucky Derby—on a much smaller scale. There are two ponds in the middle of the track, both spitting water. Lighted billboards flash the lineup of dogs, odds for each to win, a clock counting down to the race. Bing looks at the meager crowd sitting at picnic tables, men and women huddled together, scouring racing forms, swigging beers. Behind them, a wall of windows three stories high, the casino looming, and Bing sees the flashing slot machine lights even from here, practically hears the *ding-ding-ding.*

Spiderman and his brother burst through the lower doors and run toward the fence as the handlers parade the dogs, pausing briefly as the announcer describes each entry. Bing looks back for the father, but he doesn't come, and he doesn't come. Those children running loose in a place like this.

"Boys!" It's not the father calling. It's a woman sitting at one of those picnic tables rocking a bassinette on the bench seat with one hand, eating French fries with the other. "Did Dad forget my root beer?"

Spiderman says, "He's getting it now."

Bing shakes his head at this improbable family outing, but at least they're out here together. No wife up in that fancy restaurant on another man's arm, no husband banished to the lower depths, to the dogs. He imagines what kinds of excursions Susie and Glen cooked up when the kids were small. A museum, or maybe the library, if they organized any family outings at all.

Handlers and hounds saunter down the track toward the gate, and Bing can't quite make out what they're doing, if the dogs are being shoved into boxes or rammed into stalls. The handlers trot back, dogless. The animals whimper and whine, anxious about being left behind, about their predicament, whatever it is. Once the handlers clear the field, the announcer sings, "Here come Sparky and Spunky!"

Bing hears a whoosh and sees two white blurs attached to a giant electrical arm zipping along the inner rail that circles the track. The arm whips toward the starting gate and once it clears, the dogs are turned loose after those fuzzy white streaks. The crowd starts chanting: *Come on Three, Five, Eight*, or whichever they picked to bring home the bacon. Bing can't help it; he starts yelling, too: "Go! Go!" As the arm passes, Bing identifies the stuffed rabbits, the silly prize at the end of the hunt, reminding him of that bone-shaped pillow on Frida's bed. He chortles, imagining that waddling blob trying to keep up with this rumbling herd. She'd still be shuffling out of the gate even as the dogs have come full circle, passing the starting point, racing for the finish line, a piercing light that just clicked on directly across from Bing.

The energized crowd really belts it out: *Come on! Come on!* followed by cheers or wails when it's over, even though the dogs keep running until the electric arm stops and they howl and wail at Sparky and Spunky, because now the *real* race is over and they have cornered their prey.

Bing watches the huffing dogs leave the track, some in triumph, some in defeat as they pass that patch of peed-on grass and head back toward the building. A man bumps into the fence as the dogs pass. "Where is that piece of shit Six?" he howls. When Number Six scrambles by, the man throws his losing tickets at him. "Worthless piece of crap!" The dog's head ducks as if preparing for a blow, but the handler puts himself between the heckler and the dog. "Back off!" the boy snarls, and amazingly, the man does.

Bing looks back for the two boys and their mother to see if they won, hoping they did, but they are halfway to the door already, bassinette bumping against the mother's thigh as she hauls it inside toward the new lineup of dogs. Bing should go back in to look for Ricky and Johnny Ray, but he doesn't look forward to the affront of noise and despair. He prefers it out here, under the safety of these bright, bright lights.

Still, he can't stay here forever, so he turns to head in when his eyes glide all the way down to the end of the fence where three men lean against it, watching the Zamboni-like machine smoothing down the track. It's Ricky, Johnny Ray, and a third man, a three-hundred pounder, easy. Bing takes a deep breath and clears his throat. Fifty feet between him and his keys. He strides toward them, getting closer and closer, and Bing watches the fat man's mouth moving as he draws on his left palm with his right finger: a picture, or symbols, a map. Ricky watches, head nodding up and down as he absorbs whatever important instructions the fat man imparts.

When Bing is three paces away, Johnny Ray sees him and stands up straight. "I thought we ditched that son of a bitch."

Ricky pops up. "Shit."

The fat man turns his meaty neck toward Bing. "Who the hell is that?"

"Get rid of him," Johnny says. He and the fat man stomp off toward the doors.

Ricky bounces from foot to foot as he watches their receding backs. "You gotta get outta here, man."

"I intend to." Bing holds out his hand. "I just need my car keys."

Ricky puffs out his cheeks and deflates them. "Yeah. All right." He fumbles around in his coat pocket for the keys and drops them in Bing's cupped palm. "Now beat it. And don't be following us." He jabs his finger into Bing's shoulder. "I mean it."

"No problem." Bing is elated to feel the warm metal against his skin.

Ricky gallops off, and Bing waits there, giving him a wide berth, examining the assortment of keys: Susie's front door, garage, locker at the plant, until he realizes a crucial one is missing: the key to the Olds. "What?" He looks up just as Ricky catches up to Johnny Ray. Bing races forward. He will not lose them again.

"Hold on!" he says, as they pull open the glass door and head inside. Bing hoofs it, lungs wheezing, nudging people out of his way until he grabs the door handle and yanks it open. The three men have paused in front of the row of dogs standing behind the glass. Fat Man sees Bing first. "Are you boys bustin' my balls?" he says, nodding at Bing. Johnny Ray looks up and his lips pull back exposing his canines, the meanest snarl Bing's ever seen. Johnny Ray boxes Ricky's ear and points at Bing. "Get rid of him or I will."

Bing holds up his keys. "I just want my car key. That's all."

Ricky stomps down the ramp toward Bing, an odd mix of scared rabbit and snorting bull. He fiddles in his pocket for what Bing assumes is his ignition key. "Dammit, Tex," Ricky says, almost apologizing as he pulls his hand back out of his pocket, balls it into a hard-knuckled fist, and swings it like a wrecking ball.

A lightning bolt in the middle of Bing's face. A crack, a red flash, blinding white heat. Bing crumbles to his knees, face seeking the cluster of dogs yanking against their leads, distressed eyes all watching him hit the deck.

As added insult something pelts Bing's cheekbone, bounces off, and thunks against the carpeted ramp before coming to rest. The key to the Olds.

TRIAGE

Call it a miracle.

No, not anymore. Call it blind luck, or survival instinct, but Bing pulls himself together and scrambles through the casino, wobbling like a drunk man, bouncing off walls and people, trickle of blood from his bashed nose running down his lip, his chin. Passing *Thank you, Jesus* dolts and inattentive security guards and an empty table at the French Quarter where a cheating wife once sat. He bursts out under the carport, bumbling by the valet guy, through the parking lot, past lines and lines of cars, buses, Winnebagos, to locate the Olds. He actually finds it. Finds the interstate, too, and gets the hell out of there, driving like an escaped lunatic, because while he's punching the gas he's also pushing the seat back, tilting the steering wheel, adjusting the rearview—correcting the million infractions Ricky inflicted on the car. But at least Bing is heading toward Susie's, looking forward to a steaming shower and clean clothes. Daughter or not, at this moment he's got nowhere else in the entire solar system to go.

He recognizes his exit, is flabbergasted by his internal navigator that remembers to take a left at that church, a right at that flagpole. He turns onto Susie's street and sees her glorious house with the tidy yard and no pack of scrabbling dogs, no car engine dangling from a tree limb. It's lit up from tip to toe, every window lamp and outdoor light burning, people gathered on the porch. Glen's car parked in the driveway, Glen just getting out of the driver's side, shaking his head up at Susie by the front door. Bing wonders what all the excitement is for because, ultimately, he doubts they even noticed his prolonged absence. Actually hoped he could slink inside and tiptoe to the basement unnoticed.

As he nears and pulls into the driveway Susie points at him and throws up her arms in what might be a hallelujah from another person. *Me?* Bing thinks. *All this because of me?* Junior, Reenie, and Brian rush for his car before he's even got the thing in park. He turns off the engine and looks up at the kids rumbling toward him, then beyond them to the person standing on the porch beside Susie, silver hair glowing like a halo. Ellen.

Reenie opens his door. "What happened to your nose?" She punches Junior in the arm. "I told you to go with him!"

Junior helps Bing out of the car. "Mr. Butler, you're home. Thank God."

"Holy shit." Brian stoops to survey the damage to the car.

Glen darts over and squeezes Bing's shoulder. "Jesus."

God. Holy. Jesus. Religious monikers that now scrape Bing's eardrums.

Glen cups Bing's jaw in his hand, turning it this way and that to inspect Bing's nose, his cheeks, but Bing is watching Ellen hug Susie, a lingering embrace that might ensue between dear friends, or a mother and daughter.

"I'll get the first-aid kit," Glen says, already jogging toward the house.

Bing doesn't have time to rebut because Reenie drags him across the lawn. Ellen steps from the porch to offer the family some privacy at the soldier's return, and Bing does feel like

he survived a bizarre tour of duty. It was definitely a tour of
something.

He expects the first words out of Susie's mouth to be *Where
the hell have you been?* Something he might say if he were standing
in her place, probably did utter a time or ten when Susie was a
rebellious teen.

Susie stands on the porch, the lights behind her making it
difficult to gauge her anger. Then she steps down and flings out
her arms. Bing flinches, but Susie hugs him, an embrace so unexpected Bing just stands there, arms akimbo, not wanting to
transfer the feral odors from his clothes to hers—at least that's his
excuse—until the moment turns awkward, so he drapes one arm
loosely around her and pats her shoulder.

Susie pulls away and looks at him. She shakes her head, and if
the porch lights were brighter he might be able to tell if those really are tears in her eyes. "Dad," she says, mouth gaping as if more
words might spill.

But they don't, which is worse than a scolding. Bing says, "I'm
sorry." He's not exactly sure what he has to be sorry for, but he
feels that he should be sorry for something.

Reenie grabs Bing's right elbow, Junior grabs his left, Brian
pushes from behind and they heave him up the steps. Inside,
Frida picks up the alluring aromas and bangs her nose against his
ankles as he's catapulted to the kitchen where Glen has assembled
a drugstore of salves and bandages. They sit Bing in a chair and
Glen pushes up his sleeves, swabbing Bing's nose with alcohol,
which stings like the dickens. All the while he is bombarded by
questions and speculations from the kids. *So where did you go? You*

smell like a sewer. You want to talk about the car? Where'd all this cat hair come from?

Even if he wanted to—which he doesn't—Bing couldn't squeeze one syllable into the verbal barrage. After weeks of inattention he's not ready for this much consideration. He shrinks from the scrutiny, from Frida pawing at his smelly pants, from the circle of heads looming.

Susie pries the huddle apart. "That's enough," she says, shutting the interrogation down. "Let him be."

If Bing didn't offer her a proper hug before, he would like to now.

Everyone looks at Bing for confirmation. "All I want is a shower and a good night's sleep."

They groan and cluck, but trail away.

Someone has made good use of his absence, Glen, Reenie, because in those short hours between mild concern and search parties they did his laundry and packed up his junk mound, vexing Frida, no doubt. Bing has no idea where all his crap wound up, and he really doesn't care if it's back in boxes or at the bottom of the Ohio River. He really does not care.

After sloughing off layers of stink in the shower, Bing slumps on the edge of his bed, tugging on socks. Frida noses his pile of dirty clothes on the floor, grunting at the essence of foreign animals, evidence of high adventures. "If you only knew," Bing confesses, picturing one of those greyhound racing vests stretched around her. "Couldn't wrap my hands around your belly."

Bing looks at his room. In the basement, yes, but snug, no kerosene heater or decades' worth of filth. No oxygen tank chaining him to the bed. No scary Leonard with his gang of thugs plotting who-knows-what in the kitchen, no wildcat woman locked upstairs somewhere. He pictures Odell, a war hero, lying in that cave of a room, staring at the fuzzy TV, ring of purring cats his only real company.

Someone raps on the doorjamb, pulling Bing back out of Odell's dark room.

Susie leans against the wooden frame. "Feel better now?"

"A million times."

"And you're sure you're all right?"

Bing's hand goes to his face, the puffy nose, swollen cheek, tender eye. "I suffered shiners worse than this in the Navy."

Susie nods. "You want to tell me what happened?"

Bing tries to tie sentences together to describe the past several hours. A whirlwind of dark images and carnival wails shoots him back into the cave, and he spends his last bit of energy yanking himself out again. "Not really," he says, head woozy, eyelids weighted with lead sinkers.

Susie's eyes rove his face, and Bing can tell she's trying to read his mind. "Fair enough," she says, perhaps remembering all the teenage interrogations she endured when she traipsed home at two in the morning.

"Thank you." Bing is already tipping over onto the mattress, which is perfect, and the sheets smell like Downy. The pillow cradles his head, his neck. He could sleep for a decade, but he hears a crinkle under the pillow, feels a bulge, so he slides his hand underneath and pulls out a MoonPie, a welcome-home present that makes him laugh.

"What in the world?" Susie says. "Who put that there?"

Bing can't answer over the laughter caught in his throat that turns to quiet sobs, because he is that touched, and because he knows no one would leave such a gift for Odell trapped in that hollow with blood kin he would prefer not to claim. It's too sad, when all Bing wants is to sleep, to forget, so he closes his eyes and feels another gift, a familiar hand on his brow, smoothing his hair, his mother's voice whispering, *Shhhh. Shhhh. Rest now. Go to sleep, little man.*

SMALL GIFTS

Sunday morning Bing finds Susie and Reenie at the kitchen table, plotting.

Reenie flips through the newspaper, two-dozen slick Christmas inserts stacked before her. "It's his eighteenth birthday, Mom. Don't get him a stupid video game."

Susie taps a pen against her temple. "You got any better ideas?"

They both look up as Bing toddles to the coffeepot. He feels their gazes on his face, the rich array of bruises that blossomed overnight. Reenie gasps, but Susie holds up a finger. Bing is relieved they won't be interrogating him about his injuries. He wants to grab his coffee and skedaddle, but Susie pushes a vacant chair out with her foot.

"What should we get Brian for his birthday, Dad?"

Bing is compelled to sit. "Oh, I don't know." He pictures his grandson up in his room, that 9/11 shrine, or out in the driveway. "Maybe something for the Camaro?"

"We thought about that, but we have no idea what he needs." Susie solves a word jumble and etches in the letters.

"Junior could probably tell you." The steam from Bing's coffee feels medicinal.

Reenie groans. "Big blabbermouth. If we asked him he'd go tell Brian."

"Maybe you could do some reconnaissance for us?" Susie asks.

Bing's neck spasms, but this is a welcome chore. "Might could."

"We only have a couple of weeks."

"I'm on it," Bing says. "When's the big day?"

Reenie earmarks a sale page of washers and dryers, an odd Christmas wish list, Bing thinks, until he remembers her ultimate hope. "Twenty-first."

"First day of winter." Susie drops her pen to rub her hands together. "Night of the big party."

Her animation astounds Bing. "You having a birthday party for Brian?"

"Like he'd ever come to one of their snotty Christmas *soi-rees*." Reenie carves out that last word like a clench-jawed snob.

"It's not a Christmas party," Susie says.

"Oh. Right. I forgot. A snotty winter *solstice* soi-ree. And Brian would never come to that pagan-fest either."

"A *what*-fest?" Bing says, utterly confused.

Susie shakes her head at the ceiling. "It's just an end of the semester gathering of colleagues."

"With Druid chanting and tree worshipping," Reenie adds, ripping out a page of television sets.

Susie snorts. "I'm not the one who's antsy to put up a Christmas tree every year."

Mother and daughter trade barbs, a needling swap meet that reminds Bing of the thousands of bickering matches between Barbara and Susie over the years. He looks from Susie to Reenie,

their shared features: round face, creased dimples, sparse eyebrows, attributes they inherited from Barbara. They are definitely
her heirs, and Bing again wonders about their questionable gene
pool. Do they express anything of him? The cleft chin, low forehead, pronounced knuckles? No. Even their mannerisms and tics
are all Barbara's: sweeping hand gestures, ear tugging, lip nibbling.

Brian comes in and the girls clam up, visually nudging
Bing on his mission, but he watches Brian pour cereal, milk,
sort the paper looking for the sports section. All the while
Bing compares his own meaty hands to Brian's slender fingers:
pianist's hands, or a surgeon's. Ears fanned out wider than Bing's
ever did, the blunt lobes no kin to Bing's danglers. The height
is about right, but Charles was tall too, and Bing ogles Brian's
neck, his skinny pencil neck.

Glen enters. "Morning all."

Bing looks up and grins, not in welcome but because Glen
has a pencil neck, too.

"Junior and I thought we'd give the Olds a once-over if that's
okay with you."

"It's more than okay," Bing says.

"Let me wash it first."

"It's forty-five degrees out there!" Susie says, but Glen is
already bounding out the back door to fetch the bucket and
sponge.

Brian and Reenie scuttle out, leaving Susie to load the dishwasher. "What do you want for Christmas, Dad?"

"Oh, I don't know." But Bing knows exactly. He wants answers. He wants to know what really went on between Barbara and Charles. He wants desperately to know if the son he mourned and buried was his. If he rightfully owns the guilt he's been lugging all these years. If the daughter, the family whose table he now pulls up to, whose roof he sleeps under, is really his family after all. He looks at Susie's back, her rumpled shirt, baggy sweatpants, hair matted from sleep. He wants her to sit so he can ask all this, but he's afraid to dredge up the rough history, the hard feelings, the blame that might sever the tenuous lifeline she recently cast, might make her want to take back the very real hug she offered him last night, probably the first genuine embrace since she was a child.

"When you think of something, just tell me." She hangs a dish towel on the rack and walks out, leaving Bing with the unanswered questions tumbling around in his mind like rocks.

Downstairs, Bing studies his face in the mirror, appraising the odd seep of blues and purples migrating across his cheeks, the squiggly veins in his eyes. If he has relatives upstairs, they don't resemble him now. Still, he can't stand the not knowing, the feeling that his entire universe has been thrown off-kilter by one thing, one discovery, one person, really. Charles.

He swears he hears a *ping* when another name surfaces. If he can't ask Susie, he can ask Tootie, who was closer to Barbara than anyone—closer than Susie, probably even closer than Bing. He doesn't know where Charles measures up on that yardstick, but he has a nauseating suspicion.

He studies the phone for ten minutes before picking it up. *What if Dillard answers?* Maybe Bing should just ask him, but he doesn't think Dillard was privy to that infidelity. He couldn't, wouldn't have kept that treason from Bing. Dillard is too loyal a friend.

Call, you chicken shit. This self-flogging raises Bing's ire, which steadies his hand. He grabs the phone—*gutless son of a bitch*—punches in the numbers—*spineless bastard*—and it starts ringing.

Dillard picks up. "Hello?"

Bing swallows the lump in his throat. "Dillard, you ornery cuss. It's me."

"Bing!" Dillard yells off in the distance, "It's Bing!" He directs his voice back into the mouthpiece. "Me and Tootie was just talking about you."

"You were?" Bing is afraid of what they might have been discussing, or divulging.

"She said you'd probably have another heart attack if you saw the God-awful Christmas decorations on your house."

Bing is relieved. "Christmas decorations?"

"You never seen anything like it. That boy Alan strapped a fake chimney to the roof, with a giant Santa poking out the top. He's got a sleigh and reindeer propped up there somehow. I expect the whole mess to crash through the rafters any minute."

"That a fact?"

"Front yard's covered with every battery-operated snowman, and North Pole elf, and baby-Jesus doohickey you can imagine. It's like high beams blasting through my windows every night."

Bing revels in the lightness in his chest, the elation of knowing that the new neighbors have gone too far.

"So, how you doing up there?"

"Doing all right, buddy. Doing just fine." He hates to lie, but he savors Dillard's voice, the familiar, homespun drawl.

"Pick up any splinters from the outhouse yet?"

An image of Odell in his kerosene-stoked room, and the lightness in Bing's chest begins to fade, Dillard's homespun voice suddenly grating.

"Bet those gap-toothed hillbillies got you to stop brushing your teeth."

Reenie asking him to slice carrots, MoonPies tucked under his pillow. Bing refuses to laugh, and he doesn't mind the awkward pause that makes Dillard clear his throat. Bing finally says, "Could I talk to Tootie for a minute?"

"Tootie? You want to talk to Tootie?" Bing hears the puzzle in Dillard's voice.

"Just for a minute. I need, uh, a recipe of hers that Susie wants to whip up. Can't tell you what manner of weeds and soybean crud they been passing off as food up here."

"That right?" Dillard says.

"Yes sir." Bing hopes Dillard will swallow this hook without adding any commentary about roadkill.

"Well, sure," Dillard says, hurt feelings shellacking his voice, but Bing can't fret about that now. Bigger fish, and all. Dillard calls Tootie over, a rustle as the phone is passed like a baton. "Hey there, Bing. We sure miss you down here."

"I miss you, too." Bing realizes for the first time that he genuinely does miss her sweetness, her refusal to tolerate Dillard's low humor, though at the time he considered her a killjoy. Here comes that lump in his throat reminding him of the task at hand.

"Listen, Tootie," Bing tries to strain the quaver from his voice. "I need to talk to you in private."

"Okay," Tootie says, voice an octave lower than usual.

"Without Dillard hearing."

"Oh! All right, hang on a sec." Tootie calls off into the distance. "Dillard? Run over and borrow a cup of sugar from next door."

Dillard's tinny voice answers, "I don't know if I can make it across that wired-up yard. Might set off a land mine!"

"Just go," Tootie says. Bing can picture the look she's shooting Dillard. "Okay. He's gone. What's wrong, Bing?"

"Nothing," his reflexive answer, but he's got to push past reflexes, through fear, if he wants to get to the truth. "That's a lie," he admits. "Everything is wrong. I just found out about . . . I need to know about . . . Barbara and . . ." He can't say the name, can't make his tongue spit out the syllables.

Bing hears a low groan rumbling all the way from Texas, down the wires, until Tootie whispers, "Need to know about what?"

Bing bites his lower lip. "Charles."

There. It's real. Now it's all real because Bing has just uttered the name, given it breath, made the secret come to life.

A fat pause until Tootie says in a slippery voice, "Charles was her bridge partner."

"I know they were bridge partners." His tone is harsher than he intended, so he says more softly, "I need to know if that's all they were."

There's that potent pause again. "Oh, Bing. Why do you have to dredge up all of this now? They're both gone, so what does it really matter?"

"What does it matter?"

"Yes. And besides, I really don't know."

"You were her best friend, Tootie. How can you not know?"

Bing can feel her discomfort even from here as she breathes deeply in and out, in and out.

"I never asked," she says. Bing has to decide whether or not to believe her. "Maybe you should let it go," she adds, "before you find out something you may not really want to know. Maybe you should just let it all go."

A sound like waves, or rushing wind, and it's hard to hear, but he thinks Tootie says good-bye, or so long, so he pushes out a feeble farewell before clattering the phone into its cradle.

Bing stands there, teetering, Tootie's impossible advice bleating in his ears. *How the hell am I supposed to let this go?*

***

Hours later Bing tries to still his frantic brain with a Cowboys game, but he can't, especially when Burl Ives starts singing Christmas songs somewhere upstairs, that stoic voice rumbling through the heater vents, jabbing Bing's eardrums. Finally he heads upstairs where Reenie decorates an artificial tree in the living room, lights already strung and illuminated, boxes of ornaments scattered on the floor.

Frida lies on her pillow by the door. She's been squeezed into a Santa doggy sweater, furry white collar, black vinyl belt. Dumbest thing Bing's ever seen. Frida looks at him and he swears she rolls her eyes.

"Wanna help?" Reenie asks, coils of garland looped around her neck.

"Oh no, no. Your grandmother always handled that. I never could get it right."

"There is no right."

Bing perks up. That's what he tried to tell Barbara their first Christmases together, but he gave up after discovering that she rearranged his efforts after he left. Still, he doesn't have the spirit. "You're doing a fine job."

A clanging outside, metal pinging against concrete. Bing looks through the front window at Junior hovering over the freshly washed Olds, front end up on ramps, Brian underneath. Junior blows on his bare fingers, drags his coat sleeve under his nose.

"Those boys shouldn't be out in that cold," Bing says.

"You try telling them that."

Bing yanks open the door to call them in, frigid air tightening his chest. "You boys come on in now!" If they hear, they ignore him, so he steps from the porch and crunches across brittle grass in his slippers, the chill burrowing through his socks. "Come on in now!"

Brian slides out from under the Olds and shakes his head at Bing. "We drove her up on the interstate. Feels like your front end is out of alignment."

"And your tires need to be balanced," Junior adds. He points to the left front wheel. "You managed to bend a rim." Junior and Brian stare. They want to probe, but they don't, and Bing appreciates their restraint.

Brian stands, wiping his hands down his pant legs just as the sun disappears, changing the light. Bing looks up into the sky. The dense blanket of clouds just hangs there, hovering close to the horizon, blue-gray underbelly promising something. Rain, maybe.

Junior follows Bing's gaze and says, "Snow skies."

On cue, fat flakes drift down, hundreds of them, thousands, a giant saltshaker seasoning the earth. Bing holds out his hand, his neck tilted back so far it cracks, the flakes quickly glazing his face, making him blink, and he opens his mouth to let them in.

"It's sticking," Brian says.

Bing looks at snow resting on grass, already collecting, coating the lawn, the brick street, the Olds' windshield. Brian and Junior attend to the car, closing the hood, backing her off the ramps, gathering tools. Bing tilts his head back up. He stands with his hands out, and he doesn't even mind the stinging wetness on his palms, his Adam's apple, his battered face.

"It's snowing!" Reenie yells from the porch. She races down the steps, skidding in her moccasins, spinning in the grass like the five-year-old Bing remembers so well. Catching snowflakes on her tongue, giggling, and Bing giggles right along with her, even as neighbors step out onto porches to gaze into the sky.

The sound of tapping on glass. Bing turns to see Susie behind the storm door, coffee mug in her hand. He doesn't want her to call him in, to reprimand him for being out without gloves or galoshes, something his mother would do, or Barbara. But Susie holds up her mug in a toast. He is grateful for that. And for the hint of Christmas tree behind her, the way the lights shimmer in the rippled glass door, the warm glow that illuminates Susie standing there with a look that is both warm and melancholy.

Bing wonders what she is sad about, if it has anything to do with him, or her mother, or Charles. Until he realizes that she is not standing in the middle of the door, but off to the side, as if she's leaving room for Glen who probably did stand beside her year after year watching their children play in that first winter snow. Today there is no Glen. His second-floor office window is dark. Glen is not home. He is seldom home, though today, a Sunday, he should be here with his family, with his wife, watching a silly old man turn back into a child.

COLD COMFORT

Bing wakes up groggy, brain warming up like an old transformer tube. He is comforted by the sounds of toilets flushing, cereal bowls clattering, car keys clinking, until the bustle is followed by oppressive silence, no one to hear his cries for help should he need to be heard. An irrational fear that's hounded him since his run-in with Ricky and Johnny Ray.

Upstairs, the natural light filtering into the kitchen is dimmer, the air thicker. Bing heads toward the picture window in the living room to ogle the fresh layer of snow blanketing the earth, the most snow he's ever seen in his life, half a foot, maybe. A dance pattern of foot-prints on the porch, through the yard, evidence of life. *Someone ought to sweep those steps.* Bing envisions the mailman slipping, cracking his skull. *Sidewalk needs shoveling, too.* He's amazed that Glen hasn't already done it. "Cheating bastard," Bing blurts, already convicting the man even if his proof is just an empty space at the door. He rubs his chest, that scar, and knows better than to put his pumper through that. Sweeping will have to do.

Downstairs, Bing layers on socks and tugs on his work boots. Buttons a cardigan over his jumpsuit. *Winter clothes. That's what I need for Christmas.* Back upstairs he finds the kitchen broom, yanks on his coat and a pair of work gloves. Frida, still in her absurd Santa sweater, looks up at him from her pillow, brow scrunched because it's not time for her walk. "No," Bing says, "but you might as well come on out." He holds the door open and she waddles through, sniffing at snow, dipping one paw in as if she's testing the waters. "Go on," Bing urges. She eases down one step at a time, belly dragging, leaving a sluglike trail in the snow.

Bing follows her into the yard, forging his own trail as he assesses the street, also coated in snow, not a hint of brick, just a few tire tracks from these well-practiced winter drivers. It's hard on the eyes, all that blue-whiteness, heaped on bushes, and on the lawn chairs Susie never did bring in. Lining every tree limb and telephone wire, a delicate balancing act, an intricate webbing of white on black. It's quite beautiful, really. And so still. Bing looks in the distance at the hill, that once fuzzy green wall that hemmed him in. It looks naked now, snow like white flesh revealing every lump and crease, skin folds and protruding bones. Barren trees poking out like bristly hair. *Not so imposing, now*, Bing thinks, softening, because it is like a live thing, a giant animal hunkered down for the winter.

Car doors slam. Bing looks toward the curb at a Pontiac that snuck up behind him, tires muffled by snow.

Four old women disembark, pant legs tucked into ankle boots. They balance casserole dishes and cake plates in their gloved hands. Bibles tucked under their arms, some zipped in quilted cases like the ones Barbara used to sew for her church gals.

One of them points at Frida. "How cute."

Bing looks at the dog, that red-and-white tube, squatting to take a dump.

"Where'd you find that sweater?" one woman asks. The others lean in for the answer.

"Oh, uh," Bing mutters, supremely embarrassed to be remotely connected to that getup. "Something my granddaughter dug up."

"It's just darling," another one chimes.

"Yeah, well." Bing wishes they would move along, which they do, heading toward Ellen's house. *Figures.* This must be Ellen's Bible study group. He squints at the flock trying to decide if they're all lesbians. Hard to tell with their bulky coats and thick scarves. He wonders what kind of Bible they are studying, remembers mashing one around in Ellen's car with his foot. It wasn't the same version Pastor Manning preached from, with absolute-definitive-irrefutable rails against homosexuality. *Hard to gloss over that.* But it's all a bunch of hooey anyway. Still, Bing figures their perverted lifestyle is deviant by any society's standards—religious or not. He watches this line of wobbling women file up Ellen's steps, clomp the snow off their boots, and disappear into her house. *Good riddance.*

An hour later, back in the kitchen, Bing thaws his chilled hands over the teapot heating on the stove. He hates this alone time now. This absolute quiet except for Frida flopped on her pillow, rooting out snow marbles lodged between her paw pads, dog tags tinkling. Bing doesn't want to go down to the basement, that cave, and he wishes there were a TV in the kitchen that he could turn on to cover the silence.

Sudden whoops and cackles from next door, pushing through Ellen's windows, zooming across the driveway that separates the two houses, penetrating the brick wall to infiltrate this very kitchen. Bing rushes to the side window that never did have curtains and peeks over the frame. There's Ellen's kitchen window, lights inside illuminating the cluster of heads and torsos milling around. Arms raised as they toast each other with juice glasses, eat wedges of cake with bare fingers. *Having a gay old time*, Bing thinks, gratified by his clever wordplay. If there were curtains on this window he would yank them closed, lower Venetian blinds, slam shutters, stomp off to show his disgust even if it's only to himself. He starts to back away, but the laughter stills his feet, and he closes his eyes and presses his cheek against the cold wall to listen. Just listen to the muffled noise, evidence of people, of life. That makes him feel safe, somehow, even if they are twelve feet and two brick walls away. He stands there, leaning fully into the wall with every bit of his weight, his strength, and he can't move, even as the teakettle boils, that shrill whistle sounding an alarm that he doesn't want to answer, not yet, not yet, not yet.

LAND MINES

That night, during dinner, Susie calculates final grades that are due in the morning.

Bing squints at Glen, wondering if he is the kind of professor who lures coeds toward cherry desks promising good grades for certain favors. Or the other scenario of girls in tight sweaters luring noble but weak teachers toward those same cherry desks. *Which one are you?* Bing pictures his son-in-law in a gush of passion, sweeping his desk protector, pencil can, picture of Susie and the kids onto the floor. It makes Bing want to punch him, and tonight he just might call Glen out if he offers one more lame excuse about going for a jog or dashing to the library. *Going to visit a sick friend.*

But tonight after supper Glen brings them all coffee and sits back down to coordinate the upcoming party just five days away, never mind Susie's mad tabulations, the fill-in-the-bubble sheets and tattered grade book before her. Glen unfolds a piece of paper and runs through the list of hors d'oeuvres he's going to cook, dishes Bing can barely unscramble as he leans in to study Glen's neat penmanship: chevre tarts, gougère, insalata di petto cappone alle noci, that last one such a spelling test Bing gives up altogether. Bing's never seen the man so worked up about cooking. Susie offers as much distracted enthusiasm as she can, tossing out the occasional grunt. Clearly her mind is on her grading. Glen apparently knows it, too, his voice rising as he tries to divert her attention, get her to tune into his plans.

But she's got more pressing concerns, even Bing can see that. This is her livelihood, after all. Yet Glen continues nudging his menu closer and closer to Susie, covering up her bubble grades. It reminds Bing of Barbara trying to tell him some trivial household tidbit while he was figuring taxes, or balancing the checkbook. It's pathetic, Bing thinks, Glen behaving like a wife desperate for her husband's attention. *Acting just like a woman.*

Bing's chest suddenly aches, not from sweeping snow, not from choked arteries, but because he feels sad for Glen, for Barbara, two people he wants nothing but to blame, to hate. For this split second he can't, not completely, because he sees, for the first time, a hint of his own part in it all, and Susie's.

"Just look at the goddamn list!" Bing blurts to Susie, to himself, wishing he could go back and look at all the report cards and upholstery samples Barbara tried to shove under his nose over the years. Would have taken five minutes, five minutes that might have changed so much.

Susie and Glen stare at him until Susie says, "Okay!" She slaps her pencil on the table. Glen holds the paper out for her to scan, but his eyes are on Bing. Bing looks at his son-in-law's face etched with a look of appreciation. Camaraderie.

You're not off the hook. Bing pushes his chair back to let this couple have their spousal time together. He aims for the basement until Susie says, "So what does Brian want for his birthday, Dad?"

"His birthday?"

"Yeah. It's this Saturday. You were supposed to—"

"Oh! Right," Bing says, just now remembering his assignment. "Got it narrowed down to two things. In fact I was just heading up to his room to whittle it down."

He dashes into the hall before she interrogates him further. As he starts up the steps he hears Susie say to Glen, "Now can I get back to my damn grading?"

Upstairs, Bing stands before Brian's closed door, a slice of light shining beneath it. Bing knocks once and the door swings open, illuminating Brian hunched before his computer screen.

"Shit!" the boy says, pressing a key that erases whatever he was eyeballing. Brian looks up, visibly relieved that it's only Bing, waving him in with curt instructions, "Close the door!"

Bing obeys. "Sorry to interrupt."

"It's okay," Brian says, relaxing in his swivel chair.

"Listen," Bing says. "Reenie and your mother want to surprise you with a birthday present, but they have no idea what you need. They sent me up here to snoop around." Bing's eyes ricochet to the computer screen and back. "But I just don't feel right about that."

"I appreciate that."

"I told them you could probably use something for the Camaro."

Brian rubs his kneecap, and Bing detects a pained look in his eyes, like his best girl just gave back his varsity jacket. "No," he says. "I won't have much time to work on her now."

"What's that?" Bing says.

"Nothing. It's just . . . nothing."

Bing's legs feel puny, delayed fatigue from all that snow sweeping. "Mind if I sit?" he asks, but if he doesn't, he'll fall. He backs toward the unmade bed beneath that September 11th montage, hands probing out behind him. When he feels the mattress, he eases his backside down using his arms as buttresses. His right hand crumples something around on the bed, a pamphlet crinkling beneath his palm. "Sorry," he says.

"That's okay." Brian holds out his hand to retrieve it.

"No trouble." Bing reads the title as he flattens out the cover: *General Educational Development.* Fat letters in a blue starburst add: *Get Your High School Diploma Online.*

"What's this?" Bing asks. Brian looks down at his feet, and Bing thinks he knows why. "Your grades can't be that bad. I'm sure your parents would get you a tutor before they'd let you flunk out."

"I'm not flunking out! I made the honor roll, in fact, not that Mom and Dad ever asked to see a report card."

"Honor roll?" Bing is staggered. He always thought Reenie was the brains of the operation—at least that's what Susie led him to believe. "That's real good. Real good."

"I worked my ass off this year." Brian shakes his head at some internal wound. "They could care less."

"That's not true," Bing says, though he suspects, on some level, it may be. He's still gripping that pamphlet. "Then why do you need a GED?"

Brian's lips purse as he sizes Bing up. "Because somebody's got to do something about Saddam Hussein."

Bing tries, truly, to make the leap in his mind that Brian apparently has. "I don't follow."

Brian leans forward to look into Bing's eyes, man to man. "That lunatic has weapons of mass destruction. It's just a matter of time, Grandpa, and I'm not going to sit around and wait for him to blow up the Statue of Liberty or the Golden Gate Bridge."

"Okay," Bing says, a step closer to understanding, recognizing the look in Brian's eyes, a look Bing once sported when he seethed about Hirohito or Hitler. It's a soldier's hard gaze, that steely resolve, and now Bing understands Brian's fighter-pilot video games. *I have to get better*, Brian had said.

A giant hand grabs Bing's aorta and squeezes, but he manages to sputter, "You're going to take the GED and enlist before you graduate."

"Close," Brian says. "I already passed the GED, and I have an appointment with a recruiter Monday morning."

"Monday? This Monday?" That giant hand grips tighter.

Brian twists back to his computer and punches a button that restores what he had been working on. The words are too small for Bing to make out, except for the blue header: *United States Air Force: What to expect in Basic Training.*

"Gearing up for boot camp?"

"That's right."

"I was never in better shape in my life," Bing muses, remembering all those chin lifts and push-ups.

"I knew you'd understand, Grandpa." Brian takes Bing's nostalgia as approval. "You're a veteran. You've proved yourself. And Uncle Roger. Damn, he *died* for his country. Man's gotta do what a man's gotta do, right? I don't care what Mom thinks."

"Oh boy." Bing imagines the weapons detonating when Susie finds out.

The dread must be evident because Brian adds, "I know. She's going to go ballistic."

"That's a fact." Bing thinks Susie's anti-Vietnam wrath will hurtle back full force. The rage she heaved at him before Roger went. And after. After.

"What about college?"

"Fuck college!" Brian spits. "Sorry. I mean, right now this is more important. It is to me. To our country. I'll do whatever grunt work Uncle Sam needs to get that bastard out of Iraq. And we won't be over there long. A year, eighteen months, tops. Afterwards the Air Force will pay for me to become a pilot, which is all I ever wanted to be."

"I see." Bing pictures Odell up in that scary hollow, his granddaughter yanked brutally out of school and sent into harm's way. Brian has more options than she ever will, but it looks as if his mind is firmly set.

The boy thumps his knees with his fingers. "You don't know how hard it's been to keep this from my friends, and Junior."

"Junior doesn't know?"

"No one knows, so you have to promise not to say a word until after I enlist. Okay? One soldier to another, do I have your word?"

Bing ignores that punishing hand in his chest, because he's honored to be included in this select group, to be welcomed into the boy's, the *man's*, inner circle. "Course you have my word."

Brian holds out his hand and they shake to seal the deal.

"I guess I'd better leave you to your work," Bing says, standing.

"Remember, not a word."

Bing leaves and pulls the door shut behind him.

In the hall, that blasted hand in his chest will not unfurl, and now it's gripping his intestines. Can't even make it to the can in the basement. He lunges toward the second-floor latrine, locks the door, and dispatches his jumpsuit to his ankles before sitting on the pot to evacuate his bowels, his twisted, anxious bowels. Bing classifies the tremor in his gut as patriotic fervor, because he wants to be excited for the boy. Truly. Wants to send him off proudly to kick Saddam's ass. Bing would do it, too, if he could subtract sixty years. At least he thinks he would.

Bing zips up and pumps antibacterial soap into his palm to wash his hands. He shakes his head at the absurdity: he's worrying about a few germs when Brian is tucked in his bunker probably worrying about germ warfare. *Combat is meant for the young*, Bing decides, imagining Brian's bony frame strapped in the cockpit of an F-14 Tomcat flying over Iraqi sand. Or in an F-18 Hornet dropping bombs on those sun-bleached, sand-blasted cities, Saddam's henchmen scrambling for cover.

Suddenly Brian is yanked out of the sky and plopped into a different theater, a different war altogether, his face smeared with dirt, crawling on his belly through dense forest. Bing knows the vision is off-kilter, but he leaves Brian down there with soldiers who had to look into their enemies' eyes, not from a distant cockpit like a certain seersucker-wearing, pencil-necked asshole. Not miles from the action, either, on a floating dry dock in the Pacific.

Bing imagines an infantryman scrabbling on the ground in enemy jungle, the squad's gunner perhaps, a former high school linebacker struggling under the weight of an M-60 and rounds of ammo, tattered fatigues covered with muck. An untested private who just nine months before was sleeping in his Houston bed, plastering Bat Masterson decals on his headboard, fighting with his sister over the last Pop-Tart. Now he's hidden beneath a dense forest canopy, scraping toward Saigon, the last words he said to his father in that Studebaker ringing in his ears: *I don't want to go.* But he went, didn't he? Because that's what men do, that's what sons do for their fathers. And the other words he whispered: *I'm scared.*

Bing sees it clearly. Too clearly. Especially the fierce look he gave his son before sending him off, a look meant to bolster, to inflate, and the words, his parting words: *You just have to suck it up, boy.*

How Roger does suck it up, swallows his fear and crawls forward anyway, sweat stinging his eyes, dirt in his mouth, toward a sharp-shooting gook in a tree who's shouldering an AK-47, crosshairs aimed at the rustling groundcover below, the shivering leaves that give Roger's position, his very life, away.

Bing slumps at the kitchen table stirring his tea, analyzing Brian's secret, an added millstone heaped upon him, as if the world wanted to see how much ballast one old man could pack before buckling. Not much more, Bing figures.

He wants to cast off this weight, part of it at least, hand Brian's secret to Susie like a ticking bomb. But she's a moving target today, skittering around like a mad woman along with Aldine, gussying up the house for the party this weekend. Bing listens to the vacuum cleaner howling, Pledge can spritzing, Frida sneezing in the distance at raised dust and cleaning products.

Bing sits there enduring the heaviness, the still-roiling intestines, because what else can he do? He promised the boy he wouldn't tell, even shook on it. He respects Brian's gung ho vigor, his invincible innocence, but isn't that the point? Isn't that why countries send their young men to do the fighting for them? They're too green to fully know the cost. Haven't yet accumulated the life trappings that older men have difficulty giving up: wives, heirs, fortunes.

But . . .

Bing wants Brian to amass all that: a woman's love, children to propel his blood into the future. Bing's neck spasms, because Roger should have been the genetic rocket to pass along the Butler name. But perhaps it wasn't Butler flesh that Vietcong bullet tore through. Bing imagines Charles sitting in the Studebaker with Roger in the airport parking lot. Roger's cold hand gripping

Charles's wrist. Roger leaning in, and Bing leans in, too, to hear what penetrating words Charles might have offered, wondering if decades later they would ring in Charles's ears the way Bing's words are still clanging in his own. He can't hear a thing, and he realizes that putting Charles in the driver's seat, granting him paternal ownership, doesn't lessen the grief. Because right now, sitting in Susie's kitchen, the only thing that matters—in his head, maybe not in his gut—is that Roger was *somebody's* son.

For the first time Bing doesn't swallow the cluster of words that have been trying to form in his craw since 1968, a sentiment he once considered too yellow to utter, a belief that the U.S. had no business in Vietnam, fighting for vague, ballooned threats that weren't worth the lives of American sons, all sixty-thousand of them. He harbors similar doubts about Iraq.

Bing twists around as Aldine dashes in, his backbone quivering because she might be a mind reader coming to bash his treasonous thoughts, but she just asks him to lift his veteran elbows so she can wipe the table.

"How's Wayne?" Bing asks, trying to act normal, remembering her husband with the broken neck.

"Same," Aldine says, buffing out a food splotch.

Bing knows better than to pry. He's learned to respect her work ethic, her thrifty vocabulary. Normally doesn't slow her down with more than a "Morning" or "See you next time," but today he wants her to sit. She looks like she deserves a break. And while she's catching her breath, maybe he can ask her what, if anything, he should do about Brian, because he has to ask someone, some no-nonsense, cut-to-the-chase one.

But Aldine darts off to attack other stains and scuff marks, blasting through this house so she can move on to the next, and the next, by day's end her shoulders slumped beneath the weight of her own burdens.

Bing closes the door on Aldine's substantial load and reopens the door to his own. Even if he divulged Brian's secret, that likely wouldn't stop him from sprinting to the recruiters first thing Monday morning. Still, maybe Bing wouldn't be doing it for Brian. Maybe he would be doing it for Susie, who ought to have an opportunity to try and change her son's mind. After that, whether he joins up or not, Susie would be able to say that at least she got to offer her own Studebaker words, hopefully ones that won't haunt her down the line.

Bing hauls his cup to the sink, feet scuffing across the linoleum under the weight that prevents him from properly lifting his feet. As he rinses his spoon, he flips the quandary up in the air like a coin: *Keep his word or tell Susie?* The coin spinning and spinning, heads over tails, refusing to land.

MODERN BRIDE

Bing heaves upstairs to Brian's room. He has no battle plans, no strategy, isn't going to try to change the boy's mind. Just wants to . . . to . . . even he doesn't know. No light leaks from beneath Brian's door, but Bing knocks anyway, the door swaying open. The room is dark except for Brian's computer screen where two animated biplanes draw spirals across the sky. Bing tiptoes in, the winter chill piercing the windows: one facing the front yard, one facing Ellen's house.

The drapes are open, and Bing goes to shut them to cut off the draft, tackling the front window first, throwing the room deeper into blackness. The side window is trickier, Bing having to reach around Brian's bedside table and lamp to feel for the pull cord behind the curtain. As he fumbles for the string he glances outside, across the great divide, toward Ellen's house. Ellen's bedroom window is a wide-open eye, lights on, no curtains drawn, and Bing spots a dresser and mirror on the opposite wall. *Don't these people believe in privacy?* Bing thinks even as he gawks into the room, a regular Peeping Tom secluded in shadows.

A figure comes onto center stage—*Reenie!*—over in that bright room. Bing backs up, nearly tripping over his own feet as he tries to hide in shadows. *What's she doing in that woman's bedroom?* And there she is, Ellen, standing beside Reenie as the girl's mouth flaps a mile a minute, hands wigwagging. Bing kneels and hunkers down to peek over the windowsill—*Kilroy was here*—to see what these two are up to. This is Reenie, after all, in the clutches of that, well, lesbian.

Reenie's hands continue to flail until finally Ellen clasps them together in her own hands to still them. Reenie's mouth stops blabbering as Ellen utters whatever soothing words it takes to calm Reenie down.

And then it happens.

Ellen releases Reenie's hands and backs out of sight as Reenie pulls off her shirt.

Bing looks away, or tries to, not wanting to view his granddaughter's doughy belly, her pale skin, purple bra. Bing can't believe what he's seeing. Reenie unsnaps her jeans and starts to unzip. Sweat beads roll down his temples; his face tingles with fear, anger, nausea. He stands-kneels-stands, tries to scream: *Susie! Glen!* Does indeed blurt, "Hey! Stop!" Wants to bang on the window, burst through the glass, lunge across the twelve feet to stop that woman from molesting this child. Choke her to death with his bare hands, because there's Reenie in her underwear, Ellen coming at her with a white bundle in her arms: a bedspread, a parachute. As Ellen fumbles with the ball of fabric, Bing wonders what perverted ritual this is, gawking as Ellen lifts it above Reenie's head. Reenie's raised arms reach inside the knot as Ellen releases the cloth, lets it float, fall, envelope his granddaughter.

A wedding dress.

Yards and yards of creamy whiteness that Ellen smooths down, tugging and pulling. Reenie adjusts shoulders and sleeves as Ellen stands behind her to hook button after button. When she finishes she again steps out of view, leaving Reenie to study her reflection in the vanity mirror, fiddle with the collar, the bustline. Ellen returns and circles Reenie, drawing out loose material at the waist, pulling stickpins from her pinched mouth to jab into the fabric. Bing is surprisingly unsurprised that Ellen, a scrap heap welder, is also adept with delicate needle and thread.

It's a domestic scene Bing never expected to witness in his life—certainly not between this pair—a bride being fitted for her gown. Something Barbara ached to do for Susie, a precious gift offered. *Let me make your dress*, but Susie said no, preferring that hippy sack from some co-op barn because she didn't intend to look—*how did she put it?*—like an elitist meringue pie.

But here, now, is Barbara's dream come true. Her granddaughter's bridal fitting. For a minute Bing pretends that the silver-haired woman enjoying this prize is Barbara. Of course Reenie would let her grandmother make her dress. They would scan patterns together. Visit bridal stores and fabric shops. Discuss buttons and beads, flowers and hairstyles, invitations and cake designs, everything Barbara longed to do for Susie. Everything Reenie probably wants from her own mother, but Susie would never stoop to that. Even if she sanctioned this marriage, which she does not, Bing can't imagine her ever conceding to let her daughter walk down the aisle in anything remotely resembling a meringue pie, even if it is the girl's very dream.

FLAG FOLDING

Friday morning Glen clatters around the kitchen preparing dishes for the next night. So many sauce pans, measuring cups, spice jars, wine bottles, whirring contraptions in use at one time. And real butter, a cardiac no-no Bing never expected to grace Glen's countertop. Glen sashays around like that Galloping Gourmet before the Brit sobered up and got religion. He whistles and trills, taps his toes to the jazz spooling from the CD player hauled in for the occasion.

Bing pulls up a chair because this is entertainment, temporarily lifting the fog of suspicion he's rolled over Glen. Bing is also hoping for a few nibbles, but Glen offers none. Not even at noon when Bing sighs, "Guess I'll make me a peanut butter sandwich." He tries to work around Glen, respect the man's field of operations, carting the fixings to the table. He smears more jelly on his fingers than the bread, too mesmerized by Glen at the counter cutting what look like narrow strips of wax paper, or transparent dough. He drops a spoonful of green something onto the end of each strip and folds it into a triangle just like he's folding an American flag.

Bing sits there gnawing his sandwich when Susie comes in and plunks the mail on the table.

"Spanakopita!" she peals, when she sees what Glen is up to.

Glen twists around and a smile unfurls.

Susie skips over—*skips!*—to look at Glen's handiwork, strapping one arm around her husband's waist to pull their hips together, a surprising display. "You didn't tell me you were making spanako-pita. My favorite."

"I know," Glen says in such a lovey-dovey voice Bing thinks he should leave the room.

Susie cranes around to look at Bing. "They're my favorite."

"So I see." Bing is happy for her, even if he has no idea what spani-what's-its are.

Susie sits across from Bing. "What's Brian want for his birth-day, Dad?"

Crap. Bing forgot that assignment—again. He tries to scrounge up ideas, but today, brain on shore leave, he's just not up to the task.

"I don't know," he confesses. "The boy's too tight-lipped." He braces for Susie's wrath: *I asked you to do one thing, one thing!*

"That's okay," Susie says with stunning nonchalance. "He probably wants money anyway. I'll just write him a check."

"A check?" Bing says.

"That's what I gave him last year. No biggie."

No biggie? But it is a biggie. The boy's selective-service birth-day certainly deserves more forethought than a check, though Bing can't remember what he got Roger on that black day. Barbara's department, and all.

"I got him something," Glen says.

Bing and Susie swivel toward Glen and Susie blurts, "You did?"

"Of course." Glen halts his flag-folding to look at them.

"What'd you get?" Susie asks.

"It's a surprise."

"What is it?"

"If I told you it wouldn't be a surprise for long, would it?" He looks at Bing. "Be warned. The woman cannot keep a secret."

"Glen!"

Glen crosses a finger over his chest leaving a butter smear on his shirt, a shocking lapse in his fussiness. "Trust me on this, Bing."

"I will," Bing says, happy to be included in this banter, even if he thinks Susie has done a fine job safeguarding her mother's secret all these years.

A key rattles in the back door, and in comes Brian wrapped in one of those gangster coats and a watch cap.

"I thought you were still in bed," Susie says.

"Been up since five."

"Five? What on earth for?"

Brian shucks his coat and drapes it over a chair. "Went for a run."

"Why didn't you wake me?" Glen asks.

Brian shrugs and tugs off his cap, earning a gasp from Susie. The quarter-inch stubble he once sported has been completely shorn, head bald as a hardboiled egg. He runs a hand over his scalp. "Like it?"

Before Bing knows what's happening, Brian leans over and loops his elbow around Bing's neck, rubbing his knuckles into Bing's Brylcreemed hair. "How you doing, Grandpa?"

"Brian!" Susie says. "You're hurting him!"

"I am not." Brian releases his grip. "Take a lot more than this to bring the old sailor down."

"That's right." Bing is awed by the unexpected affection, respect, even if his neck feels pinched.

Susie opens her mouth, but Brian cuts her off: "Gotta run." He dashes into the hall, thunders upstairs, leaving the three in the kitchen with their mouths agape, and Bing trying to rearrange his hair.

They order pizza for supper and Bing groans when he lifts the lid on a vegetarian mishmash, not a hint of pepperoni or sausage. After eating Glen stands to slot his plate in the dishwasher. "I have some shopping to do."

Susie's forehead scrunches. "You've been cooking all day. Can't it wait until morning?"

"Some of it needs to marinate overnight."

Hard to argue with that, though Bing thinks Susie would like to. She rolls a pizza crust between her fingers. "I was going to write tonight anyway."

"Your migrant worker article?" Glen asks.

Susie nods, ripping that crust into pieces.

"Maybe you'll finish it soon," Glen says. "That's great."

But it's not great, even Bing can see that, deceitful fog rolling back in, rolling all over Glen.

Hours later Glen still isn't home, and the kids are gone, exercising their Friday night prerogatives. Brian especially, Bing figures, given his Monday morning call. Susie is upstairs doing who-knows-what. Perhaps waiting at a window for Glen's headlights, ear cocked for the sound of his key in the lock, or hunched over her desk carrying out her life's work, occupying her brain so it won't have time to put two plus two together, trying to remain oblivious to her husband's extracurricular activities, or her children's. Maybe that's what Bing was doing night after night in his workshop back home. He certainly never waited by a window for Barbara.

Bing hasn't decided whether to tell Susie about Brian, but he feels drawn to her, the other lonely soul in this too-big house. He heads upstairs, pausing at the landing to look toward Brian's room, wondering if there is already a duffle bag packed in his closet. If he enlists, Bing knows just how quiet that room will soon be, a howling silence that may last forever.

And there's Reenie's door. Right now she's probably scouting out churches or reception halls with Junior. Or maybe she's over at Ellen's trying on her wedding dress, dancing in circles, satin skimming the floor, Ellen clapping her hands in delight.

Susie's office is dark, which brings a gush of relief to Bing. Maybe she isn't so oblivious after all. Isn't so bound up in migrant workers that she can't hear the roof above her sliding off like a silo door, her children, her husband, missiles preparing to fire.

Bing leans in the master bedroom where Susie sits propped up in bed, books and papers scattered before her, raised coffee mug in one hand as if she's about to take a sip. Bing opens his mouth, but Susie's eyes are closed, the dark wedges underneath betraying her fatigue. She could be sleeping except for the mug hovering there, waiting for however long, the once-hot coffee probably tepid.

He wonders if in her mind she's imagining her husband feeding spani-what's-it to some twenty-year-old student. Or maybe Susie has carted Glen off to a tropical island where they bury their feet in the sand, drink cocktails speared with paper umbrellas. Or perhaps they are back in Austin, two college students in the first bloom of love, debating for hours and hours in the library over some heady subject. Wherever she is, Bing hopes she has no battle-bound son to contend with. No marriage-minded daughter to try and keep in school. No ornery old man in the basement to hide secrets from.

Still, at this moment, Bing realizes this is his chance. One *ahem* would yank her back from that tropical island or U.T. library so he could warn her about Brian. Quiz her about Glen. Barrage her with questions about Barbara.

A piercing vision of Barbara feeding spani-what's-it to Charles.

The image makes Bing's teeth chatter, limbs chill, bowels lurch. He doesn't want to do it, doesn't want to make a sound, not a board creaking beneath his feet, though it has nothing to do with disturbing Susie's reverie. Maybe not knowing wouldn't be so bad. Maybe he could live with the uncertainty rather than face up to the truth.

He starts to back quietly away until he sees a face staring at him from Susie's nightstand. Roger. Standing there in an eight-by-ten glossy, smiling like there was no Vietnam, one arm strapped around skinny Susie with her long-long hair and peasant blouse. Roger not wearing a dress uniform, but jeans and a t-shirt, shock of bangs that nearly got him kicked off the football team. His one act of defiance. How Roger used to shake his hair out of his eyes, that perpetual head jerk that drove Bing crazy.

Bing watches Roger's grin magically morph into a sneer. Arm undraping from his sister, finger now pointing at Bing. The boy jeering as he stares Bing down.

What? Bing asks in his mind.

The answer fires back in Roger's nasal voice: *Coward!*

What?

Do it! Talk to her!

Bing is staggered by Roger's directive, his once-sheepish son no longer so timid. *I can't.*

It's your patriotic duty.

What's that got to do with it?

A man's gotta do what a man's gotta do.

Bing's head dips down. *I can't.* A thorny admission, but not as wrenching as the one that tumbles unbidden from his mouth: "I'm afraid."

Susie's eyes snap open, and Bing backs into the hall, wondering if she heard him, if she also hears the raspy laughter scraping the back of Roger's throat, his taunt: *Suck it up, boy. Isn't that what you said?*

Bing stumbles backward.

Suck it up, old man. Suck it the hell up!

Bing turns away from this Roger he no longer knows, a man, a stranger whose scoffing sends Bing tripping down the stairs, no longer caring about noise, about disturbing Susie, who calls out, "That you, Glen?"

All night Bing whips sheets around with his legs, flips from belly to back, wanting to sleep, not wanting to, because every time he sinks into that shut-eyed cesspool, Roger's face surfaces, contorted mouth garbling those damning words.

Why now? Bing wonders. *After all this time.* It's not as if Roger didn't have ample opportunity to berate Bing before this. How many times did the image of Roger's last minutes ambush Bing over the years? How he tried to squelch it, squeeze it out, but it played and replayed: those rustling bushes, that whizzing bullet. And after, after, Bing imagined Roger's buddies dragging his body out of the jungle. A weary medic shaking his head before moving on to the next lifeless soldier, and the next. Shadowy flashes of a coffin tucked in the belly of a transport charging back home along with dozens of other parents' worst nightmares. After landing, the plane's cargo door opens and a churning conveyor belt delivers that box back to Texas soil.

And there it is, that flag-draped coffin at the funeral home crowded with Roger's high school friends, his football teammates, the ones who were left that is, the ones who hadn't yet traded one uniform for another. And the girls, all that sniffing and weeping, pros by now, itinerant wailers who traveled from funeral to funeral during those horrible years, all their white-picket dreams buried along with the boys who might have made them come true. At the cemetery, the sharp report of saluting gun fire, as if Roger were being shot all over again, and again, and again. Bing watched the young soldiers in dress blues and white gloves undrape Roger's coffin and fold the hallowed fabric into a neat triangle, a bundle of bitter, unpalatable grief, so Bing likewise folded those feelings into a tight triangle in his mind, shoved it down so far he wouldn't feel the sharp corners jabbing into his soul. Barbara sat in her mourner's chair weeping, shoulders shaking as she held out her own trembling black-gloved hands to accept the star-splattered bundle as if it were her due, or her ticket into the sad club of mothers who had all offered up their sons.

Roger had plenty of time to seethe whenever Bing tiptoed into his son's room, a shrine dedicated solely to him, the entire space, not just one wall over a bed memorializing a black September Tuesday. Every bit left undisturbed because it was too hard, just too hard to box up his football trophies, to unmake his bed, unpack his dresser, undo his life. But someone finally had to do it, had to suck it up: Barbara, a decade later while Bing was at the plant. Hauled Roger's clothes, shoes, board games off to whoever accepts those sad remains. Donated his flag to the veteran's cemetery. Leaving only one shelf for Bing to deal with thirty-some years later when he dismantled the house for good. One shelf for a shoe box full of baseball cards, a globe-shaped piggy bank, a bundle of blue airmail letters.

Why now? Bing wonders again. Right now Roger offers nothing but sullen silence, and besides, Bing knows why now: Brian, who may be marching down the same life-snuffing path.

SHRAPNEL

Bing wakes at noon and plows through his groggy ritual: slippers, robe, toilet, breakfast. In the kitchen he is assaulted by decorations: streamers crisscrossing the ceiling, balloons dangling from light fixtures, a hand-scrawled poster taped to the wall: HAPPY BIRTHDAY BRIAN. An uneaten bakery cake sits in the middle of the table along with a couple of wrapped gifts and an envelope containing Susie's fat check, no doubt. Bing should have gotten the boy a present, something that might mean more than a fistful of cash.

Susie comes in and gives Bing the once-over. "Rough night?"

Bing wants to blurt, *Yes.* Wants to ask if Roger dogs her sleepless nights, too. "Pizza didn't agree with me," he says instead, flapping a hand toward the decorations. "When's the party?"

Susie sets the teakettle on the stove. "Three hours ago."

Bing scans the unopened gifts, uneaten cake. "You weren't waiting for me, I hope."

Susie eyes the balloons hanging there, the crepe streamers fluttering in the air whooshing from the heater vent. "No. Brian apparently prefers to play paintball with his friends."

"Where's Glen?" It's a brave inquiry. Bing thinks he is ready for the answer even if it's *He never came home last night.*

"Clearing snow off the sidewalk. Wouldn't want the guests falling on their asses."

Bing's head pivots at the unexpected crassness, or humor. He's not sure which. "What time's this other shindig start?" Bing asks, calculating how much time he'll have to put in, or if he's expected to put in an appearance at all. Maybe they would prefer he stay hidden in the basement, the Texas galoot who might embarrass them in front of their Queen's-English guests.

"About eight." Susie pulls a tea bag from a canister, drops it into a mug. "One of Glen's students is coming at seven to help set up."

"Glen's student?" Bing says, radar alerted.

"Grad assistant." As if that should ease his mind. "Glen likes to throw her a few bucks when he can."

I bet, Bing thinks, wondering what else he throws her.

"I have something for you." Susie goes to the hall closet and returns with a garment bag. "For tonight. I hope you don't mind."

Bing envisions a tweed jacket with elbow patches, a starched button-down that'll pinch his neck. Maybe even a tie. A month ago he might have coughed up some attitude. *If people don't like the way I dress, they can just blah, blah, blah.* But Susie looks weary and the fun hasn't even started, so he decides to offer moral support any way he can, even if it means donning a new suit.

"Much obliged," he says.

"Reenie and Junior picked it out."

"They did?" Bing asks, itchy tweed transforming into black leather and chains.

Bing unzips the bag, and it's not a suit coat or studded leather pants. It's a navy pullover sweater with three buttons at the neck. A red Polo jockey over the breast, but Bing doesn't mind that because the knit is so cushy. Behind the sweater is a pair of pleated khakis.

Susie holds up the waist. "With elastic in the sides so they'll give a little."

Bing pictures his combat-boot-wearing granddaughter and her pierced near-fiancé sauntering around the men's department of some stodgy store, enduring salesclerks' snubs.

Susie says, "What do you think?"

"They did good." Bing is so touched he wants to put the clothes on this very minute.

Instead he takes them to the basement, hangs them in his closet, and decides that tonight he'll wear his Sunday shoes. Even burnish them to a high gloss. He drags his kit from under the sink and sits on the bed with his shoes and well-used shammy. While his buffing hand falls into the spit-shine rhythm he picked up in the Navy, he tries to think of a gift for Brian. Mentally runs through the valuables he hauled up from Texas, the few remaining ones he can place, that is: his retirement watch; his Army discharge papers. Then he knows what to give Brian, a meaningful gift that now has double meaning. Bing looks toward his bedside table, that drawer, the bundle of blue envelopes resting there in the dark.

He drops the shoe polish and reaches, fingers pausing over the paint-worn knob. He tugs it open, reaches in, gropes around his spare glasses, amber prescription bottles, until he feels the crinkly Safeway sack, the plastic sheath for his son's last words. Bing draws it out, holding it in both hands as if it's a wounded bird, or a live grenade.

He starts to unfold the wrapping and reach inside to read, reread the letters that he knows so well. Letters he pored over nightly in his workshop after Barbara went to bed, words he tried to interpret more reverently than his Bible. But here, now, his hands start to quiver, plastic bag shivering. He can't do it, can't pull out those fragile sheets, doesn't want to flip open brittle pages that might also release Roger's venom. Afraid he might read even deeper between the lines than he did when they arrived, one by one, fresh, when the author was still alive.

Barbara would read them aloud at the kitchen table, Susie cupping her face in her hands, brow furrowed as her mother gave voice to Roger's penned descriptions. Mundane details suddenly exotic given Roger's locale. A yearning for his mother's pot roast and peach cobbler. His Yankee bunkmates from Vermont, Pennsylvania, Michigan, and the hooch they shared. The squint-eyed mamasan they paid seven dollars a month to tidy up and do laundry, the squint-eyed babysan who toddled after her. The typhoon season, the predictable, set-your-watch-by-it daily rain. The constant wetness that turned rice paddies into lakes, the perpetual damp that rotted fatigues. How he stopped wearing boxers, but stockpiled socks. Whole paragraphs about leeches and mosquitoes and weekly malaria pills. About missing the Texas heat. About spending weeks in those wrinkled mountains, his only cover a rubber poncho strapped to bamboo poles. Of going days without bathing, red dirt caking his skin. Sleep deprivation. He wrote very little about the actual war, only offering odd glimpses. The strange beauty of green and purple tracers swooshing across the night sky. The way the wounded dirt seemed to glow in the dark. Of soldiers brandishing NVA souvenirs: engraved belt buckles and canteens. Bing often pictured the men who once drank from those canteens, their undecipherable initials, dead Vietcong rotting in the jungle, but in his mind they often turned into Japs.

At the end of every letter, every single one, Roger carved a postscript in hard capital letters: *I AM NOT AFRAID!* A stoic motto meant to bolster Barbara and Susie, but Bing understood this secret code was especially for him. Roger, still very much afraid, wanted to show his father just how far he could suck it up.

Bing wondered, after, if that sharp-shooting gook climbed down from his tree and carried off Roger's canteen. Wagged it like a trophy in front of his comrades. If it's propped even now on a shelf in some shack, Roger's eroding initials, RBB, fading, perhaps worn down by a squint-eyed Vietnamese kid galloping by it every day, every day, running his grimy finger across those foreign symbols, wondering about the dead GI his father, his grandfather, killed.

GRACE

Bing showers, shaves, spends twenty minutes sculpting his hair because tonight it has to be perfect. This is his coming-out party, Susie finally introducing him to her colleagues. The doorbell chimes, Frida barking alarm as Glen's student arrives. Bing wants to rush upstairs and appraise this woman who may be the temptress luring Glen away from his wife, his home. Bing hustles, snipping price tags from his new clothes before putting them on—careful around the hair. He wishes he had a full-length mirror to consider the effect, but everything appears to fit: no snugness in the crotch or underarms; plenty of give in the waistband to accommodate a hearty meal.

He lifts Roger's letters from his bedside table, secures the Safeway sack with a rubber band and heads upstairs.

In the kitchen, the birthday decorations still adorn the ceiling and walls, but the cake, the gifts, are nowhere in sight. The table now serves as a bar with rows of wine and liquor bottles and mixers, an assortment of glassware. Trays of olives, pearl onions, cherries. Whole limes waiting to be sliced.

Bing hears crunching and looks toward Frida, nose in her bowl. Santa sweater replaced by a green felt affair with pointy court-jester collar and cuffs. *Pitiful.*

Glen dashes in wearing his own pullover sweater, all zigzaggy pastels. "Hey there, Bing." He jogs to the stove to slide a tray of brown something into the oven.

Susie stampedes in, going straight to the fridge to pull out a platter of what looks like raw bacon strapped around cantaloupe balls, a dish Bing reckons he'll avoid. She starts to haul it to the dining room but stops when she sees Bing. "You look nice."

Susie is slicked up in a burgundy pantsuit, floral scarf tied around her throat. Lipstick and rouge, though there's not enough under-eye goop in the world to hide the purple wedges.

"Did Brian make it home?" Bing asks.

"Nope." She exits with the tray.

R&R, Bing thinks, picturing Brian gallivanting with his buddies, chugging beer in a bar, Stew's Place, maybe, *Reginaaaa* pouring him shot after shot. Bing hopes not, wouldn't want Brian being hijacked by Ricky and Johnny Ray to god-knows-where— though a visit with Odell might do the boy good. Let him see how war heroes really wind up. Or maybe Brian is out joyriding in his Camaro, burning rubber, letting out his last few whoops and hollers. Perhaps he's parked in a dead-end lane, snuggling a girl in the backseat, smooching like there is no tomorrow, be- cause for him, it's a distinct possibility. Bing remembers necking with Barbara on her parents' divan before he shipped out, how she tucked a lacy handkerchief into his pocket. Later he found a snip of her hair folded inside that he kept near his heart dur- ing his Navy tour. Bing wonders if Roger had that chance, got to find comfort in an honorable girl's arms. If she wrote to him over there, if he lived for her letters scented with rose water and sealed with a kiss. Bing hopes so.

When Susie bolts back in, Bing holds out the Safeway sack. "I have a present for Brian."

Susie stops short, studies the sad-looking gift. "You didn't have to do that."

"I wanted to do something for the boy."

"That's very sweet." Sweet isn't the right word given the weighty contents, the desired effect. "Just put it on the shelf in the hall closet with the rest of his gifts."

"Okeydokey," Bing says. "Where's the helper?"

"The what?" Susie says.

Bing looks at Glen standing at the counter, the back of his well-combed head and whispers, "Glen's student."

"Oh. Crystal's in the dining room. *Crystal!*"

"No!" Bing says, not ready to face her.

"Yes?" Crystal calls.

Footsteps approach, and Bing prepares for a face-off with a seductress as sparkly as her name.

There she is in the doorway between the kitchen and dining room, can of mixed nuts in her hand. A short hunk of a girl, mushy and bulbous, glasses too small for her wide-wide face. There is nothing sparkly about her, at least not to him.

"This is my dad," Susie says. "Bing Butler."

"Pleased to meet you, Mr. Butler."

"Likewise."

Suddenly there's another person in the doorway behind Crystal, a towering man with a pelt of dirt-colored hair.

"This is my husband, Scott."

"Your husband?" Bing says, suspicions gurgling down the pipes. "Nice to meet you, too."

The pair saunters away and Bing wonders, *If not Crystal, then who?*

The doorbell sounds and Frida again scrabbles toward it, yowling. Susie runs after her, grabbing Roger's letters from Bing's grip. "I'll put this away if you'll cut the limes." Bing stands there, hands out, still feeling the weight of Roger's words in his palm as Susie tosses the bundle into the closet like a worn-out sneaker. She passes the stairwell and shouts up, "Reenie, I told you to take Frida over to Ellen's! Now move it!"

Ellen. Just the sound of her name makes Bing's mouth crimp. He pictures her over there preparing to baby-sit. Probably fixed chicken livers or meatballs to coddle the dog with.

He looks toward the front door at Susie bending down to keep Frida from gumming a black woman wearing a swishy red cape, carrying a foil-covered platter like it's the crown jewels.

"It's Francine!" Susie calls to Glen as the woman whips toward the kitchen, toward Bing, who scuttles backward and falls into a chair to attack those limes, maybe get so lost in the task he won't be noticed.

"Hi there," Francine says to Bing, Susie on her heels, snarling Frida bringing up the rear. Francine rushes past to offer Glen a hurried kiss-kiss. "I know I'm early, but I wanted these to be here when Madeleine arrives. She's not here yet, is she?"

Madeleine?

"Not yet. Ned's picking her up." Glen peels a corner of foil from the crown jewels. "Bing, you better grab one of these now because they go fast."

Francine walks over and stoops so Bing can reach in for what he hopes is a chicken wing or corn fritter, some Southern home cooking, but when she pulls the foil all the way back what he sees are—egg rolls. Dozens and dozens of them.

"These are shrimp," Francine says, nodding toward a row. "Those are pork."

Bing tweezes one out before Francine whisks the platter into the dining room.

Reenie slogs in, hair braided into a dozen skinny whips, ends tipped with red and green beads that clack together, and he wonders what Francine will think about that. Reenie stops in front of Bing. "Let's see," she says. "Stand up."

Bing cranes his neck to make sure that strange woman is nowhere in sight before standing. Even turns in a circle, a small reward for Reenie's efforts.

"You look nice, Grandpa. You really do."

Bing is touched by her attention, feels he should offer something in return, some compliment on her holiday hair, her t-shirt that reads: *Eve was framed.* He finds the thing he can talk about honestly: Barbara's dime-store brooch shaped like a Christmas tree, multi-colored stones twinkling in the light.

"Barbara wore that pin every Christmas."

Reenie's hand flies to the pin, probing it as if she's reading Braille, trying to decode a message from her grandmother.

Bing wants to deliver that message, tell her that Barbara would approve of her wedding dress, of Junior, but he can't, not here, so he says, "She always liked your style."

"Really?" Reenie's face tips up to fully receive this gift.

Bing starts to say yes, but the doorbell sounds again, and so does Frida, skittering toward the intruders, shattering this moment.

Susie slaps a spatula on the stove. "Reenie! Get that dog over to Ellen's!"

"I'm going." Reenie darts after the dog, followed by Susie who grumbles, "Take her out the back door."

Bing sits to man his lime post. He watches Reenie scoop Frida up, haul her through the kitchen, the dog belly-up in Reenie's arms, limp paws bouncing with every step. Frida eyeballs Bing as she passes, elf collar crowding her face.

Voices from the living room, Susie asking, "Can I take your coats?" Bing hopes she isn't going to toss them in the closet with Roger's letters, bury his words so deep under layers of bomber jackets and houndstooth fabrics they'll never be found, but Susie says, "I'll put these upstairs on our bed."

A man and woman ask, "Is Madeleine here?"

"Not yet," Susie says, voice weary.

The doorbell chimes again. Bursts of laughter and revelry. A woman yodeling, "Terry and Kim just pulled up, too."

And they're off! Bing thinks, though there's no Sparky and Spunky whipping around the house on a mechanical arm. The hallway and living room fill with partiers: *Your tree is beautiful! The house is lovely!* All that hugging and cooing. Bing hunkers down to slice limes, hoping to disappear as people file into the kitchen to offer gifts of wine. "Glen, you son of a bitch. Where've you been keeping yourself?" *That's what I'd like to know*, Bing thinks, just as Glen draws everyone's attention to Bing. "This is my father-in-law, Bing Butler." All eyes bear down, and he feels them burning through the Polo-shirted façade into his blue-collar, high-school-educated soul. Bing nods, eyes on his hands. A chorus of greetings until the revelers see the spirits lined up. They scramble to pour themselves drinks, except for one pinched-faced woman who asks Bing for a vodka tonic with a twist.

"I'm just slicing the limes," Bing says, though he thinks he could pull off a vodka tonic.

The woman's mouth puckers. "Okay." She fixes her own cocktail. "Is Madeleine here yet?"

He shakes his head and offers a lime wedge, which she drops into her glass. Bing now understands that despite his new clothes, his well-crafted hair, this isn't his coming-out party.

The chatter grows along with the crowd, not as snooty as Bing envisioned. Some are Glen-like, bookish and tidy; others are artsy with asymmetrical haircuts and rings on their thumbs; still others could use a hot shower and an ironing board. They press in on Bing, the only seated person in the room, his face confronted with elbows and rear ends until he feels as if he's stuck in a crowded elevator gasping for breath, heart flip-flopping. Thankfully, Susie clears the room, shouting: "Vittles are in the dining room!" Bing is warmed by her phrasing.

A mad rush toward the food, someone gasping, "Francine's egg rolls!" leaving a handful of shy-eyed stragglers. Bing notices one shaggy-haired fellow wearing an unbuttoned shirt over a t-shirt printed with the image of a bearded man; fat letters underneath spell a name Bing can only partly read: CHE GUEV. Bing knows who that dead commie is.

Susie returns and pours herself a glass of wine. "I think that's enough limes," she says, eyeing one pulverized into mush. "Why don't you go fix a plate?"

A heat wave flashes across Bing's face at the notion of having to go in there to offer *howdy*s, reach his hands through the throng to grab a handful of this, spoonful of that, too afraid to ask what the heck anything is. "I'd rather, uh—"

"How about I bring you something?"

"'Preciate it," he says.

"Let me put on some music first." Susie dashes out.

Bing doesn't know what to do with himself, if he should offer to help Glen. There appear to be enough hands on deck, especially with Che over there, but soon they all file into the dining room leaving Bing alone.

Then he isn't alone, because Glenn Miller music wafts in, one of Barbara's favorite songs. Bing can't remember the title, but the lyrics make him sigh. *You are always in my heart, even though you're far away.* He can almost feel Barbara's hands on his shoulders, how she would drape them there whenever a song she loved drifted from the radio. "Dance with me." Early on, Bing obliged with his stiff gait. Barbara didn't care if they just swayed in slow circles around the kitchen linoleum, pot of beans in the hissing pressure cooker on the stove. *I remember that you care, and then and there, the sun breaks through.* Over the years Bing felt less and less inclined to dance, felt foolish in front of the children, felt he had to relinquish such playfulness when his waistband thickened, temples grayed. How Barbara pouted when he said no. She pressed her back against the kitchen wall with her arms crossed over her chest, listening to the music herself.

She's over there right now in Susie's kitchen by the back door, a tender illusion leaning into the wall. Thirty-something Barbara in that orange chiffon dress Bing liked so much, with the belt that cinched her waist, soft auburn hair framing her face. It hurts to see her there, pouting. *Just before I go to sleep, there's a rendezvous I keep.* Why did he ever stop dancing with her? Why would any sane man stop dancing with her?

Susie returns and hands Bing a plate piled up with Glen's spani-what's-its, egg rolls, lumps of brown goop, and tiny disks of bread. "I have a surprise for you." Bing thinks there are enough surprises already until Susie grabs a beer from the refrigerator. Not just any beer—a Lone Star.

"Where'd you get that?"

"I have my ways." Susie digs a bottle opener from the drawer.

Bing accepts the bottle and takes a long pull. "Hits the spot."

Susie sidles off and Bing tips his beer toward Barbara who only glares. *Why did you stop dancing with me?*

Junior bolts through the back door carrying a grocery sack, a whoosh of cold air blasting in with him. He peels off his coat and he's wearing his work clothes. *Atta boy.*

"Mr. Butler!" Junior clomps forward, meaty hand outstretched. Bing takes it and offers a sincere pump, tries not to stare at the Aunt Jemima bandanna strapped around the boy's head. He's doubly thankful when Junior sits beside him so he no longer feels like he's treading water alone and so he won't have to endure Barbara's rebuffs by himself.

Junior glances overhead at the streamers and balloons. "Where's the birthday boy?"

Bing shrugs, again wondering where his grandson is. Hoping he hasn't already signed on the dotted line.

Junior holds up the grocery sack. "I have a present for him. Where should I put it?"

Bing looks toward the hall closet, but he doesn't want Junior near Roger's letters. "No idea." Bing takes a pinch of sweater between his finger and thumb. "Thanks for picking out my, uh—"

"No trouble, Mr. Butler."

Bing pushes his plate forward—an acceptable display of gratitude. "Help yourself."

Junior goes right for the spani-what's-it, angling the entire wedge in his mouth. "Oh, man," he garbles. "I have to get me some more of those." He bolts up and darts into the dining room in his grease-smeared dungarees to cavort with all those eggheads. "Hey, everyone!" A smattering of hellos, Susie offering a tepid, "This is Reenie's boyfriend, Junior."

"Excellent spanakopita, Dr. Babcock," Junior bellows, syllables dripping effortlessly from his no-college, junkyard-owning tongue. "Your best batch yet."

"Hear, hear!" someone echoes.

The back door pushes open again, Reenie, carrying a casserole dish, followed by Ellen hauling a foil-covered tray.

Bing wishes someone had warned him. "Aren't you looking after the dog?"

Ellen sets the tray on the table and tugs off her gloves. "She's quite capable of looking after herself." She sheds her coat and folds it over a chair back, smooths down a blue satin tunic that comes to her knees, matching shimmering slacks, Chinaman slippers. Ellen instructs Reenie to take her casserole dish into the dining room. Ellen's eyes skim the table, resting on Bing's plate. "I made something I think you'll prefer." She peels foil off her tray, and Bing eyeballs miles and miles of tamales in real cornhusks. Ellen bends to serve him four. One of her handmade pendants dangles around her neck, a cylinder of brushed silver and hammered brass. Bing stares at the tamales, hoping Ellen will leave, but she just hovers there in an excruciating pause that lasts for an hour, a day, until Bing says to the plate, "Looks good."

The pause continues a hair longer, a taut bubble stretching until Ellen bursts it. "Well, enjoy." She carts her tray to the dining room. Bing watches her straight shoulders, silver braid upswept in a swirly coil though he thinks he prefers it dangling loose. He looks at Barbara, expecting a red-faced sneer, but Barbara stares at Ellen, or through her, face noncommittal, and Bing wonders if they could have been friends. If these women had enough in common to share a cup of tea. The image of those two nibbling finger sandwiches together makes Bing feel oddly possessive. Ellen was *his* friend, after all. Ellen and Barbara certainly couldn't discuss welding or chess. He can't imagine Barbara grunging through a junkyard in her chiffon dress and satin pumps. Besides, Barbara had Tootie, and all her church gals. All Bing had was Dillard, a good enough friend, but he couldn't cook like Ellen, certainly couldn't play chess, couldn't have a meaningful conversation without it turning into off-color jokes, which was fine with Bing once upon a time. But now, well. Bing is surprised by his agitation. When he looks back toward Barbara, she is in her own dream world, swaying to Glenn Miller, eyes closed, arms looped around an imaginary dance partner's neck. Bing's, or someone else's, someone who probably never refused to dance.

Bing wants to take his plate and settle in his recliner downstairs with a good war movie, so he can forget about Barbara dancing over there. About Charles. About clench-jawed, finger-pointing Roger. But Bing knows he can't, so he uncaps another beer and sits back down, unwrapping his tamales. With every forkful he allows himself to be hypnotized by the aroma. He's lured back to Rosie's, that restaurant in Houston, and is so happy to be there with Janey the waitress sashaying off to fetch his Tabasco. The only missing ingredient is the melodic Spanish background chatter, the cackling babies. He isn't even rankled when Susie's guests come in to refill drinks, to form a trio not by Rosie's cash register, but by Susie's stove.

The two men, one of them Che, and a blonde woman, are apparently new to each other. The woman's hair is cut too short, black horn-rimmed glasses just like Bing's mother wore, a dozen wristwatches running up her left arm. He wonders what she is so afraid to be late for. She holds a glass of wine in one hand, plate of food in the other, but that doesn't stop her from wagging her hands up and down, right and left, the men's heads following them as if she's a conductor. She blabbers about being a new hire at Marshall and still reeling from culture shock. She'd been warned about what she'd encounter in the southern coal fields. It occurs to Bing that in all the time he's lived here he hasn't seen a coal mine yet. Not even a glistening black lump on the side of the road.

"Where are you from?" Che asks.

Bing expects her to bleat *Baaaaston* or *Chicaaaago*, but she says, "Wheeling."

"Is that in West Virginia?" the other fellow asks.

"Yes, but I consider myself from Pittsburgh since we're practically a suburb." She flaps a hand to dismiss her hillbilly heritage altogether. Bing wants to say, *Why don't you just say you're from Pittsburgh and be done with it?* She yaps on and on about her dismal students, about their poor grammar and undecipherable twangs, about podunk K-Marshall and this hick town with no decent restaurants. Bing recognizes some of her mocking jabs from his own repertoire, but today, listening to her, he finds his blood beginning to simmer, jugular pulsing, especially when he hears Reenie laughing in the next room. His brilliant granddaughter a West Virginia hillbilly born and raised. And Brian, wherever he is, ready to fly off and put his podunk life on the line.

A soft voice counters: "I love my students." It's Che. "I love Huntington, too. Wouldn't move back home for a million bucks."

Snooty Girl folds her arms across her chest. "And where are you from?" she asks, no doubt expecting him to offer up some hamlet even dinkier than Huntington.

"Born in Berlin, raised in Manhattan. Couldn't stand the pretension."

Ha!

Blondie huffs and frowns into the dining room. "There's Glenda," she says, leaving, followed by one of the men, but not Che, who watches her retreat.

Communist or not, Bing holds up his plate. "Tamale?"

Che accepts. "Thank you, Mr. Butler."

"Madeleine's here!" someone calls from the living room. A thunder of shoes as people scamper to pay homage to the queen.

Che doesn't budge, and Bing feels at ease enough to ask, "Who is this Madeleine, anyway?"

"Visiting professor. Expert on everything from Native American literature to queer theory."

Bing spins around. Even he knows better than to utter *that* word these days, especially with Ellen roaming around.

Bing cranes his neck for a glimpse, but Madeleine's fans are piled too deep, a unified body that moves into the living room, out of Bing's view. Glen rushes into the kitchen, digging through the pantry to pull out a liquor bottle and glass that he must have squirreled away earlier. He looks at Bing, Che, and holds up the bottle. "It's her favorite."

Bing and Che shrug.

Susie comes in. "Acting like a bunch of idiots." She isn't discombobulated, but maybe she should be. This could be the Other Woman sitting on Susie's sofa. Bing doesn't know how he would react if he were in Susie's shoes. Or perhaps he *is* wearing them, but at least Barbara never paraded Charles under Bing's nose. He looks toward the back door, toward Barbara, but she's no longer there.

Bing stands, no formulated plan, and walks toward the living room. He peeks in at the guests pressed around the sofa. Bing sneezes—*shoot*—and several people turn to look, sending him scrambling up the stairs. He climbs up to the landing, but when he pivots to make his final ascent he hears chatter up there. *Which way to go: up or down?* He keeps climbing, softly, ear tipped forward to identify voices. He pauses at the very top and peers around the corner. There, in the hall, stand Reenie, Junior, and Ellen, three other souls who are not all agog over Madeleine.

Ellen is saying, "I wanted to give these to you in private." She pulls two tiny gifts from her tunic pocket. They waste no time peeling off the paper, lifting the lids. "Cool," says Junior. Reenie says, "Awesome." They lift something out of their respective boxes and dangle them in the light before sliding them into their pierced ears.

"Remember our deal," Ellen says.

Deal?

Reenie fiddles with her earring. "We will, but it won't be easy."

"I never said it would be," Ellen says. "But if you wait until you're at least a senior, I'll design and make your rings."

"That's worth the wait," Junior says.

Reenie hugs Ellen as if she's hugging her own grandmother. She might as well be, because only trusted kin could draw such a promise from this girl.

All three turn to head back downstairs. Bing hits reverse as fast as he can without stumbling. He makes it to the landing before Reenie catches him. "Grandpa!"

"I was just heading up to use the can. Is it occupied?"

Ellen looks down at him standing there, caught. "It's free."

"That's good," Bing says, lumbering up the steps he just descended.

Junior bounces to him trying to offer excuses. "We were just, uh . . . Ellen just made us . . . We weren't—"

Reenie nudges Junior along to stop his babbling. She tilts her jaw toward Bing. "Look what Ellen gave us."

Bing holds his hand up to steady the inch-long silver cross. Five red stones run vertically down the shaft, four run horizontally, a tiny seed pearl at the intersection.

"Pretty," he says.

Reenie thunders down, followed by Ellen, who passes with a nod. Bing is awed by her quiet poise, this woman who is as comfortable in satin as she is in butter-colored work boots.

Bing heads down too, forgetting his bathroom lie, following Reenie into the kitchen where she flashes her new earring at Susie. Bing can only imagine how his daughter views this sacred symbol. He's not sure how he regards it anymore. Even so, he doubts that Susie appreciates what an ally she has in Ellen.

But Susie has other matters on her mind as she dismisses her daughter and looks at the wall clock. "Where is Brian?" she mutters to no one, not even to Reenie, who's standing right in front of her begging for undivided attention. "So inconsiderate." Susie goes for the corkscrew to open more wine, oblivious to her daughter who leaves, chin to her chest.

Guests saunter back to the kitchen having offered their curtsies to Madeleine. Bing might as well take a gander, too. He chugs the last of his Lone Star for courage and inhales before passing the closet door, passing Roger in there doing who-knows-what, maybe shredding his letters into confetti. Bing stares into the living room from the hall, the little bit he can see: the front door, the marble table beside it. But something is missing. Some prominent thing. Frida's pillow. The *real* queen's throne banished along with her majesty. No evidence of her whatsoever, not even the stink.

Bing leans forward to assess Madeleine seated in the very center of the couch. He knows it's her because of the semicircle of guests who have pulled chairs around her. She's older than he expected, in her sixties maybe, with hints of the beauty she once was, plus a self-possessed air. Intense eyes with hard-won wrinkles: a woman to be reckoned with.

Directly across from her sits Glen, eyes welded onto this woman's face.

Madeleine yaks about a paper she presented in New Mexico, another she's preparing for a conference in South Dakota. She spiels on and on about a collection of essays she and Glen have been editing—*so that's where he's been spending his time.* About their heated debates over whether to include a piece by a scholar who gathered his research from books and journals, not actual field work, a mortal sin in Madeleine's view, not so unforgivable in Glen's.

"A debate we haven't yet settled," Glen says.

"I thought we had! The man doesn't even speak Lakota!"

And soon they go at it, both leaning forward, posturing for the spectators. Their voices rise, and Glen begins to spit just as he used to when Susie fired him up. As Glen and Madeleine go head-to-head, Bing studies their eyes for clues. Glen, indeed, is utterly enamored, but Madeleine's eyes flit from guest to guest making sure they are fully engaged. Still, Bing understands that this is the woman Glen has been entangled with lately, maybe as a sexual being, maybe not, but certainly as a respected adversary. But if it isn't physical, why all the lame excuses about trips to the store and last-minute jogs? Certainly Susie couldn't be jealous about this working relationship. But Bing can't deny Glen's spark-ing eyes, which is exactly the way he used to look at Susie, years ago. Bing is profoundly embarrassed when he understands that what they were up to back then was intellectual lovemaking.

That's what Glen and Madeleine are up to right now. Never mind stolen kisses and dingy hotel rooms; their witty banter is the equivalent of foreplay, of sex. Something once reserved solely for Susie. A different kind of betrayal, but betrayal nonetheless.

Bing cranes backward to look in the kitchen. Susie is pouring her third glass of wine, or fourth. He should go and offer support, but she comes to him instead with a fresh Lone Star. "Bottoms up," she says. As he tips the bottle, Reenie and Junior settle on the stairs behind him. He's surprised they haven't bolted to Reenie's room to escape her parents' stodgy friends. But they look as if they're enjoying themselves, as if they are not out of their league.

Susie takes a slug of wine. "How you doing there, Dad?"

"Good. Real good." Bing eyeballs Glen and Madeleine. "How are you holding up?"

"Fine. Why wouldn't I be?"

Bing looks at his daughter, who may believe her own lie, a trick she learned from her father. "When's this Madeleine leaving?"

"She just got here."

"I mean Huntington. When's she hightailing it back to wherever she belongs?"

Susie shakes her head. "Not until May."

"May!" Bing blurts so loud that not only does Susie gape at him, but several guests turn to gawk at him, too. "Not soon enough," he whispers.

"I hear you," Susie says, a look on her face that is so un-Susie like, almost vulnerable. "I need a refill," she says, stomping off.

Bing twists back around and leans forward to glare at Madeleine, the source of his daughter's suffering, wondering if

Susie can survive five more months of this. Hoping her marriage can take it, too.

If only there was something he could do to snap Glen out of his trance, catapult his awe back to Susie where it belongs. But Bing thinks Madeleine is going to do it herself as the conversation shifts to a topic that won't float in this godless house: religion.

Not *real* religion, but close enough as she gabbles on about Indian creation stories, *Native Peoples*, she calls them. Humans entering the world through a hollow log, or popping out of clam shells, or being fashioned out of mud pies, or how a woman's snot dripped onto a mussel that turned into a baby. Ridiculous, and Bing can't wait for Glen's retort, can remember too well how Glen and Susie berated Barbara for believing in Adam and Eve, another creation story involving mud pies and spare ribs.

Glen sits there, hands draped over his knees as he waits for the right moment, Bing guesses, allowing Madeleine to quarry her own tomb. Bing moves closer, watching for Glen's mouth to form the first denouncing word, because he doesn't want to miss a single syllable when this woman is sent packing.

Someone coughs, breaking Bing's concentration. Ellen stands by the French doors leading into the dining room, sipping wine as she listens to Madeleine, not spellbound like Glen, but obviously intrigued. What does she think about all this gibberish, this lesbian *Christian*?

Bing looks back at Glen, and finally his lips part. *Here we go.* But what comes out of Glen's mouth is "Fascinating!"

Fascinating?

"What rich cultural lore." Glen offers more affirming blather, but Bing is too shocked to follow. Wants to shout, *Now wait a minute!* Wants to ask how Glen can listen to this claptrap when he wouldn't offer the same respect to Barbara. Ultimately, however, clam shell or Garden of Eden, it's all drivel.

Bing cringes at his blasphemy: doubting the creation story he was weaned on. Lumping it together with some tribal nonsense. Regardless of his recent uncertainties, his large questions, faith is a hard habit to break. He looks behind him at Reenie and Junior on the stairs, prominent crucifix earrings dangling, still so sure of their God's existence, which makes life easier; Bing grants them that. Where everything can be neatly shelved under Right and Wrong, Black and White, Good and Evil. How Bing envies their righteous view, an uppity outlook he wore like a second skin for seventy-seven years. But it's not that cut and dried as he remembers his wife, a person of purer faith than he ever had, and look what she was up to. And Reenie and Junior aren't exactly model Christians hanging out of windows smoking pot. Hasn't Reenie chosen a homosexual as her confidante, her stand-in grandma? And why wouldn't she? Ellen is probably the only woman Reenie can turn to about issues of faith.

What an odd puzzle, Bing decides, glancing at Ellen standing there listening to Madeleine, not captivated, but respectful, as if these creation stories do not contradict her biblical story, as if there is room in her mind for a variety of views. And there must be, because somehow she has found a deity who is not appalled by her sexuality, who can tolerate it, and maybe even more than just that.

Bing scratches his head at the mystery. It's an odd God-puzzle, one he wants to hunker over and piece together, but not tonight.

Because at the moment he is perplexed by the smaller mystery of Ellen standing solidly there, not a fidgety mess, just utterly relaxed in her singleness even in the midst of couples, a mocking reminder of her spouseless state, and Bing's. Bing assesses the room for pairs, picking that painful scab. Glen and Madeleine dueling it out. Another couple wedged together on the love seat. Reenie and Junior cackling on the stairs, conspiring the way young couples do, maybe spinning the same hopeful visions Bing and Barbara spun way back when about their future twined lives.

Bing feels so alone surrounded by matched sets, missing Barbara, his other half, his soft echo.

It is a pain so palpable he leans back to look in the kitchen at Susie, essentially spouseless. And Ellen over there, striking up a conversation with Che, who is admiring her pendant. Effortless. She makes it look effortless, this interacting with strangers, getting on with her life when her husband, or whatever she called her other half, her echo, died.

Bing grazes his shoes against the hardwood floor, eminently self-conscious, so *un*Ellen-like, a wallflower caught in the middle of the dance floor and desperate to sprint back to the wall. *I hate this*, he thinks, and immediately hears a familiar *clack-clack,* the source hidden by the Christmas tree.

Bing rounds the tree and sees a hint of shapely leg, foot encased in an orange, bow-topped pump. Barbara, that glorious chiffon blur sitting at a café table in the corner where there's never been a café table before. She's a beautiful sight—even if it is wishful thinking and Lone Star induced—right heel tapping the wooden floor, *clack-clack*, a tic that only manifested when she was keyed up.

Bing starts to lunge toward her; she's rescuing him again. But a shadowy shape emerges in the chair opposite Barbara: young pencil-necked Charles in a seersucker jacket. Both studying tight fans of playing cards in their hands, a smattering of clubs and diamonds faceup on the table. Bridge, Bing guesses, though he really wouldn't know, never bothered to learn, doesn't even know if it can be played by just two people. The way Charles looks at her, rapt, the same way Glen worships Madeleine. The way Junior moons over Reenie. The way Bing pined for Barbara decades ago.

It is an ache so exquisite all Bing can do is amble to the wall by the door where Frida's pillow should be and lean back against the cold plaster, let the chill bite his shoulder blades, small penance for his sin of neglect. The more excruciating penance is hearing Barbara's clacking heel, watching her and Charles embroiled in some intense dialogue, both fully engaged, so equal, so even, her face soaking up Charles's respect like a sponge.

The party carries on as if there is no bridge-playing mirage in the corner, no very real old man trying to press himself through a wall to hide behind drywall and studs. Voices blare as conversations grow more animated. Bing nurses his beer, picking up words and fragments, mostly highbrow gobbledygook, but also discussions about the Steelers and Cowboys and beer making. Someone exchanges Big Band music for drum-thumping racket. The din hurts his ears, but Bing stays put because he wants to be near Barbara.

Glen takes leave of Madeleine every so often to fluff up the guests: "And how are you doing? So glad you could come. You people need to eat more prosciutto." He flits in and out of the kitchen to refill drinks, grab napkins and lime wedges. Dangerous maneuvers, Bing thinks, like sticking his hand into a tiger's cage since Susie leans against the sink baring her teeth. Glen is ignorant of her ire, uttering stupidities like "It's going well, don't you think?"

When it's Susie's turn to make the rounds—a scarier prospect in Bing's view—she bobbles through the living room with a tray, canapés about to slide off as she steals peeks of her husband and Madeleine in the center of this boxing ring, both oblivious to Susie's clumsy footwork.

She circles the room once, twice, muttering under her breath at the guests who just smile weirdly when she nods toward Glen and Madeleine. "Aren't they ever coming up for air? Somebody get the hose!" By round three she's an annoying mosquito with an empty tray buzzing about their ears. This time Susie stops and plants her feet behind her husband. It takes a second for her torso to stop swaying. "Madeleine!"

Madeleine lifts her head and Glen twists to look at his wife, his titillated blush draining. "Oh, god."

Susie opens her mouth and there's a collective hush as the spectators' eyes pivot between Madeleine and Susie.

Susie belts, "Can I get you anything?"

"No, dear," Madeleine says.

"Well, okay then!" Susie lopes off, signaling that the danger is over. A communal exhale. There will be no hair pulling or fingernail scratching. Susie slinks back to the kitchen, her corner, to lick her wounds.

Eventually Glen is sent on an expedition for his queen, ginger ale, and heads for the kitchen where Susie still guards the sink, wineglass in hand. Bing wishes Susie would really let Glen have it. Regardless of the ugly scene, at least it would release some of the pressure building in this house.

Bing stares as Susie watches her husband pour. *Say something.*

She raises her glass above her head as if she's going to hurl it to the floor to let the shards speak for her.

Now we're talking.

Instead she brings the glass to her lips and drains it as Glen struts back out to deliver his offerings.

Bing watches his slumped daughter. He's never seen her so deflated, defeated, perhaps regretting her missed opportunity. He looks over at Barbara and wonders if she ever slumped against a counter regretting missed opportunities to admonish—or confess—because Bing now understands that either would have been better than the silence they both practiced, the pretense. But maybe Bing defeated, deflated her, too.

Bing's legs grow weary, his bum sore from pressing into the wall, empty beer bottle now resting on the floor. He wants to sneak off for another. Barbara wouldn't notice. Nobody would. Just as he's about to tiptoe off, the front door eases open and in slips Brian.

"Hey, Grandpa," he whispers.

"Have a good leave?" Bing wonders if there are signed marching orders in his back pocket. He has to strain to hear Brian's answer, since a new noise has been added to the music blaring, heels clacking, guests gaggling: a thumping, or knocking, someone hard at work with a ball peen hammer.

"I had a great day," Brian says.

Bing sniffs the boy's breath for a hint of alcohol. There is none, so Bing wonders if Brian is sporting any new tattoos: an American flag, a bald eagle, a tribute to his mom—*right*. He spots a different kind of tattoo on the boy's neck—a hickey. Seems he did find comfort in some girl's arms, if comfort is the right word.

"Best day of my life," Brian says.

Bing thinks he understands why. He tries to talk over the incessant pounding that grows louder and louder. "You didn't meet with your—"

"No," Brian says. "First thing Monday." He waves a hand at the party. "I'm going to my room. I hate these things. Leftist assholes."

"I hear ya," Bing says, hoping his grandson doesn't get a look at Che over there.

"Brian!" Glen says, standing.

"Shit," Brian growls, exit thwarted.

Glen excuses himself from Madeleine. "We've been worried about you."

Brian assesses the well-tended guests. "Yeah, right."

"Where were you?"

"Out with my friends."

"All day?"

"Yeah." Brian tries to step past his father but is confronted by Susie stumbling from the kitchen. "Is that my Brian?" She clamps one arm around his neck. "How's my baby?"

Brian leans away from her wine-coated words, peeling her arm from his neck. "You're drunk."

"I am not!" Susie scans her guests for validation, but they look at the rugs. She thwacks her palm against Brian's shoulder. "We had a whole birthday breakfast ready for you, and presents."

A closet full of presents.

The hammering grows faster. Bing wonders if Junior and Reenie hear it. They jump off those steps and rush toward Brian crooning, "Birthday boy!"

Brian tries to push his way through the family, a tangled net that will not let him pass.

"Come on, everybody," Susie says. "Let's sing 'Happy Birthday' to Brian!"

"No!" Brian says, face scrunched at being the center of so much attention. But it's too late. The guests stand, even Madeleine, and press in around Brian to start singing.

The melody grates against the garbled wails blaring from the stereo, plus the ball peen hammer. The ceaseless *clack-clack* of Barbara's heels. Bing looks at her in the corner, leaning forward in her chair singing *"Happy Birthday"* to her grandson, Charles right beside her, glowing, as if Brian is his heir, and maybe he is, an agonizing reminder that pisses Bing off.

Where the hell were you when Roger and Susie were growing up? Why weren't you putting food on the table, paying doctor bills? Where were you when Susie got married? Where the hell were you when Roger got himself killed?

The pounding explodes into jack hammering, someone trying to break through a concrete wall: *Let me out!* Now Bing can pinpoint the source: Roger, in the closet, pummeling his fists against the door, wanting out so he can get at Bing. *You son of a bitch!*

Bing looks at the closet door rattling, the knob shaking, hinges straining while these idiots sing to a boy, a man, who wants none of it. Bing thinks Brian would like nothing better than to dive in that closet, too, where Roger rails at Bing. *You son of a bitch. It's all your fault!*

Bing starts to rush to the door to lean back against it, keep Roger from breaking through. Keep Brian from getting in. But he doesn't, because he is afraid of his own son.

You should have let me go to Mexico! I'd still be alive if you'd let me go!

A tiny voice in Bing's head: *I know.* He turns around to see his wife staring at the closet, hands now encased in black gloves, lap burdened with a star-splattered flag.

And Charles scooting his chair close, draping his seersucker arm around her shoulders to offer comfort in ways Bing never did. Bing turns toward the closet, pictures his son inside clawing at the door in the dark, no longer angry, but scared. *Let me go!*

Let him go.

"Let me go!"

The words are too clear, too present, and Bing realizes they aren't coming from Roger, but from Brian, held in place by Reenie and Junior, having too much fun with this playful torture that isn't playful to Brian. And Susie, arm looped through her son's so he can't bolt, her only ally, making him suffer the excruciating gaiety until it looks as if he'll explode.

"Let him go!" Bing bellows from his station at the wall, a shout so penetrating it shuts everything down: the singing, Roger's clawing, leaving only the discordant noise pouring from the stereo.

Everyone's eyes shift from Brian to Bing, a diversion that allows Brian to burst through the throng to clatter upstairs, his feet hammering the wooden slats. Reenie and Junior clip up after him. "We were just kidding!"

But Bing is stuck there, eyes burning with regret over Roger, Barbara. And suddenly, without warning, he is crying. Face drawn into a haggard grimace, mouth open, eyes crimped against the tears that will not be stopped.

His chest heaves as he stands there sobbing, real shoulder-shaking, throat-aching howls. Not in the privacy of his basement, not in some dim alcove, but right in Susie's living room packed with strangers ogling the spectacle of an old man falling apart. The way Susie stares at him, like she's never seen him before in her life, and maybe she hasn't.

Bing can't stop wailing, and he can't move either, doesn't want to leave Barbara over there, though she's looking at him, too, eyes anguished. Bing wants to tell her he's sorry, *I'm sorry*, but Charles is right beside her. Charles, lover or nonsexual soul mate, it doesn't matter, because apparently he won after all.

All Bing can do is clamp his hands onto his wet face, a curtain of fingers closing him off from this world. He wants to escape, but his feet are two-ton anchors dug into the floor.

So he hides inside himself, and what a dark, empty cave it now is.

A hand on his wrist. Ellen, not too embarrassed to aid a weeping man, pulling Bing back out of himself, dissolving the images of Barbara and Charles, and soon there's only a bookshelf over by the Christmas tree where his wife once sat.

Ellen whispers, "Let it all out."

He does.

Finally Ellen hands him a wad of napkins, and he lifts his glasses to blot his eyes, blow his nose. When he settles the frames back into place he looks at the stunned guests, pained expressions on their faces as they watch this pathetic display.

As they scrutinize him, Bing's heart doesn't cartwheel, adrenaline doesn't surge. He does not feel inclined to bolt and bury his head in the dirt, because at this moment, in one freeing *whoosh*, he doesn't give a fuck what anyone thinks—not even red-faced Glen who gapes at his father-in-law before looking contritely at Madeleine. And what a colossal *whoosh* that is.

Susie sidles over. "Are you all right?"

"He'll be fine," Ellen answers for him.

The guests offer abrupt farewells: *It's getting late. It was a lovely party. And where are our coats?*

Ellen steers Bing toward the kitchen, but he stops at the stairs. "Here's fine," he says. His legs feel rubbery and he plops down on the third step, never mind the guests stampeding up and down to get their coats. It feels so good to sit after so much standing and weeping, his energy spent.

"I'll be right back," Ellen says, slipping into the kitchen as Bing breathes, just breathes in and out as if he's inflating his soul, bringing it back to life.

Ellen returns with a tumbler of water. "Drink this."

He obeys, appreciating the tint of whiskey biting the back of his throat, draining it.

Bing stares at the empty glass a moment, then looks back at Ellen, upswept hairdo coming loose, coiled braid threatening to spring free any second. He hopes that it does.

"Here," Ellen says, taking the glass from him. She stands there, looking at him, and he can only imagine the sight he must be. "I'm heading home now," she says, lingering, as if she wants to add a few more words.

She doesn't, but as she starts to walk off Bing puts his hand on her wrist to still her. He looks at her pendant, the seamless soldering, the blending of two distinct metals, and fumbles for the right words to express gratitude. Not just for the drink, the rescue, but for Reenie, the wedding dress, the bond she and this stand-in grandma share. He can only think of two words, two insignificant words that catch in his throat, but he forces his chin up to look into Ellen's eyes. "Thank you."

Ellen covers his hand with hers, and her fingers are so warm. "You're welcome, Bing." She turns to leave, takes one step, and another, his fingers slipping from her wrist, but she pauses. "I'm having trouble with one of my torches."

"Your Mig?"

"As a matter of fact. If someone wanted to drop by and take a look at it tomorrow, he would be richly rewarded."

Holding a torch in his hands again would be reward enough.

"I have a mind to make beef stew," Ellen adds. "Maybe a batch of yeast rolls to sop up the gravy."

Ah, the reward. "I reckon I can manage that."

Ellen looks at him, eyes glinting. "Well, all right." This time she does leave, but not before Bing catches a flash of coiled bun springing free, silver braid bouncing against blue satin.

Bing's eyes pivot to the mass exodus at the door, guests begging farewell blessings, not from Susie, but from Madeleine standing beside Glen.

Susie hovers in the corner where her mother once sat, helping folks with their coats, her swaying impeding the process.

Francine swishes by Bing, red cape fluttering, platter depleted of egg rolls. She kisses Glen and practically genuflects before the queen. "Lunch next week?"

"I look forward to it," Madeleine decrees.

Francine chirrups and flits out the door.

Che is next, shaking Glen's hand, and Madeleine's. No words. Before leaving he turns to the real hostess. "Great party, Suz." He looks at Bing on the stairs. "Pleasure to meet you, sir."

Bing nods.

The last one left, besides Crystal and Scott who are already repositioning the living room chairs, is Madeleine. She looks blankly around the room. "I seem to have lost my ride. Has anyone seen Ned?"

Susie squawks, "He was the first one out the door."

"I'll take you home," Glen says.

Bing watches Susie's eyes snap open, and he offers his second surprise of the night: "I'll take her." Glen, Madeleine, and Susie gawp at him.

"Don't be ridiculous," Glen says. "I'll take her."

As if that settles that, Madeleine says, "I'd like to use the facilities first." She walks to the hall closet and puts her hand on the knob.

"Wait!" Bing shouts, imagining Roger in there ready to burst free or tumble out. Whichever, Bing doesn't want Madeleine anywhere near his son.

"What?" Madeleine says, even as she turns the knob and opens the door an inch, two inches, Bing bending forward to squint into the dark space to see if he can catch a hint of Roger's hand, of Roger. But as the door opens wider all he sees is the edge of the vacuum cleaner, a bag of Sno Melt, and beside them, on the floor, a crinkly Safeway sack wound with a rubber band.

"He's gone," Bing whispers.

"What's that?" Madeleine bends to hear his words.

Bing looks up at her, a profound emptiness in his gut. "The bathroom is upstairs."

"Oh." She closes the closet door almost all the way, almost, leaving Bing on the steps staring into that one-inch gap.

Susie collects glasses and plates, pressing them sloppily to her chest, staining her scarf.

"Give me those." Glen unburdens her, hefting the dishes to the kitchen where Crystal loads the dishwasher, plates clattering and clanking.

Bing wishes he had a handful of darts to hurl at Glen's back. Or head.

Glen settles his dishes on the counter as Crystal reaches under the sink to pull out not the Cascade but Bing's box of MoonPies. "What in the world are these doing down there?"

"Give me those." Glen grabs the box so roughly the disks fly out and scatter across the floor. He frantically scoops them up and peers behind him as Bing looks down to study that mole on his wrist.

"You keep them under the sink?" Crystal asks.

Glen bends to stow the contraband behind the lineup of Windex and Pledge that Bing knows so well.

Bing is flummoxed. Of all the people in this house, Bing never would have suspected his weed-eating, low-sodium son-in-law. *I'll be jiggered*, he thinks, looking up at the ceiling as Glen passes, not wanting to risk shutting the operation down. Imagining Glen sneaking down to the kitchen in the middle of the night to sate his sugar jones.

Shoot, Bing thinks, disgusted for allowing a box of MoonPies to so easily thaw his anger.

Madeleine eases down the steps, buttoning her coat. Bing would like to reach his hand out and give her ankle a good yank.

Glen opens the door for her. "Be back soon," he says to no one.

Madeleine looks at Susie's back as she bends to collect crumpled napkins.

"I had a lovely time," Madeleine says.

Susie doesn't utter one peep.

A needling pause until Glen cups Madeleine's elbow. "After you."

***

More thunder on the stairs, enough racket to make Bing stand and move aside. Junior hops down three steps at a time. Reenie clomps more slowly, carrying Frida's pillow, a ring bearer with an oversized load. She squats to settle the bed back where it belongs. "That's better," she says, standing to appraise the smelly cog that puts her weird world back together. And Bing's.

Junior grabs the doorknob. "We're going to Stamford Park to look at Christmas lights, Mr. Butler. Wanna come?"

"Stamford Park?"

"It's a fancy subdivision lit up like you wouldn't believe."

Bing thinks an invitation to join this cuddling opportunity must be a joke, since that's what he and Barbara did whenever they drove around gazing at holiday lights. *There were tender moments. There were.*

Bing expects Reenie to jab Junior in the ribs. *Why'd you invite him?* What she says is, "Come on, Grandpa. It's so pretty."

For the second time tonight Bing thinks he could cry, but he doesn't. "No, you two go on ahead. You don't need a third wheel on a ride like that."

"Okay," Reenie says. "Will you wait on the porch while I go get Frida?"

"Sure thing." Bing follows them out, storm door slamming behind him. He pauses at the top step as the kids dart through the snow.

It's frosty without a coat, his breath coming out in white puffs, and Bing tries to blow smoke rings, but he can't. Never could. He rubs his hands up and down his arms, surveying the neighborhood which is quite beautiful with the streetlights humming, circles of light up and down the road. Christmas trees lighting folks' windows. Strands of electric white icicles dangling from porches. How he wishes Barbara were standing beside him, holding his hand, looking at these decorations. She didn't need a fancy subdivision to make her happy, never mind Charles's River Oaks mansion. No, it was the little things. That's what he loved about her. Still does.

The night sky is as blue as Ellen's tunic, stars twinkling their hearts out. He looks over at Ellen's porch, sees Junior's and Reenie's dark figures, watches the door open as they collect their charge, Ellen's silhouette leaning out, going back in. Bing imagines her inside waiting for them to clear the steps before turning off the porch light. And there it goes, the porch light, as they herd slowpoke Frida back home. Bing hears her snuffling the snow, snorting it out.

Junior and Reenie urge Frida toward the porch steps. She climbs them one at a time; arthritic paws and cataracts and elf getup make the going slow.

"See you later," Reenie calls. She and Junior sprint to his truck by the curb, white letters on the door advertising *Plymale's Salvage and Scrap*. Junior opens the passenger door and Reenie hops in, sliding to the center. Junior races around to his own side. The engine rumbles to life and off they go, red taillights shrinking.

Frida sniffs at Bing's feet, *friend or foe?* Her stumpy tail thumps as if she is genuinely happy to see the old man.

"How you doing there, stinky?" Bing squats to pet her, no longer fearing a snarl or snip. He gets a lick, not out of affection, he's sure, but for a hint of what the old buzzard's been eating.

A train clatters in the distance, *clackety-clack*, Barbara's happy heels, a racket so thunderous Bing imagines the sound rippling through the valley, up hollows, maybe all the way to Odell's house where that frail soldier lies in his bed, listening, dreaming of distant places, distant times. Bing envisions miles and miles of moonlit track, alluring rails that lead to New England, probably. California, maybe. Texas.

Bing feels the light penetrating through Susie's front window on the back of his head, his shoulders, imagines it warming him all the way to his bones. He can't see it, but he knows that looming behind him is that hunkered-down hill coated in snow. He wonders what it will look like come spring, all those limbs greening up, coming back to life.

He could stay out here all night, but Frida paws at the door, anxious to reclaim her throne. He opens the door for the real queen and follows her in because he has one more chore left to do.

BRAVERY

Frida waddles from room to room, sniffing foreign odors, rooting for crumbs. Satisfied, she ambles to her pillow and lies down, tries to settle in, but her costume makes it difficult, pinching her neck, her tumors, eyes bulging even more than usual.

"Let's get that stupid thing off." Bing kneels, rolling her this way and that to figure out how in blazes the thing works. Velcro, he discovers, unsticking the fabric from around her belly, working her paws through the dumb sleeves. Frida sighs when he's finished and closes her eyes.

Bing wishes he had someone to attend to him. Help him downstairs to swap his party clothes for PJs, nestle covers under his chin, set a glass of water on his bedside table before he closes his eyes to let the dreams come. But there is no one, and besides, he knows there will be no shut-eye until he's completed his mission.

Crystal and Scott stuff leftovers into the fridge, wash wine glasses and serving trays. Susie is humped over the kitchen table, slurping coffee. Bing points at her ceramic mug. "Won't that keep you awake?"

Susie studies the brew. "I can never sleep after these parties anyway."

She picks a morsel from a plate of hors d'oeuvres. Bing is happy to see her toss solid food down her gullet to absorb some of that wine. He sits across from her as she pokes her finger into one of those mystery dips. She's picking really, pushing scraps around, until she comes to Glen's spani-what's-its. She's not timid with that, not jamming it into her mouth, but stabbing it with a fork over and over until it's a punctured mess.

Atta girl, Bing thinks, feeling very close to her, feeling like he can take that first step. Now's the time, while Glen is gone. Bing glares at Crystal and Scott, fingers thrumming. *Hurry the hell up and leave.*

Susie gets up to rummage through a cabinet for Alka-Seltzer. She plops two in a glass of water and watches the fizz. Bing thinks she's going to need more than that to divert tomorrow's hangover. Still, she's not staggering anymore, not swaying, voice isn't as slurred, and Bing wonders if she was ever really very drunk.

"I'm going up," she says, heading toward the stairs.

"You're going to bed?" Bing asks, alarmed. He's not ready for her to call it a night.

"Just let yourselves out," she says to Crystal and Scott.

"Will do," they chime.

Bing wants to stall her, needs to stall her. "Aren't you going to wait up for Glen?"

"Ha!"

Scott and Crystal scrub those trays like they're trying to burnish off the silver plating.

Susie grabs the handrail and hauls herself up one step at a time. *Just like an old woman*, Bing thinks as she slips out of sight.

Bing's innards twitch as the hired help bustles about. He stares at the wall clock counting the interminable minutes: five, ten, fifteen, one ear perked listening for Glen's car. He'll be here any minute, any second, which would ruin everything, because Bing feels he has to make his move tonight while he's got the gumption—at least he thinks he has the gumption—or forever hold his peace.

He stands, sits, stands, paces from room to room rubbing his hands together, trying not to think about the erratic thump in his chest.

Finally Scott stows the broom, Crystal drapes a washrag over the spigot, and they leave, taking all sound with them. The house becomes a vacuum, unmercifully quiet compared to the recent symphony of discordant clamor, Bing's weeping the most jarring instrument of all.

Bing shuffles to the stairs, and when he passes the closet door, ajar, he knows he can't leave Roger's letters on the floor in the dark. They deserve a better place, higher ground. He opens the door wide, wider, looking at the back panel for hammer marks or clawing. Of course there are none. He bends to scoop up his son's words. He knows just the spot for them.

Bing clutches the letters to his chest with his left hand, puts his right hand on the rail to start climbing. *This is it.*

But he can't move.

It is an involuntary stupor, his body rebelling against his mind, on strike against anticipated danger.

Bing looks over at Frida. "Come on, girl," he calls, hoping some company might calm his gut, bolster his courage, as if a blind guide dog could manage that.

Frida's right eyelid cracks open.

"Come on."

She closes her eye and nestles her muzzle deeper into her pillow. *You're on your own.*

Traitor. Bing looks at his feet, his ridiculous spit-shined shoes. A car rumbles out front but continues driving past, rattling the front windows. It's not Glen. *Where the hell is he?* Bing is certain the next car will be his son-in-law's, wanting it to be, not wanting it to be. He urges his feet, his muscles, his nerves into action. *Come on.* They will not obey.

Bing's head goes down and his shoulders sag. Defeated, deflated as Susie was a few hours ago. He's ready to skulk to the basement, let this window close for good.

A voice whispers in his ear, firm and steady. *You can do this.*

Electricity zaps through Bing, scalp tingling, skin pimpling. *Who is that?* He wants to swivel around, see if Glen came home and snuck up behind him. But he's frozen solid. Lungs stopped in midbreath.

You can do this, the voice whispers again, and Bing knows who it is. *Oh, God.* Roger, resurrected for one last act.

I've got you, Roger promises, enough support to fortify Bing, to frighten him into action, and he climbs up one step, two, legs wobbly, his heart running away in his chest, and that's what Bing would like to do, too.

You're doing fine.

What do you want?

Just to help you.

Why? Why would you want to help me when I was the one who— Bing falters under the guilt bearing down, sole slipping off the wooden slats, torso pitching forward. He grips the handrail, knuckles blanching. *That goddamn Studebaker.*

None of that matters anymore.

Bing feels a hand on his back; he really *feels* it, his son's sturdy palm, and his forgiving words: *It wasn't your fault. I could have run if I'd wanted. It was my decision to go.*

Yours?

All mine.

Bing slumps further, not under the burden of blame, but under the weight of forgiveness. He wants to turn around and look at his son, to fully accept this gift, but he feels Roger pressing him on, his dear son who embarrassed so easily, who is trying to sideline gratitude even now by urging his father forward.

Bing straightens up to take one slow step, and another. As they move deeper and deeper into the shadowy stairwell, Bing feels as blind and arthritic as Frida down there. But with his son's hand on his back he feels surprisingly safe. As he climbs toward Susie's room, however, the fear becomes so tangible it nearly flies out of his mouth. *I don't know how to talk to her. I never knew how to talk to her.*

I know.

There are so many things, too many things.

The reassuring whisper: *Just a few more steps.*

Bing looks up into the hall, sees the light from Susie's room and his throat swells, making it difficult to breathe. He stops climbing. *I can't.*

Yes, you can. We're almost there.

This is the hardest thing I've ever done in my life.

You can do it.

Bing forces his right foot up, his left, finally reaching the top. He steps into the hall and looks at Brian's door sealed shut, no light.

Bing holds up Roger's letters, relieved to have a legitimate detour. *Let me just . . .*

Okay.

Bing tiptoes to Brian's door and presses his palm against it. The door sways open and Bing leans in, eyes going right to the bulletin board above the bed, newspaper and magazine photos fluttering, World Trade Center victims falling out of windows. Bing can almost hear their moans. Agonizing wails that rain down on Brian, who sleeps beneath them. Painful pleas tumbling into his ears night after night. No wonder the boy is so driven. But tonight he has collapsed in delirious bliss. *He'd better enjoy this kind of contented exhaustion. He'll be enduring a different kind very soon, unless—*

I need to tell Susie about Brian.

Yes.

Bing eases in and rests Roger's letters on Brian's keyboard, letters on letters. He imagines Brian waking up tomorrow, Sunday morning, that holy day, and opening the fragile envelopes one by one as if they are sacred text. Reverently reading them in this room that is as hallowed as any church.

Whatever happens, it's his decision, Roger says.

Bing knows that it's true. He nods and backs out, closing the door behind him.

He faces Susie's room and begins tallying up all the other things he needs to talk to her about. Glen and Madeleine. Barbara and Charles. The questions. The lies. Bing's breathing becomes erratic as the impossible list grows and grows, each item weightier than the next. His jaw trembles at the daunting task. *It's too much. It's just too much. How can I have a lifetime of discussions in one night?*

You don't have to do it all tonight. You just have to make the first move.

Susie coughs in her room and she could be ten years old again with a sore throat, calling out for her mother to bring her a glass of water. How pathetic she looked, a scrawny kid with swollen glands, Vicks-coated kerchief tied around her throat.

The first move, that's all. Bing nods, tiptoes to her doorway, and peeks in, the king's pawn, exposed.

Susie sits up in bed, covers pulled to her waist, dim bedside lamp casting meager light on the pile of books and papers scattered around her comforter. Glen's side of the bed is still regulation-made. The chicken or the egg. Bing wonders which came first: Susie burying herself in her work to fill—*how'd that jukebox song go?*—the husband-shaped hole in her heart, or Glen packing his own workaholic-wife void with an outside life. Whichever, Bing doubts Susie can focus on this highbrow business, busyness, at the moment, but that isn't the point, after all.

Susie yanks a tissue from the box on her bedside table beside that picture of Roger, smiling. A grin so welcoming and large Bing turns around to fully face it, though he has to close his eyes to really see.

And there he is, Roger, not in fatigues, not dirt-smeared and helmeted, but wearing the same t-shirt and jeans as in the photo, the shock of bangs Bing wants to push out of his son's eyes.

And I need to talk to her about you, Bing adds, finishing the long, long list.

Roger nods, the shy linebacker shoving his fists in his pockets, a gesture Bing remembers so well. A nervous tic Bing tried to break: *Get your hands out of your pockets.* Tonight he sees just how precious it is, and he wants to take it all back. Everything.

But Roger already knows that. He looks at his father, eyes full of grace.

Still, Bing needs to say the words for Roger, for himself. "I'm sorry," the aching admission vibrating off the walls.

"Glen?" Susie calls.

Bing sucks in his breath and squeezes his eyes shut even tighter, trying to tunnel inside himself again.

But he can't, not anymore, and Roger says, *Answer her.*

Bing exhales and says in a trembling voice, "No, honey. It's me." He turns around and leans in, a fidgeting mess in the doorway.

"Are you all right?" she asks.

"Yup. Just coming to check on you. Are *you* all right?"

Susie scratches her earlobe. "Sure. Fine. Never better."

His shoes melt into tar balls sticking to the floor. All he can do is look at Susie as she practices her own bravery.

Go on, Roger says, giving Bing a final nudge. He bumbles into Susie's room.

She sits up straighter as Bing sits at the foot of her bed, mattress creaking.

He clears his throat once, twice, trying to swallow the golf ball lodged there. "You're not all right."

"What?" Susie asks, shoulders pulling back.

For the first time in his life Bing sees her, really sees her: his brilliant, feisty, fragile little girl. He sees the fear they both share, his legacy to her, and he wants to switch it off for good, a motive that gives him the courage to say, "I think it's time we had a long talk."

Susie opens her mouth to rebut, her eyes darting, looking for an exit, another twitch he recognizes, so he does the only thing he can to keep her from bolting. Revives a ritual that Barbara performed night after night when she tucked their daughter into bed, a custom Bing observed from the doorway. He doubts Susie remembers. Still, he reaches his hand toward the fabric teepee covering her left foot and wraps his hand around it so he can toggle it back and forth, back and forth, an odd metronome. At first her foot tightens in his grip, then it relaxes. She closes her eyes, probably wishing that the hand clasping her foot was her mother's, not Bing's, and that's all right with him. It really is. Because he imagines Barbara sitting beside him, her hand covering his as together they console their daughter. But Susie is not consoled as she opens her eyes and looks at Bing, eyes pleading. Her mouth opens, lips quiver, and what she says is, "Dad."

"Go ahead," Bing says, because he knows what she needs, now it's her turn to cry, not in a living room full of colleagues, but in the privacy of her room with her father to relieve her.

"Just let it all go," he says, scooting forward to catch her as her head goes down, her hands fly to her face, shoulders shake.

"Everything's going to be all right," he says, and truly, no matter what happens with Brian, with Glen, with anything, Bing believes it.

ACKNOWLEDGMENTS

I am indebted to Daniel Wallace for selecting *Shrapnel* as winner
of the Fred Bonnie Award. Thank you to the folks at River City
Publishing for bringing the novel in for a landing: Carolyn Newman,
Shari Smith, and Robin Miura, editor extraordinaire. I owe choco-
late-covered strawberries to my writer pals whose astute sensibilities
made this a much better novel: Laura Bentley, Zoë Ferraris, Paul
Martin, John Van Kirk, Mary Sansom, Leslie Birdwell Shortlidge,
and Shannon Butler. Muchas gracias to Michele Schiavone, the best
proofreader on several continents. A shout-out to the dude at the
Waffle House in Richmond, Kentucky, who gave me the inside scoop
on welders' torches and lore. Deep appreciation goes to the veterans
in my family: my father, Charles Manilla; my brothers Steve and
Phil; and my nephew Jason. A special thank you to my brother-in-
law, Dave Palmer, who shared with me his memories of serving in
Vietnam, as well as the landscape and jargon. As always, heartfelt
gratitude to my mother, Elaine Manilla, and my husband, Don
Primerano, my biggest fans.